# Burton's Solo

## An Elder Darrow Mystery

# Burton's Solo

## An Elder Darrow Mystery

# Richard J. Cass

Encircle Publications, LLC
Farmington, Maine U.S.A.

Paperback ISBN 13: 978-1-948338-30-1
E-book  ISBN 13:978-1-948338-31-8
Kindle ISBN 13: 978-1-948338-32-5

Library of Congress Control Number: 2018911034

Editor: Cynthia Brackett-Vincent
Book design: Eddie Vincent
Cover design and composite illustration by Deirdre Wait
Cover images © Getty Images
Author photo by Philip McCarty

Published by: Encircle Publications, LLC
PO Box 187
Farmington, ME 04938

Visit: http://encirclepub.com

Printed in U.S.A.

"People don't realize you're blowing over changes, time changes, harmony, different keys. I mark a point in my solo where it's got to peak at point D I go to A, B, C D then I'm home."

—James McBride

# Dedication

*For Anne, Ever and Always*

# Acknowledgements

As always, it takes a much bigger team to send Elder and Burton out into the world than it might appear.

First, thanks once again to the folks at Encircle Publications, Ed Vincent and Cynthia Brackett-Vincent, for ongoing support and believing that my two strange wounded men have good lives to live and good stories to tell. And for Deirdre Wait at High Pines Creative, for another exceptional cover. Long may we publish together.

Thanks also to important early readers:

• Brian Thiem and Bruce Coffin, for making sure Burton acts like a cop and not some over-imaginative TV-watcher's version thereof,

• Brenda Buchanan, Rick Smith, and Tom Jipson for important and challenging early feedback that made *Burton's Solo* far better than it might have been.

Also, thanks to:

• Tim Glidden, for the very cool Spotify playlists that accompany the first two books (https://tinyurl.com/In-Solo-Time and https://tinyurl.com/Solo-Act), and

• Maine Writers and Publishers Alliance for their support and the fine work they do for all the various writing communities in all parts of the state of Maine. Proud to be a member.

I can't say enough how important the encouragement of the Maine literary community and, specifically, the Maine Crime Writing faction, is. It's unusual in my experience to find so many writers devoted to each others' successes, and I am proud and pleased to be part of it. I only hope I give back as much as I receive.

And, not least, a special shoutout to the spouses and partners who hold us all up. Thank you—you all know who I'm talking about.

Above all, of course, for Anne, my anchor and my sail. Thirty-four years in the boat, dear. Still sailing, still bailing.

# 1

"**B**urton said the perp walk would make the six o'clock news,"
I said. "What time is it?"

Marina looked at her watch.

"Five forty-six."

She picked up my dirty dishes off the bar and carried them back into the kitchen.

To cut down on drunken arguments about whether it really was last call, I didn't keep a clock out front in the Esposito. It also worked the way not having windows helped the Las Vegas casinos. People forgot whether it was day or night and kept doing what they were doing. In the three years I'd owned the Esposito, I'd learned a few tricks.

I pointed the remote at the small TV, mounted up in the corner solely for the use of the occasional Red Sox fan. The dust on the glass surface crackled and the screen brightened.

I lowered the volume, though it wouldn't bother my only two customers on this cold Monday evening in February, house painters working in a brownstone on Shawmut Ave. Neither one of them was within five feet of sober and they'd been bitching out their foreman so unimaginatively, listening to something else would be a relief.

WCVB was already down to the sports and weather, so I'd missed the five-thirty report. The six o'clock newscast usually led with the big local story of the day and the arrest of Antoine Bousquet for double murder was a very big story. I muted the commercials until AnnaLise Jacobs appeared on the dot of six.

She bestowed her professionally friendly smile on all of us out in TV land and launched right in.

1

"Violence erupted today outside Boston Police Headquarters as Antoine Bousquet, the Belgian clothing designer, was arrested on suspicion of murder in the deaths of two of his employees."

AnnaLise favored us all with a gypsy-dark look of caution, almost hidden under all that hair.

"We do need to caution you that the film we're about to show may be disturbing to some viewers."

The footage panned, locating the camera in a scrum of media held back by the boundary of the concrete bollards on the Tremont Street side of Boston Police Headquarters. A clot of plainclothes officers and one uniform escorted a slim, medium-tall man in a beige two-piece suit, black shirt, and silver tie along the sidewalk toward the building entrance. A topcoat draped over his wrists in front, drawing attention to the fact he was handcuffed.

Burton walked closest to Bousquet, only fitting since he'd been the primary investigator. He'd bucked public and political pressure to build the case for arresting the civic icon and he'd earned whatever credit he got.

The print reporters and still photographers pushed and shoved, but TV is king in Boston, as it is everywhere else, and the camera maintained its focus.

Burton kept the group moving. He'd be the first to admit the perp walk was a made-for-TV event but he wasn't going to stop to answer questions. As the group approached the glass and steel doors, though, he steered Antoine Bousquet around so his face—narrow, planed, overly tanned for winter—squared up to the mob. The designer winced at the harsh lights and the barking crowd, then said something to Burton out of one side of his mouth.

"Oh, shit," I said.

Burton and I had been through enough together for me to recognize when he was about to blow: the hard set to his jaw, the swell in his chest. He grabbed the handcuffs with his left hand, whirled Bousquet, and quick as a gun—bam, bam, bam—fired three jabs into Bousquet's face.

The press noise exploded, baying for the blood of the news. Bousquet tried to slump onto his knees to protect himself but Burton hoisted him by the cuffs and stared into his face as if contemplating further ass-kicking.

The uniform separated them. Bousquet knelt on the sidewalk. The camera zoomed in on his face, the split lip, the blood dripping from both nostrils onto the concrete sidewalk, the darkening flush of what would be a spectacular black eye in a couple of hours.

Burton stepped back and stared at his hands, as if appalled by what they'd done, though it might only have been regret that he'd used them on the hard bones of someone's head. He always told me if I needed to punch someone, go for the soft parts.

I closed my eyes and shook my head. He was always running along the thin edge of fuck-up, usually because he invested himself so heavily in his cases. This was not going to help his shaky standing in the department. It might even jeopardize the case against Bousquet.

The film cut away to a severely disappointed AnnaLise.

"There you have it. Again," she said. "Even more evidence that the Boston Police Department is a wee bit out of control." She smirked at her co-host. "Not much presumption of innocence there, eh, Derek?"

She brightened.

"In other news, the Duck Pond will be opening for the season . . ."

I shut the TV off and cursed, loudly enough for the house painters to look down the bar. Marina was out in the kitchen but she'd hear about it soon enough, probably from her mother. Carmen did not approve of the fact that Marina and Burton had been dating, off and on, for more than a year.

I sipped my coffee, which had gone cold, and wished it were Scotch. Did Burton have some kind of professional death wish? He always went his own way, but the fact that he cleared homicides at a higher rate than anyone else in the department usually saved him. It wasn't clear if that would be enough to save him from a public fuck-up like this.

Marina's phone rang out in the kitchen, the first few bars of Nelly Furtado's *Powerless*. No doubt that was Carmen, carrying the bad news to Marina. Which meant it was all beginning.

# 2

If I'd known Burton was going to disappear on me, I might have paid more attention to his mood on that Tuesday afternoon when he came into the Esposito for the first time in weeks. Predictably, the department had suspended him for punching out Antoine Bousquet, but Burton's attitude didn't seem anymore down today than on one of his usual crawls up the slopes of Mount Drunk.

Besides, I was too involved in my own problems to notice too much. Being sober for the last six months had pretty much trashed my reactions: I got angry more quickly, cried more easily, and was generally touchier than a sunburned Chihuahua in a room full of cactus. Then there was the money my father Thomas had left me and what that meant for my future. And the bar's.

"Publicly funded trash-talk radio." I balled up the Style section of the Globe and pitched it into the trashcan. "Morons."

WGBH was canceling *Eric in the Evening*, one of the few all-jazz radio shows left on the air anywhere, let alone in rock and roll crazy Boston. All the big brains over on Guest Street had determined that the public radio airwaves needed more rehashed political commentary, more puff pieces on the local politicians and real estate developers, more and more words, that is, at the expense of the complex beautiful music that, except for some petroglyphs carved into rocks somewhere, was America's only native art form.

The notion that I wasn't going to be able to turn on the radio at eight every night and hear the sweet lilt of Horace Silver playing "Peace" and then Eric Jackson's molasses tones introducing the evening's theme annoyed me past reason.

4

"They didn't shitcan him altogether." Burton spoke over the top of his fourth whiskey sour of the afternoon. "He still has the weekend slot."

"Ten to midnight on Saturday night? Deadest time on the radio dial. And anyone who listens to jazz is probably out in a club, hearing live music."

"Always assuming there's anyone left in the world who remembers what a radio dial is."

I poured myself a glass of tonic water and squeezed a wedge of lime into it, drank it so fast the bubbles got up my nose and made me sneeze. Shuffling through the iPad, I picked the Tommy Flanagan version of "Peace" and turned the volume up, disgusted.

Most of the gossip said the drivers of the decision were two members of the station's board, the big-wallet, big-stick Hope brothers, long practitioners of the version of the Golden Rule that says that he who has the gold makes the rules.

Their mouthpiece was one Marty Laird, a big-mouthed TV interviewer who rarely stopped talking long enough to hear the answers to his questions. He reminded me of other media personalities the city had spawned over the years—a certain faux-populist newspaper columnist and a much unloved baseball writer came to mind—both of whom focused on their own visibility more than anything useful they might report.

"You know I'm not one of these nostalgia freaks," I said. "But they did the same thing to Ron Della Chiesa with *Music America*. 'GBH has its monthly identity crisis and all of a sudden the only place you can hear Sinatra on the radio is down in Plymouth."

Burton was happy enough to play along. The last thing he wanted to talk about was what had happened with Bousquet yesterday, anymore than he intended to end this day sober.

"Fuck me," he said. "When I was a kid, I was listening to the Stones. Joe Cocker. The Beatles. What were you, Duke Ellington's youngest fanboy?"

I might have been, if I'd discovered the Duke before he died in 1974.

" 'California Dreamin' '," I said.

Burton snorted part of his drink, coughed, then laughed.

"I don't really see you as a folkie."

I leaned on the bar, trying to gauge if he was going to get drunk enough for me to cut him off, something I'd only had to do twice before. I'd bought myself a season's pass on the slope of sobriety this winter but even before all the Bousquet business kicked up, I worried about him. He'd had an ugly winter, starting when his divorce from Sharon started to limp a little closer to finality. Add in the fact that we'd averaged two snowstorms a week since mid-December and it was now the first week of February and he'd been whacking the bottle hard, even for a boy from Charlestown with a lot of practice.

Having him around the bar in this frame of mind always tensed me up, not that he was the kind of cop who threw his weight around when he got loaded. No, the more Burton drank, the heavier he got, until the space around his stool became a black hole, dragging all good cheer and conviviality down into the void with him. The only brake I had on that was making him pay for all his drinks. No freebies for that kind of mood. Not in my bar.

"Not the Mamas and the Papas," I said. "Wes Montgomery."

Burton faked some air guitar.

"It was the dead of fucking winter and you liked the idea of someplace warm," he said.

I nodded.

"Surfing, zoris, baggy shorts, and Hawaiian shirts. Bleached blondes in French bikinis."

"You know the two-piece suit was a sartorial invention of the third century AD?"

"You know a lot of strange shit, Burton."

"But you didn't leave town, did you?" He slammed the rest of the drink, wiped his lips, and pushed the glass back over the bar.

"Boston boy," I said. "One more?"

He shook his head.

"Pretrial conference. On the Bousquet case. It helps my meetings go better if I'm coherent." He smirked. "If not entirely sober."

"I thought you were on suspension."

"DA doesn't give a shit. She's still got to put the case together."

Antoine Bousquet had emigrated to the United States with a European reputation as a clothing designer and built a local empire out of rendering his designs into clothes in factories he established down in Chinatown. Eventually, though, instead of employing locals, he started importing illegal immigrants to sew the shirts, suits, and dresses. For the price of passage and a bed in a three-decker firetrap, a person could make his or her way to the golden pathways of America. Or Boston, at least. The story was as old as the city itself, down to the hints of violent intimidation that kept the workers in line. None of it was very far from slavery.

Then came the beating deaths of two young women working in Bousquet's sweat shops, both of whom had separately opened complaints about working conditions with the city's Office for Immigrant Advancement. Bousquet's mistress, Viktoriya Lin, had come out of the sweat shops too, but when her cousin, another seamstress, became the third person to disappear, Viktoriya had added to the police pressure on Bousquet by filing a missing persons report.

Burton was assigned the homicide case originally, though his bosses at Schroeder Plaza were no doubt holding their heads in pain by now. The beat-down of Bousquet had muddied things to the point that a friendly judge had allowed Bousquet to bail himself out, almost unheard of for a murder charge.

I reached under the bar and pushed a can of Altoids across to him. He slid them right back.

"Dead giveaway," he said. "I've got a toothbrush in the car."

"That's about as subtle." I hesitated. "Any word on whether the investigation is continuing?"

I'd read that the DA now wanted even more evidence of Bousquet's guilt than Burton had developed.

"Oh, it's going. I got people chomping at the bit to take over my case." He lifted one shoulder. "I'm more worried about the disciplinary hearing. I know I fucked up but I can't go back and fix it. All I can do is ride the trolley to the end of the line."

He was pretending not to care but losing his job would drive him permanently into that deep black hole he sometimes visited. His case against Bousquet had no doubt been tight and by the book, but because of the way his temper took hold, his judgment was suspect.

"Be smart, Burton. You know there are people out there who'd love to take you down."

"Wouldn't be the first time someone tried." His smile was tight. "Some of them think I'm halfway there already."

He backed off the stool, sketched me a salute, and headed for the stairs up to the street.

I watched him go, wishing there was more I could do for him, then knelt down to rummage in the music drawer for that old Wes Montgomery CD. Until the pall over Burton lifted, all of us were going to need a little dreamin'.

# 3

Marina walked out of the kitchen as the steel door at the top of the stairs clanged shut.

"Is he doing all right?"

It was an odd question to ask me, since the two of them had been dating—if anyone knew how he was doing she ought to. I frowned at her.

"He'll talk to you," she said. "He doesn't talk to anyone else."

"He knows he's in trouble. But he still thinks the case is solid. The rest of it is all distraction, as far as he's concerned: the media, his bosses. Lawyers and politicians."

She squeezed her lips together, making her look even more unhappy.

"Did he tell you we're not seeing each other anymore?"

"Really."

"The divorce. Sharon. It's dragging on. I don't think he really wants to go through with it."

Marina was exactly the stabilizing influence I needed in the kitchen after Jacquie Robillard got herself murdered. Marina was a creative cook and managed to stay calm even in the weeds of a busy Saturday night. And she'd turned out to be a fierce haggler with my suppliers, some of whom had been cheating me and kicking back money to Jacquie. I couldn't imagine running the Esposito without Marina. The only downside was that she'd given up taking classes at the community college so she could work full-time, something else her mother Carmen wasn't happy about.

"And you started smoking again."

The odor clung to her clothes. Stress, no doubt. Another thing for Carmen to blame on me if she ever found out.

"I wash my hands right afterward."

Her sharp tone was intended to remind me that she and her mother both managed their lives fine without input from any male authority figures. Marina's father was an unknown and never-mentioned ghost in their story. But even though at forty-seven I was only six or seven years older than her, I couldn't help feeling avuncular.

"It stinks," I said. "But you know that." It was too early in the week to start an argument. "If the stories about Bousquet's sweat shops are true, I can't say I blame Burton for smacking the guy. Even if it does get him in trouble."

She grinned and pumped her fist.

"He didn't smack him. He fucking whaled on him."

"Language." I laughed, which is what she'd intended. She knew I worried about Burton, felt like I owed him.

"And Bousquet provoked him," she said. "Asked him how many of his designer dresses Sharon owned."

That was a detail Burton hadn't shared with me. It seemed like a weak taunt.

"I would have nailed him for it too. Not that I have to ask which side of the question you come down on."

Marina's dark eyes flashed.

"Even if I didn't know what Bousquet did? I'll tell you about sweat shops. My mother, before she went to work for your parents? She came over from Sicily, seventeen years old. The first people she worked for, she cooked, cleaned, took care of the babies twelve or fifteen hours a day. Six and a half days a week. For her room and board only."

Before my mother died, she occasionally alluded to the fact that Carmen had lived a rough life before she came to our house on Louisburg Square but this was the first time I'd heard details. No wonder Marina was so self-sufficient.

"Disgraceful," I said. "You know my mother loved her."

"I know. Your father, too."

Her eyes were wet, which made me uncomfortable. From bits

and pieces of conversation over the last few months, a couple asides from Burton, I gathered that Carmen was slipping, both physically and mentally. There had been ER trips for heart palpitations and a tentative diagnosis of incipient dementia. Soon enough, Marina would be dealing with what everyone who outlived their parents did, caring for someone who couldn't care for themselves anymore.

My father's will included a trust for Carmen, though its terms bound me not to tell anyone until two years after his death. On that date, a month or so from now, I would come into my own inheritance too, an amount of money that meant I'd have to make some serious decisions about the future, whether I wanted to stay in the bar business, what else I might owe the world.

Marina wiped her eyes with the corner of her apron. A pot sizzled in the kitchen, probably peppers and onions and celery for the white bean chili, since it was Tuesday.

I cut off Wes Montgomery and thought about what music to play for the dinner crowd that would filter in soon. Nothing too heavy, maybe some Beach Boys, since Burton had gotten me thinking about California. It was still only thirty-one degrees outside. *Pet Sounds*.

# 4

About seven-thirty on Thursday night, the street door opened and let in two customers and a blast of icy air. I was in the process of turning down the volume on the music and switching the TV on to NESN for the pregame show—the Sox were playing a split-squad spring training game in Fort Myers and several diehard fans asked very nicely if I would turn on the tube. Since they represented a majority of the current clientele, I agreed.

My two new customers jogged down the stairs as if late for a meeting. Both of them wore very nice suits, though probably not Antoine Bousquet originals. One was a solid dark green wool two-piece, the other a navy with a very thin raspberry pinstripe. Neither man wore an overcoat, despite the temperatures, and whatever they'd come to the Esposito for, it wasn't to watch baseball.

Green Suit—thin, tight as his ivory shirt, and brown-skinned as an acorn—called out as they passed the stage on the way to the bar.

"Darrow? Are you Elder Darrow?"

Pete Inklin, a drywall installer from Southie who sold a little pot on the side, though not in my bar, peeled off the end stool and up the stairs, from which I inferred he had something in his pockets he shouldn't have.

The two were clearly cops, with the arrogant certainty and the over-hard glares. The second one stood a couple paces to the left of Green Suit, as if worried I might take them out with one shot. He looked like a whisky barrel stuck onto two skinny legs.

I sipped my coffee and made a face—it was cold. Navy Suit took the expression personally.

"Don't start us out with the attitude, son."

He wasn't old enough to talk to me that way but before I could tee off on him, Green Suit held up a palm.

"We're from the Boston Police Department, Mr. Darrow. I'm Murray, he's Biggs. We understand you're a friend of Daniel Burton's."

Enough of a friend I knew no one ever called him by his entire first name, even his mother. I tilted my head.

"He drinks here. Once in a while."

"We'd like to ask you some questions about him," Murray said. "His hair was a thin layer of steel wool over his scalp, his lips almost invisibly thin."

"Here?" I looked around the bar. "Now?"

"Please."

Biggs glared at me, tiny eyes in folds of flesh, his head a smaller keg. I assumed it was police theater, good cop/bad cop.

"Don't I need a lawyer for something like that?"

I knew I didn't but I was playing for time. Biggs shook his head and snorted, predictable as a TV character.

"It's just questions," Murray said. "You don't have anything to worry about."

The implication being that he could find something, if I forced him to.

"You're not arresting me? You don't have anything to compel my cooperation?"

The skin around Murray's eyes tightened when he recognized the legalistic phrasing. I hadn't been hanging around Burton all this time without learning something.

The pair of baseball fans at the far end of the bar were signaling for refills.

"I'm running a business here, gentlemen. I can't drop everything because it's convenient for you."

Biggs rolled his eyes now, the sideshow of the brains and brawn pair.

"Saying no won't make it less likely we'll have to interrogate you." Murray tapped his fingers on the bar in a paradiddle.

The word was supposed to frighten me, the way the word had been deployed to frighten countless people, guilty and not, since September 2001. Except that, with the adventures Burton and I had come through, the death of Alison Somers and the murder of Timmy McGuire, I knew a good deal more than your average citizen about how the cops worked and what, in legal terms, I did and did not have to do. And I wasn't going to say another word to them until I talked to Burton.

"I'm afraid you're out of luck tonight," I said. "Unless you want to watch some baseball. Maybe it would be acceptable if I came in voluntarily, tomorrow or the next day? Say around ten?"

Murray didn't like me outflanking him. He pulled the cuffs of his shirt down.

"You know where to go?"

I quashed my impulse to be a smartass and nodded.

"Nine o'clock tomorrow morning," he said. "If I don't see you, there will be consequences."

I allowed him the last word and walked down the bar to serve my thirsty customers. What the hell kind of trouble was Burton in now? Or was this just part of the investigation into his beating up Bousquet?

# 5

The Cougar's engine turned over on the first try, which it damn well ought to after I'd dropped three grand at the mechanical restoration place in West Roxbury. The paint was faded from its original yellow to a characterless beige and measled with rust. The upholstery, where the vinyl had cracked, was patched with colored duct tape. But the engine now ran, as an oenophile had said about a cabernet I served him one night in the bar, as smooth as Baby Jesus in velvet pants.

I'd called Burton repeatedly last night and again this morning, but the fact he wasn't answering was no surprise. His opinion was that the best a phone call could bring him was information and the worst was bad news, which meant he never picked up. I understood how he felt about it but that didn't keep me from cursing him out. I wanted some direction from him before Murray and Biggs asked me anything. Whatever they wanted, it was unlikely to be favorable to Burton, though I didn't see what I could add to a discussion of his punching out Bousquet.

I circled the austere glass and steel building at Schroeder Plaza four or five times, looking for a space. Building police headquarters in a neighborhood where parking was almost nonexistent sent a message to the city, or at least I took it that way.

Finally, I squeezed the Cougar into a space vacated by a yellow Mini. Tight fit, but I'd driven a car in the city for too long to give a shit about bumpers, mine or anyone else's. Why would you call them that if they weren't supposed to bump?

Inside, the security line into the building wasn't too long. The officer on the stool at the metal detector was busting the balls of a Hispanic kid with about seventeen piercings, making him remove the studs and rings and balls one at a time until he quit alerting. The old woman with the boy wore an age-shiny black coat and carried a plastic purse. Her teenage charge sighed and rolled his eyes.

"I know. Right?" he said when he saw me watching.

Grandma cuffed him on the ear and once they were through the detector, dragged him in the direction of a sign that read "Fingerprints—This Way."

When I asked for Detective Murray at reception, the office had to scroll through an online directory to find his name. Over her shoulder, I saw him listed in the section for Professional Standards, which surprised me not at all. Maybe Murray and Biggs were fact-finding for Burton's disciplinary hearing. Unless they wanted my opinion on how not to arrest someone.

He didn't make me wait long. I'd barely gotten through the first article in the *Sports Illustrated* swimsuit edition some wag had slipped between the pages of a *Forbes* with Donald Trump on the cover. Murray stepped through a frosted glass door and beckoned. I handed him the magazine.

"Probably ought to keep this locked up, don't you think?"

He took it without comment and dropped it on the desk officer's blotter.

"Your bad-cop pal not sitting in today?"

I run my mouth when I'm nervous.

"Detective Biggs is busy this morning. It's just you and me." He opened the door to a small bare conference room. "You're not under any obligation to be here. I appreciate your coming in."

A flip-flop from last night's attitude. I looked up into the corners of the room.

"So. No recording, then."

He didn't replay, which was my answer.

He sat down across the table and pushed a bottle of water in my direction. I'd watched too much TV to even touch the bottle. I couldn't imagine what they might want my DNA but I was taking no chances.

"So what can I do for you, Detective?"

"Describe your relationship with Daniel Burton."

"Asked and answered about fifteen hours ago. He's a patron at a bar I own."

Murray mocked his disappointment.

"It's a little more than that, isn't it? I read the papers. I can use the Google just like anyone else."

I shrugged.

"There were a couple situations where our interests aligned. He helped me out."

"So you're friends."

"He comes to my bar, I serve him drinks. We talk. We don't go out on the town together."

Murray's eyes drew together, creating a horizontal wrinkle above his fleshy nose.

"Last time you spoke to him?"

"Couple days ago, maybe? He stopped in for a drink."

"After the Bousquet arrest?"

"After you suspended him, you mean?"

"Was he angry? Antsy? Talking about what he was going to do?"

"Are you and Biggs Anti-Corruption or Internal Affairs?" I said.

Murray seemed surprised I'd know the difference but Burton had dealt with Professional Standards before. Anti-Corruption investigated a cop's alleged criminal activity; Internal Affairs looked into complaints of misconduct.

"Neither here nor there," he said. "Though it does beg the question. Ever see Burton misuse his position?"

"Never."

And unless someone confronted me with incontrovertible evidence, I wouldn't believe it, either.

"So. How did he seem, then? The last time you saw him."

"Fine. Chastened a little. Preoccupied."

"With?"

"I think he said he was on his way to a pretrial conference. About the Antoine Bousquet thing."

Murray had a tell, a small flicker on the outer edge of his left

17

eyebrow. I'd seen it when I asked what division of Professional Standards he was in and I saw it again now. Was he surprised?

"And you haven't seen him since."

"Since Tuesday. Didn't you ask me that already?"

I understood the technique, re-asking questions to compare the answers, but he didn't show a lot of interest in my answers.

"What kind of trouble is he in?" I didn't expect an honest answer but maybe a hint.

"He ever talk about moonlighting? Paying work outside the job?"

This was the big worry?

"Nope. The only time we discussed his work was when I had an interest."

"Like the Alison Somers case."

Even now, hearing her name was like a knife to the gut. I nodded.

"Did he say anything about the Bousquet episode to you?"

"Only that he knew he'd screwed up. Look, I don't know where you're going but you ought to talk to some cops who know Burton. He's a good cop."

"He punched out someone during an arrest," Murray said.

"You don't have a temper? You know Bousquet said something to provoke him. OK, he took the bait. Doesn't make him a bad cop."

"This division of the police force, Mr. Darrow? We don't do the thin blue line." His voice was sharp, clinical.

"But I'm sure you run into people with an ax to grind. People high and low in the hierarchy might hate him but no one's going to say he's crooked."

Murray frowned, as if I'd insulted him somehow.

"OK. Let's get formal here. This is an interview, no jeopardy attached. I'd appreciate some answers for the record. No editorials."

"Law school, right? Suffolk, probably, since Harvard doesn't do nights."

He started to retort, then pinched his lips together. The recording.

"Agreed?"

"Sure. Ask your questions, officer."

"Detective."

His ego couldn't let the demotion slide.

"Would you like anything before we continue? Water? Coffee? Herbal tea?"

I smirked.

"Nothing, thanks. Fire away, metaphorically speaking."

"Your name is Elder Darrow?"

"Correct. No middle initial."

"You own and operate an eating and drinking establishment known as the Esposito."

"Also a jazz bar. But yes. I thought this conversation was about Burton."

He moved his fingertip to the next question on his printed list.

"You've known Daniel Burton how long?"

"Two and a half, three years."

"Nature of the relationship."

"I pour the drinks and he pays for them. We don't date, if that's what you're asking."

"Does he always pay?"

He looked eager for that answer but if they were trying to job Burton for taking a free drink, this was even more trivial than I thought.

"It's not unusual for a bartender to buy a patron a drink once in a while," I said carefully. "I'm sure it's happened to you."

"I don't drink."

Of course.

"He's never solicited a freebie or offered anything but money as payment."

"Does he ever work for you? Behind the bar? As a bouncer?"

I shook my head. This could not be about anything as silly as Burton moonlighting. Could it?

"Not even as a volunteer."

"Does he talk to you about his cases?"

"No. Except the Somers case, where I knew the victim. Oh. And the one where the guitar player was stabbed to death in my bar? Part of his duties, I assume."

Murray's robotic delivery made me wonder if I were undergoing some kind of high-tech lie detector test. I'd read about ones that analyzed voice patterns.

"And are you acquainted with Burton's wife?"

Was I ever.

"Sharon? Sure. We've met a few times."

Including a brief pre-Burton affair ten years ago. I'd never mentioned it to him and wouldn't tell Murray, either. His eyebrow twitched again.

"Nature of your relationship with her?"

"None." He was irritating me. "Are you trying to manufacture trouble here?"

He looked at his list.

"No relationship, then."

"Burton brought her by a couple of times. Four of us went out to dinner once at Jacob Wirth's. Outstanding spaetzli."

"That was it?"

"Are we done here, Murray? Because I don't get the sense I'm telling you anything you don't already know. What am I doing here?"

"Your friend never showed up for his pretrial conference. And he's been missing ever since. Just wondering if you could help us find him."

Burton was missing?

"Wait." I kept my face flat. "You guys suspended him, am I right? Which means you took his gun, his badge, and his ID. So he's not supposed to be working. But you're trying to keep track of him?"

Murray closed the folder on his list of questions and rested his hands on top, knuckles gnarled and misshapen: karate hands.

"We can make it easier on him if he just comes in," he said. "Let him know we want to talk to him. No one's trying to fuck him over."

Hard for me to believe missing a meeting was grounds for the threat but who knew?

I stood up and slid my chair back under the table, fishing for an exit line. If history held, I'd think of a great one on my way out of the building.

Murray escorted me out without another word. At the front desk I peeled off my visitor's badge and signed myself out. As I stepped out into the raw morning air, buttoning my coat, I couldn't decide if I should be worried. Burton wouldn't miss a meeting without good reason but Murray's focus on moonlighting added a darker tinge to his questions, too.

"Shit." I walked up to the Cougar.

An orange ticket was tucked under the wiper, an MBTA citation. When had the transit police started to enforce the parking laws in front of police headquarters?

I threw the ticket on the seat, climbed in, and drove back across the city to the Esposito.

OK, if Murray were investigating whether Burton moonlighted, why had he forced me to come into headquarters to talk? Because he would have known, if he hadn't come on heavy last night at the bar, I would have answered his questions then and there. Was it because he wanted me on record for something? Or maybe he wanted to talk while his partner wasn't around.

I turned down Mercy Street and into the alley behind my building, trying to wipe my mind. Time to get to work. Burton would have to take care of himself for now.

# 6

I tried calling Burton from the car again but he still didn't answer. It wasn't like him to disappear completely—usually he'd at least respond to a voice mail. I was curious if he knew why Professional Standards seemed more worried about whether he was working as a bouncer than whether he'd screwed the case against Antoine Bousquet.

I slotted the Cougar into my reserved spot next to the big green dumpster behind my building and walked up the alley to the front door, jingling my keys. The pleasures of owning the Esposito, of transforming it from a dive bar into something more classy, were still new enough to enjoy, though I wondered sometimes whether I'd still enjoy it when the transformation was done.

More importantly, in all the time I'd owned the place, I'd only slipped into a bad drunk once and that made me superstitious about the benefits. When I bought it, I'd taken the chance that something productive to do with my days might help settle my life, give me the stability to control my drinking. I hadn't expected to come to enjoy the daily routine, having a schedule, knowing my customers and Marina depended on me.

All those warm and fuzzy feelings dissipated when I rounded the corner out of the alley onto Mercy Street and saw who was waiting for me by the front door. The only positive I could think of in seeing Sharon there was that she might know where Burton was and why he wasn't talking to anyone.

Sharon Burton, née Jansky, leaned against the Esposito's steel front door as if to make sure no one got inside ahead of her. I wondered if she was going to revert to what she liked to call her "Hunky maiden name" once the divorce was final. Assuming it ever was.

At five-six, she was seven or eight inches shorter than me. Except for the spectacularly large breasts, she was leaner and tighter, too. Though now that I looked, the breasts seemed less spectacular than I remembered.

She wore a dark green wool jumpsuit with epaulets that looked like a uniform from the flight deck of the Starship Enterprise under an open sheepskin vest, a costume so odd it had to be fashionable. She slapped an eight-by-ten manila envelope against her thigh like an instrument of domination.

"Sharon."

"Do you have any idea where the Super Cop's gotten himself to? He's not sleeping at his apartment and he's not answering his phone."

"Nice to see you too," I said. "Come in and I'll make you some coffee."

"That's still your solution to everything? A nice cup of coffee?"

Better than the bottle of Scotch it used to be, I thought. I couldn't say now what had attracted me to her almost eleven years ago. I'd been drinking hard but that was no excuse for my lowering my guard that far. We'd been together a grand total of eleven days, with minimal emotional involvement and maximum sexual. It all blew up into a slap-fighting argument in the middle of the FleetCenter that almost got both of us arrested.

Burton didn't know any of this, unless Sharon had told him. Her extroverted nature must have been what attracted him but if I'd known him when they'd gotten together, I would have tried to warn him. She was the most self-involved woman I'd ever met, an absolute sleight-of-hand artist at getting whatever she wanted.

As we walked inside and then down the steel stairs, she caught me looking at her breasts. Something *was* different.

"I had the reduction done," she said. "What do you think?"

Discussing her breasts with the wife of one of my few good friends was not on my agenda today, even if she would soon be his ex-wife. At the bottom of the staircase, she grabbed my arm. I was worried that she was going to offer to let me test their heft but she only handed me a photo.

"Old on the left, new on the right. What do you think?"

She didn't have to tell me which was which. It was obvious why someone who cared about appearance as much as she did had undergone the surgery. The oversized originals were slumped and striated where weight had stretched the skin. In a museum, the picture would have been called The Inevitability of Gravity. On the right hand side, they were a more appropriate size for her body, turned up pertly at the tips.

"The doc did an amazing job." She wet her lips. "All the scars are underneath, so nothing shows. Unless I want it to."

I tossed the photo onto the bar, more saddened by her neediness than titillated. Burton had probably paid for the pectoral update, another reason I was glad he was getting out from under. They'd been married for seven years but only in the last eighteen months had he been talking about the marriage as a net loss in terms of intimacy.

I went back to the original question.

"I have no idea where he's gotten himself to. I saw him Tuesday, in here. He was on his way to a meeting."

"Shit." She bit a collagen-thickened lip and laid the envelope on the bar. "Look, hon. When you see him? These are the final papers. He needs to sign them and have them notarized."

I stepped behind the bar and started to assemble a pot of coffee. Looked like the divorce was back on.

Marina came in the door, down the stairs, and walked into the kitchen without acknowledging Sharon. The burners on the grill snapped on and the fryer started to sizzle.

I emptied the glass carafe into the coffeemaker and flicked on the button.

"You know he was suspended, right? I don't know the next time I'm going to see him."

I didn't like her assuming I'd do her work for her.

"You're still asshole buddies, though. Just hold onto them. He'll be in sooner or later, if I know him. They need to get to the lawyer by the end of the month."

Sharon did not settle for a no once she'd decided something should happen a certain way. Either she'd heard the word a lot as a child or not enough.

"No guarantees," I said. "If and when he shows, I'll pass them on."

Burton wasn't kidding himself about the state of his marriage but pleasing Sharon wouldn't be high on his list of priorities. Not signing would screw her up more than him.

"Good enough." She sniffed. "I suppose."

Marina stepped out of the kitchen.

"Elder. That halibut from J. J. Hook. Did it come yet?"

She stiffened when she saw Sharon was still there. Marina knew who she was but I doubted she had anything to say to her.

To prove me wrong, Marina picked up the photo of Sharon's breasts from the bar.

"Must have been a relief to unload all that silicone." She placed the photo face down on the bar with a grimace, as if it was more pornographic than clinical, and returned to the kitchen without waiting for my answer to her question.

I pulled in the corners of my mouth, which were threatening to smile.

"Bitch." Sharon looked at me with her luminous green-blue eyes—colored contacts—shimmering. "Why is he always telling people bad things about me?"

"Cut it out, Sharon."

Her sorrow dried like a puddle in the sun.

"Is he fucking her yet?" she said. "She looks like one of those nice Catholic girls."

The curse dropped from her lips like chewing tobacco drool, unexpected and disgusting. For someone who worried so much about how she looked, her speech and her manners could be pure white trash.

"Did you want some coffee, Sharon?" I was sure my try at being civil would be lost.

"I don't drink in dive bars, sweetie." She pulled the sheepskin vest in tight around her new equipment and pointed with her chin at the envelope on the bar.

25

"Get him to sign the fucking papers, please. Before the twenty-eighth? I'm sure he doesn't want this shit show to drag on any longer than it already has."

Finally. Something we could agree on.

# 7

Several hours later, in the afternoon doldrums, my only customer an unemployed long-haul trucker from Cotuit, I was still feeling bruised by my collision with Sharon. She was a reminder of my lousy record with relationships and the fact that my current romantic life was dead.

Since Susan Voisine had broken it off last year, I'd conducted a run of one- and two-night stands that made me wonder if being an alcoholic had left me capable of only glancing versions of love. Sober now, for however long I managed, I thought I might be able to handle a little more emotional complexity. Sharon only reminded me how little I'd been doing to find someone who agreed.

The beginning chords of Nelly Furtado sounded out in the kitchen. A few seconds later, Marina stepped out, untying her apron. Her sallow face was flushed with the heat. She looked grim.

"I need to step out for an hour," she said. "I'll be back in time for the dinner rush."

I ducked my head to see the kitchen clock. Four-ten. Nothing got going until six or so.

"Fine," I said. "Is Carmen all right?"

She hung her apron on a hook.

"An hour at the most. All the prep is done."

As she climbed the stairs, buttoning her coat, I wondered if I shouldn't ignore the terms of my father's will and tell her about the bequest, even if she wouldn't have access to it yet. If Carmen was going to need outside care, at least Marina would know there'd be funds to cover it. Thomas had delayed my inheritance to give me the chance to make the Esposito succeed but I didn't understand why he'd held back Carmen's.

And thinking about what would happen saddened me—Marina worked here mainly because the schedule let her look after Carmen during the mornings. The money from Thomas meant I'd lose her too. I knew she wanted to go back to school.

I refilled the trucker's beer and slid the shaker down to him when he asked for it, though the practice of using salt to raise the head on draft beer appalled me. Anyone who did that deserved hypertension. I tried not to get irritated about things like that anymore, like people putting ice cubes in their wine. If I let everything that irked me get to me, I'd always be got.

The landline at the Esposito existed on the assumption that anyone looking for someone in my bar wanted an actual Yellow Pages number to call. It rarely rang but when I saw the caller ID this time, I felt relieved. If he was in trouble, at least he was in touch.

"Danny B. Where in the northeastern quadrant of hell have you been?"

He sneezed in my ear, then laughed gratingly.

"Wouldn't you like to know. I take it that means people are wondering what's become of me?"

"Where are you?"

"So someone has been looking?"

"Only your soon-to-be ex-wife. And the Boston Police Department."

"Sharon? Fuck her. All she wants from me is the ink from my pen. So to speak. Did she show you the new tits?"

"Pictures. Burton . . ."

"And surely the whole department isn't looking for me? They were the ones who took away my toys and told me to go home."

My irritation swelled. When he got off onto one of those manic rants, it was useless to try and interrupt. He'd probably been on a bender.

"Actually it was just the cops who investigate the fuckup cops. Or the ones who do bad things. Which one were you again?"

"Oh, those cops." I heard him grin. "So basically nothing important's happened."

"They did haul me down to the station for an interview."

If I thought that would make him feel guilty, I was wrong.

"Ought to be more careful who you hang out with, then. But seriously. No gorgeous women come looking for me? Russian models?"

"Seriously? No. I thought Professional Standards was going to push me about Bousquet but it was something else. What are they after?"

Silence, then a dry laugh.

"I am done with that asshole. I couldn't care less if he falls into a pothole and drowns. Talk to you."

Then he hung up. It was all I could do not to slam the receiver down. He hadn't even acknowledged the question, let alone tried to answer it. So why had he called? To find out if a Russian model really had come looking for him? The joke was flat and though I'd always feel like I owed him something for helping out in the Alison Somers case, I was beginning to lose interest in the games he played.

\* \* \* \* \*

Marina wasn't back by six-fifteen. My irritation with Burton had faded somewhat—he wasn't my brother and half the time I wasn't even sure he thought I was his friend. What I owed him wasn't going to float the relationship forever.

As the dinner hour approached, my clientele increased to a couple dozen people scattered around the tables, eating bar snacks and drinking, listening to Christian McBride play with SuperBass, a live recording from the bar I'd like to be some day, Sculler's. At least one obvious tourist couple was scanning the paper menu and the chalkboard and I was either going to have to tell them the kitchen was closed or go out back and try and cook myself.

But as the male member of the pair, a sixtyish gent in full L.L. Bean—khaki pants, madras shirt, boat shoes with no socks—waved me over, the street door opened up and Marina descended the stairs, wearing a long-billed cap she hadn't had on when she left.

Relieved, I only paid her half a look as she passed, wondering more what month of the year the old guy in his boating attire thought it was.

"We'll split the calamari appetizer," he said. "Separate plates. And I'll have a bowl of the clam chowder. Be sure it's hot."

"Just a salad for me." His female companion was less brand-identified, in black wool slacks, a red turtleneck sweater, and suede ankle boots. "And another round. Please."

"Oyster crackers," he said. "Several bags."

Nothing I couldn't have handled myself. I made another Rob Roy and poured a glass of chardonnay—guess who got what—and walked back into the kitchen.

Marina's back was to me. She stirred a steaming pot. The hat hung on the coat rack.

"Couple orders," I said. "Nothing complicated."

I clipped the slip into the metal ring and rotated it to her side of the counter. She didn't turn around but when she dropped her free hand, I saw she was holding a bag of ice.

"Marina?"

She laid the long wooden spoon across the top of the pot and turned around. The left side of her face, from the middle of her cheek up to her fast-closing eye, was swollen, turning dark.

"Holy shit. What happened to you?"

She shook her head and repacked the ice in a dish towel.

"It was an accident," she said.

Had Carmen whacked her? Intentionally or not? Marina had made it sound as if the old woman might be losing her marbles but this was a worrisome escalation of that. And knowing Carmen, she'd feel terrible if she understood what she'd done.

"Carmen?" I said.

Marina half-shrugged, as if to say I could think what I wanted, and turned back to stir the chowder.

"Calamari will be about three minutes," she said. "They want that first, right?"

# 8

In the Esposito's earliest days, when I closed on Sundays, I used to try and fill the day with a catering gig or a private party, as much to keep myself busy and the bottle out of my mouth as for the extra cash. These days, I tried to take the day off to relax, though I preferred to get up and out of the apartment. An hour at the kitchen table with the newspaper and coffee was about all the sitting I could stand. This morning, I was less relaxed than usual since I had an actual date, the first in a while.

Mid-February is always iffy in southern New England, with precipitation as likely to fall as icy rain as in a snowstorm. Blizzards were not unheard of. But once in a great while, a gorgeous clear blue sky day like today snuck in like a bastard child and teased everyone's late winter mood away. That the bonus fell on a weekend day was lagniappe, and everyone and his dog was out walking on Mass. Ave.

Pedro's was on the Red Line near Central Square but on a day like this, the two and a half miles didn't seem like too long a walk. Even the melting slush seemed hopeful as I crossed the Longfellow Bridge. Some people called it the MIT Bridge but I'd spent a year and a half matriculating at that other Cambridge college and preferred to call it the Harvard Bridge.

The restaurant was small and dim, an unprepossessing storefront on the corner of Albany Street, its wide picture windows steamed opaque. I stepped inside and shucked my jacket, sweating lightly from the walk, and raised my hand to Kathleen, holding down a booth in back against the feral stares of people waiting in line.

"Hey." I slid in opposite her.

31

We'd met over the counter at the bank she worked at, when I'd brought the weekend receipts in one Monday morning. Over the course of a couple of months, we'd traded pleasantries until I got adventurous enough to ask her out. She'd checked out my left hand, smiled, and wrote her phone number on the back of my deposit receipt. This was the first time we'd met outside the bank and my stomach felt pleasantly tight.

Kathleen chose the restaurant, which suggested she lived somewhere within walking distance—parking anywhere nearby was practically impossible and the T wasn't reliable on Sundays. I assumed she might live in Cambridge from the way she was dressed today in a long rust-colored skirt, a chunky gray sweater, and dangling silver earrings. Her long black hair, threaded with silver, was braided down her back.

It was ten-fifteen but I thought we'd agreed on ten-thirty.

"Hope I'm not late."

She raised her mug with both hands, elbows propped on the table.

"Two sips' worth, maybe. I got here early. I didn't know how busy they were going to be." She smiled at the line by the door. "It just filled up."

"Everybody loves Sunday brunch," I said. "Plus the T station's right down the street."

I was babbling, out of practice with light conversation that didn't take place with a bar between me and the person I was talking to.

Her eyes were an unusual shade between lavender and blue. The earrings tinkled softly as she turned the smile on me.

"I'm not going to make a run for it, though." She pushed one of the menus in my direction. "We should probably order."

My throat was dry. I reached for the water glass and drank.

"Uh, Elder. That was mine."

I blushed. There was only one on the table.

"Sorry. I'll buy you another one."

The waitress spared me further embarrassment by appearing. I nodded to Kathleen.

"Cheese omelet with mushrooms and onions," she said. "Side of the hash. Wheat toast."

The mute waitress turned to me.

"Two poached on the hash, please. Blueberry muffin, tomato juice. And more water. Thanks."

She nodded, swiveled for the kitchen.

"Confess," Kathleen said. "You were worried I was going to order the vegan scramble."

I smiled as she retrieved her water glass and took a sip.

"I may live in Cambridge," she said. "But I'm not exactly of it."

I had no snappy reply to that and the conversation stalled for a moment. Then we both spoke at once.

"No," she said. "Go ahead."

"I was going to ask what you do when you're not working. Hobbies? Knitting, sailing, raising miniature Chihuahuas?"

The waitress slid a mug of black coffee and a glass of water in front of me, sloshing but not spilling. She refilled Kathleen's.

"Actually, I'm a competitive shooter—trap and skeet. Some pistol but mostly long guns."

So much for the Cambridge clichés.

"Interesting. Were you in the service?"

She gave me a lopsided smirk.

"As in, how did a nice girl like you end up with such a macho pursuit? Would you believe my father taught me?"

Talking about fathers on a first date seemed a little fraught but I went with it.

"You're young enough . ." I fumbled with what I meant to say. "Your father would have been Vietnam era, then?"

"He wasn't military either, Elder. We used to go out to the quarries in Milford to shoot."

"Was he a cop?"

Her face closed up and her eyes got cold.

"You know, there are other people who like guns and shooting." She put down the mug and stared at me. "Actually, my father was a criminal. You remember the Quincy Armored robbery?"

It had been a year ago, maybe two, a much smaller job than the famous Plymouth Mail Truck robbery in the sixties.

"Your father robbed armored trucks for a living?"

33

Burton was going to get a laugh out of this.

Kathleen frowned as the waitress placed our food in front of us. She reached for the salt, shook it over her omelet, then picked up the wooden-topped Cholula bottle.

"No. He wasn't involved at all but they accused him of it."

I broke the yolks of my poached eggs into the hash and waited for the rest of the story. Her voice was husky, reliving some injustice.

"They claimed he was the financier. That he would supply the money up front for people who needed equipment: guns, uniforms, explosives. And get paid a percentage of the take."

"They sent him to jail?"

Her head was down, concentrating on her breakfast. The story interested me, though I wasn't going to press for details. Even as a child, no one would have found it strange if her father worked odd hours. Lots of people worked shifts for the gas company or the phone company or the paper mills.

"It was a misunderstanding. He was killed in an arrest—wrong place at the wrong time."

"I'm sorry."

I wasn't sure I could have imagined a brunch date getting weirder faster. She whipped her head up, eyes shiny.

"He wasn't a thief, Elder."

"I believe you. We can't always pick how our family stories come out, can we?"

Not that my history was anything to brag about, despite a family tree that stretched back to the Mayflower. I'd been a degenerate alcoholic for a very long time before scratching my way back toward some normalcy.

Kathleen ate several bites of hash before she spoke, more lightly this time.

"Sorry. I don't usually go all confessional on a first date." She smiled and my chest eased. "You have a nice way of listening."

"Bartender's secret. They teach it the first year."

She nodded for the attempt if not for the joke.

"Give yourself a little credit. On me." She wiped her mouth with a napkin. "So what you're doing . . you like it? The bar and the people?

The music?"

I'd talked about the Esposito on my trips to the bank and I was sure I'd said more than she wanted to hear about auditioning bands and putting on the shows. What I hadn't said anything about was the aggravation of dealing with drunks, the slim profits, the many slow nights.

"Most of what I care about is the music. The bar's really just an excuse to get the music out there."

She was a good listener too and I wanted to think of a way to see her again. She mopped up the remains of the hash and ketchup with a toast corner, eating as if it were a pleasure.

"I'm more of a rock and roll girl myself. You ever get to the Tea Party? Or the Rat, when it was open?"

I shook my head. Even if I had, I probably wouldn't remember.

"Different crowd than yours, I'm sure." She smiled at me. "Not that I'm not musically catholic."

I took that as a hint of future interest. We'd drunk as much coffee as we could, prolonging our exit until the waitress slapped a paper check down in front of me and spoke her first words.

"You guys are all done, right?"

Kathleen nodded at the crowd in the doorway. I laid down some bills on the check.

"We'd best get out of here before someone lynches us. You like to walk?"

"Good idea. Especially since we'll be back to sleet and snow tomorrow."

"Thank you, Mr. Weather Channel." She tucked her hand in the crook of my arm as we slipped out through the doorway.

"It is kind of funny, you working in a bank, though."

The warm sun, a full stomach, the pleasure of her company had lulled me. As soon as I said it, I wished I could recall the words.

She dropped my arm, stopped dead on the sidewalk.

"What do you mean? Because my father was a criminal? I told you he didn't do anything."

"Nothing. I didn't mean anything at all."

"So I shouldn't be trusted around money? Is that it? Or am I trying to make amends in some twisted way?"

She stared at me, her breathing obvious.

"I'm sorry," I said. "Mouth over mind. Just ignore me."

She shook her head.

"Do you have any idea how long it took me to understand that being a crook wasn't some kind of genetic gift? Can you imagine being six years old and trying to shoplift a doll because you thought you were supposed to?"

I shook my head, in full retreat now. "No. I can't."

"Let me tell you, then." She squared up to face me. A passing couple moved away from us, whispering.

"I imagine it's like being born to a father who expected you to go into the family business when you grew up. Like maybe investment banking. Something like that?"

I didn't know whether to be impressed or pissed off as she wheeled and stalked off down the sidewalk.

# 9

I didn't ask Kathleen how she knew so much about me and my family, though I had to assume some Googling was involved. The Darrow surname had been all over Boston for centuries, both in the eponymous bank of my parents' families and in Thomas's behind-the-scenes involvement in running the city. Of course, my escapades with Burton had gotten some minor press too and biographical details showed up in those reports. Not that it was possible to hide anymore. People were more suspicious if they couldn't find you online.

After we parted on the sidewalk—she hadn't answered the question of whether she'd come to the Esposito next week to hear music—the walk back to my apartment felt much longer than the walk to Pedro's had been.

As if I needed more things to worry about, the street-level door to my apartment building was wide open. I kept reminding Mrs. Rinaldi to pull the door tight when she came in because the latch was loose. Given the prevalence of street crime all over the city, I didn't take safety, mine or my tenants', for granted.

A brick sat behind the foot of the black iron railing. The cleaners used it to prop the door open when they mopped the hallway. I hefted it and pushed open the door with my other hand. The sunlight had faded under the weight of the afternoon clouds but I had to wait for my eyes to adjust—the light bulb in the foyer had burned out last week and I hadn't gotten around to replacing it.

"Don't brick me, bro'." A high-intensity flashlight beam shot out from under the staircase, blinding me.

"Jesus Christ, Burton. Get that out of my eyes. Where have you been?"

He clicked it off, leaving sparks in my vision, and stepped out of the shadows. I reached behind me and pulled the door to, hard.

"Come on upstairs. I don't want to disturb Mrs. Rinaldi."

"Won't she be at Mass?"

"She goes to the early one."

Up on the third floor landing, I fished out my keys and undid the locks, including the dead bolt I'd installed last year. As I flicked on the lights, Burton pushed past me toward the bathroom, unzipping as he went. His stream splashed loudly and unmusically in the bowl.

"Shut the door, will you please? I'm not your wife."

The afternoon nap I'd been contemplating was clearly off the agenda, but Burton wouldn't have shown up here if he didn't have something on his mind. I was glad to see he'd surfaced but wondered what he wanted from me.

The commode flushed and he limped out into the kitchen.

"What happened to you?" I said.

He moved gingerly, and a wide scrape decorated the side of his right cheek. Bandages covered the knuckles of his left hand, not the one he'd punched Antoine Bousquet with. His eyes were red-rimmed and his face was pale, as if there wasn't enough oxygen in his blood. Either exhaustion or hangover. He yawned and his jaw cracked.

"You got anything to eat? I'm so hungry my belt buckle's carving initials into my backbone."

The cornpone shtick made me roll my eyes. He was trying to misdirect a conversation we hadn't even started.

I walked into the living room, punched the remote for the Bose, and Johnny Hartman started singing "Lush Life." Good enough. When I walked back into the kitchen, Burton was rummaging in the refrigerator drawers.

"Come out of there," I said. "We both know you can barely cook a hot dog."

He pulled his head out of the vegetable crisper and grinned.

"Baked, boiled, or fried?"

I inspected the shelves. I usually did my grocery shopping on Sundays but not today.

"I got nothing. Oatmeal, probably."

"Whatever. I'm empty."

I pulled out a sauce pan, measured in three parts of water, one part steel cut oats, and wondered if I could get him to be straight with me.

"Half an hour. In the meantime, you can tell me what you've been doing. The Professional Standards guys were pretty put out that they didn't know where you were."

He turned his back, walked over to the coffee maker, and filled the carafe.

"I'm suspended, remember? If I can't work, they can't tell me what to do. If you really want to know, I was helping out a friend."

"Which is why you look like someone tossed you out of the back of a moving pickup?"

He poured in the water and looked at me over his shoulder.

"Sorry, Elder. Personal business."

His twisted grin suggested I wouldn't like what he would say if he did explain. He took the grinder out of the drawer and the canister of coffee beans—Blue Mountain, the good stuff—out of the freezer. He measured out enough to wake the whole block.

"If it's personal, why are Murray and Biggs so concerned about it? Sounded like they were worried you were moonlighting."

"Those the IA guys? Because if it's those two? They couldn't find each other's dick in a porno theater. None of this is official business."

Burton's lone ranger history was too rich and varied for me to believe his bullshit. I salted the water to make it boil faster.

"You're moonlighting while you're on suspension? Is that allowed?"

"Just helping out a friend," he insisted. "Her cousin's gone missing."

"OK." I gave up. "You're not going into detail. Yet here you are. For what?"

He flicked the switch on the coffee maker and it started to gurgle.

"I know it's a pain in the ass. But I need you to keep covering for me. If anyone else comes looking?"

"More than I already have, you mean. What does that look like?"

"You still own that camp on the lake? You didn't sell it off when the old man died?"

"Told you any number of times. You're welcome to use it. You don't want anyone to know you're there?"

The coffee burbled to a stop and the machine peeped.

"I only need it for a couple nights."

I stirred the oatmeal, added raisins and walnuts, covered it up again.

"Have at it," I said. "You know where the keys are?"

"I've been up there already. These past couple weeks."

Typical Burton. Ask forgiveness, don't ask permission.

"I hope you've been enjoying yourself."

"Not exactly."

"You don't want to tell me what this is about?"

"Better you don't know," he said.

I'd always trusted him before, though his tendency to go solo worried me. The only way I found out Alison Somers was murdered was through his willingness to buck the department's command structure. That had cost him, and so could this, whatever it was.

"You can tell people I was there," he said.

"Past tense? Including the people who've already quizzed me about where you were?"

"All you have to say to anybody is that you agreed to let me stay there. You didn't know if I actually went."

"OK. That's all you need?"

He poured coffee for both of us.

"You're going to be hearing more negative shit about me in the next week or so. I'd rather it be a surprise, in case anyone comes asking questions. That way no one can claim you knew more than you do."

Murray and Biggs were still my primary candidates for making Burton-related trouble.

"Mushroom time," I said.

He nodded.

"But I won't feed you shit. Just keep you in the dark."

"You prepared Marina for any of this?"

He shook his head.

"We're all done. She refuses to come near me until I quit the booze. And that's not going to happen."

I suspected Marina's problem had more to do with Burton's inability to let go of Sharon. Marina had enough to worry about with Carmen. She didn't need another dependent.

I turned off the burner, spooned cereal into bowls, set out butter, maple syrup, milk. We sat down.

"Another topic. Sharon came by."

"You told me that." He plunged his spoon into the oatmeal. "Like I need her bullshit in the middle of all this. What's the latest?"

I'd brought the papers home with me. Burton stared at the return address, the six-part name of a law firm in Norwood.

"Seriously. She got around to drawing up the papers."

He lapsed into deepest silence, staring out the kitchen window at the blue-gray sky. The two of them had been backing and forthing for a year and a half and my guess was that Burton was still ambivalent. I had no idea what Sharon might be thinking, papers notwithstanding.

Her complaints about the marriage, what Burton had shared, were typical of public service spouses—a focus on the welfare of others over family, strange hours, low pay—but she had to have known what she was marrying into. Both her father and grandfather had been firefighters and her brother was a State Trooper in Maine.

Burton's spoon clanked in the bottom of the bowl. He picked up the envelope and, straining with its thickness, tore it in half.

"I don't have time for this right now."

"All righty, then." Nothing I could think of to say seemed helpful.

He leaned across the table, serious as a priest.

"I'm trying to keep everybody clear, Elder. Remember. All you know is what I told you. You lent me the camp on Otter Lake. I can clear things up with IA—they're used to me being a flake."

"Shit, Burton."

I felt loyalty to the man and it pissed me off that he wouldn't let me show it.

"Shit could hit the fan as early as tomorrow," he said. "Stick to what you know and you'll be fine."

He stood up and arched his back, massaged his kidneys.

"Better get going." He flashed teeth. "Long drive back to New Hampshire."

"What do I say to Marina?"

She was going to worry, regardless what he thought.

"Whatever you think she needs to hear. She can do better than me. I know it and she knows it."

That sounded a little fatalistic for my taste. I hoped he wasn't launching himself into another professionally suicidal operation. He'd done his job on the Bousquet case, regardless of the aftermath; I hoped what he was doing didn't have anything to do with that.

"Don't be stupid, Burton. All right? None of this is worth your job."

"That option might be long gone by now." He started for the front hall. "You're only safe if you never open a door."

"What are you, now, Yoda?"

He shook his head and closed the door behind him. As I cleaned up the kitchen, I had a gut-deep sense that he was in worse trouble than he knew. And listening to his resignation about it gave me no confidence he was going to handle it well. The question for me was what, if anything, I could do to help.

\* \* \* \* \*

After Burton left, I finished the pot of coffee and thought about whether I'd screwed up things with Kathleen beyond repair. She was sharp and funny and I had the sense we might be able to connect if we could get over my clumsiness. I decided to give her a few days before I called her.

The phone rang and I cursed under my breath for the loss of a quiet Sunday afternoon.

"Mickey Barksdale," Murray said into my ear. He hadn't apologized for calling me on Sunday.

"Heard the name. Can't place it offhand."

Now I really hoped he didn't have me on some kind of high-tech lie detector.

Mickey Barksdale was what I liked to think of as Burton's evil doppelganger. They'd grown up down the street from each other in Charlestown and were right about the same age. Mickey had, to put it politely, taken a divergent path: he was the closest thing to a native-born mob boss left in the city.

Not that Boston had much left in the way of serious organized crime. A series of internecine rivalries a dozen years or so ago had chopped the city into smaller territories. No one was in total charge the way an old-time regional crime boss like Raymond Patriarca had been. Whitey Bulger was the closest historically to Mickey—a homegrown thug—but Whitey had turned out to be as greedy, disloyal, and amoral as Donald Trump. According to Burton, Mickey owned an actual passion for the welfare of the people in his neighborhoods, most of whom had little other power in the city. Kind of a Tip O'Neill of the underworld. Micky maintained a ruthless focus on local control of most of the city's criminal activity.

"Burton's childhood pal," Murray said. "Grew up in the same parish, went to grade school together."

"Sounds like you're trying to write the Bulger-FBI story all over again." I sat down in an armchair and looked out the bay window at Commonwealth Avenue. "Burton lived in Charlestown. That's as close as they get."

Though I knew better.

Murray couldn't have lived in the city long if he didn't understand how neighborhoods worked. Twenty-first century Boston was as Balkanized as it had ever been. The ethnic makeup of an area might have changed—Latinos in East Boston instead of Italians, Caribbeans in Hyde Park instead of middle-class whites—but the boundaries were rigid. You might hate your neighbor but you'd still stick up for him over someone from another part of the city.

"It wouldn't be," Murray said. "As you point out, the first time someone in law enforcement decided their personal ties were more important than a sworn oath."

Murray's voice took on a prissy messianic edge, like one of the street preachers on the Common. Maybe working in a division that investigated other cops attracted self-anointed defenders of the faith. He was that, and a prick to boot, but the questions about Mickey opened up what IA was investigating all over again.

"That's not the Burton I know," I said. "But I don't suppose you guys put too much stock in loyalty."

"Maybe loyalty to something bigger than your schoolyard chum."

Apparently we weren't going to move beyond that. I pressed the button that dropped the call and cut him off.

# 10

I got into the bar a little early the next morning because I was out of coffee at home. A little after nine, the street door opened, surprising me, and Marina walked in almost two hours before she normally arrived. The lights were up as high was they went and from my perch on the stool behind the bar, the bruising on her face looked worse than Friday, more purple and yellow. The swelling around her eye had gone down.

She set a brown paper shopping bag from Whole Foods on the bar, shucked her windbreaker, and hung it up. Today she wore a sleeveless black jersey top and a loose pair of beige cotton pants, as if she expected the kitchen to be hotter than usual. When she picked up the bag again, she winced.

When she looked at me, I saw the broken capillaries in her eye.

"How's Carmen?" I said.

"She's fine." Snapping was unusual for her—she was more likely to sulk when she was pissed. "She didn't have anything to do with this."

I touched my own cheek, under the eye.

"Did you get a doctor to look at it?"

"Subconjunctive hemorrhage," she said. "Ugly but harmless."

A round imprint showed in the middle of the bruise, like a ring. But if Marina didn't want to talk about something, I couldn't force it.

"We need to talk about something else," I said. "Once you get the kitchen set up."

I'd decided to tell her about Thomas's bequest to Carmen. Even though she wouldn't have access to it right away, knowing it was

45

coming would make life easier. She'd have more options for dealing with Carmen's diminishing states. If it meant she left the Esposito, I'd have to roll with it.

"Whatever." She disappeared into the kitchen.

The rubber seal on the refrigerator cracked as she yanked it open to store what she'd bought. I unfolded the newspaper on the bar to see if anything exciting was happening in Spring Training. And in the back of my mind, I turned over the easiest possible way to break the news that she was soon going to have a couple million dollars at her disposal.

\* \* \* \* \*

I trusted Marina enough at this point that sometimes in the middle of the day, if I felt like I needed to get out, I'd head up to the coffee bar on the corner of Mercy and Holbrook, see some other people than the solo sad-sacks who drank in the afternoon. I was coming to a new stage in my sobriety, where I judged people harshly for things I'd been guilty of myself for so long.

"Mr. Giaccobi."

I nodded to the short old man behind the counter as I walked in. The café looked as if it had been dropped into place from the North End, though we were miles from that neighborhood. The wall was covered with aerial photographs of Sicily and tourist posters of Rome and Firenze. One whole section was devoted to tacked-up crayon drawings of stick figures and houses. Giaccobi's granddaughter had studied early childhood at Smith and returned to the old neighborhood to teach first grade.

Giaccobi himself, brown as a walnut and gnarled, carried over a tiny white cup with a doppio espresso and two miniature biscotti balanced on the edge of the saucer.

"Mr. Darrow. You are well today?"

I'd asked him several times to call me Elder, small businessman to small businessman, but Giaccobi had a very formal nature. I handed him a five, waved off the change, took that first fine sip, and chased the bitterness with a bite of cookie. I was still considering the least intrusive way to tell Marina about the money when a man and a woman walked into the café, stepped to my table, and seated themselves as if I'd been waiting for them.

Giaccobi raised an eyebrow as he looked at me. I shook my head, though I recognized the woman from newspaper photos. Not her companion, though he shared similar enough features to be a sibling.

"You know who I am, then." Her voice was a caw, dark and sharp.

I took another sip and finished the first biscotti, chasing the crumb lodged in my throat with a slug of sparkling water.

"Viktoriya Lin. Antoine Bousquet's . . . friend."

Her eyes turned up at the outside and her mouth was generous. I guessed she was Chinese but a prep school classmate had assured me once that only another Asian could distinguish for sure. Whatever her ethnicity, the woman was exquisite: smooth white skin unmarred by moles or blemishes, a tight lithe body sheathed in a one-piece black cat suit with an embroidered vest layered over the top. The bleached yellow straw of her prickly hairdo was a jarring note, maybe an attempt to distract from her stunning beauty.

"His whore," she said. "You can be frank. That's what I was to him. For a time."

My heart rate was jacked, nothing to do with the espresso. I toyed with the almost-empty cup.

"But you can call me Vicky." She pouted. "Will you? No one ever calls me what I want to be called."

Her male companion was either high or intellectually challenged. Maybe both. The light in his eyes was dim and he twitched in his chair as if he found it difficult to sit still. Thick through the shoulders and thighs, he wore cheap jeans and a stretched out T-shirt from a local radio station, a bone Hawaiian fish hook pendant on a cord around his neck. His features were Asian too, but coarser, as if his side of the family sprang from the other side of the tracks.

"You feel like you need a body guard," I said.

I nodded at the hulk, tilted the last of the espresso into my mouth, and shuddered at the cold bitterness. Vicky looked surprised.

"He's my brother."

And he's heavy. But no explanation of his presence beyond that.

"Edward," she said, as if talking to a trained dog. "Meet Mr. Elder Darrow."

He emitted a sound partway between a cough and a grunt. She beckoned at Mr. Giaccobi.

"Tea, please. Green."

The old man's face showed nothing but I'd bet nothing had surprised him since World War II. He trundled off behind the counter. Vicky turned back to me.

"Your cook is very loyal. She did not want to tell us where to find you."

I tensed. Vicky was some kind of threat, though I didn't understand how yet.

"I'm going to assume you didn't try and bully her. Considering that you seem to want something from me."

She laughed airily, dismissing my concerns.

"She was quite amenable."

Deliberately not saying how they'd persuaded her. My stomach muscles tightened.

"You've found me. What do you want?"

She held up a polished pearl fingernail as Mr. Giaccobi set a celadon teapot and two handle-less cups on the table. Vicky inclined her head in thanks like a queen. He wiped his hands on his apron and walked away.

"I have found you. Yes. Whom I have not found is Daniel Burton."

I'd anticipated something like this, because of the connection to Bousquet. Anger bubbled in the back of my head, some of it at Burton.

"I don't keep his calendar," I said. "And I haven't seen him in quite a while. What do you want with him?"

Edward looked up sharply, as if he'd recognized a word or two. He lifted the lid of the teapot and stirred the water and leaves with his forefinger, watching me the whole time.

"Well, Mr. Darrow. I don't think I believe you." Vicky sighed like a bad child actor and nodded at Edward.

Edward pinned my wrist to the table with a forearm like an iron bar and used his other hand to pour tea over mine.

I stifled a scream but not because I was being macho. Mr. Giaccobi was shielded by Edwards' body from seeing and I didn't want to drag him into this. He wouldn't be a match for Vicky, let alone brother Edward.

Edward let go. I retrieved my hand and set it in my lap, the pain like a glove, the damaged skin turning pink and pulling. My head felt light.

"That doesn't change my answer." I was surprised my voice stayed steady. "I still don't know where he is. Believe me—if his own bosses don't know where he is? He has to be off the grid."

She didn't look surprised that the BPD did not know where Burton was—maybe that's where she'd started.

Mr. Giaccobi had seen more than I thought. He carried a stainless steel bowl full of ice cubes to the table, handed it to me, and glared at Edward. I plunged my hand in, gasped at the chill. Vicky eyed the old man as if she might have underestimated him.

"I suppose it would be intrusive of me to ask why you need to find him so badly?" I said.

Vicky poured tea into the two cups and pushed one toward her brother, who smiled, revealing stained and broken teeth. He tossed off the boiling tea as if it were a shot of booze. He smiled at the bowl in my lap as if he wanted to call me a wimp but couldn't think of the word.

"I have been employing Mr. Burton on a personal project," she said. "It is very time-sensitive and I need to know what progress he's made."

Something to do with the Bousquet case, no doubt. She'd been one of the sources for the information that got him arrested.

"Burton works for the Boston Police. I don't believe he freelances."

Though as I said that, I remembered Detective Murray's questions about what Burton had been doing. I still found it hard to believe that IA would bother him over a moonlighting gig, when scores of rank and file officers padded their paychecks with detail work.

I raised my hand, dripping, from the ice water, the pain throttled down to a minor throb. The skin was the pink of overcooked shrimp.

"Since I haven't been able to locate your friend," she said. "Perhaps I can convince you to help me find him."

49

Her looks generated not a single spark in me.

"I cannot help you. As I said, we haven't been in touch."

I set the steel bowl back on the table, careful not to slosh ice water over the side. Blisters rose on the back of my hand and the throb converted itself to a stinging pain. I wanted to shake it out but I didn't want to let them see how much it hurt.

"You will find him for me," Vicky said. "I happen to know you're his best friend. Maybe his only one." She scaled a business card across the table at me. "This is my private number. Call me when you know where he is."

She gathered herself to leave. With my fingernail, I flicked the card back at her, the glossy cardboard skidding off onto the floor. Edward humped himself up out of the chair and cocked a fist the size of a coconut. I braced myself.

Edward grunted, dropped his hand, and went very still. Mr. Giaccobi stood behind him with the barrel of a silver revolver pressed into the side of Edward's neck.

"The two of you." Giaccobi's accent disappeared like clouds from an August sky. "Out."

Vicky eye-fucked me as she rose from the chair, trying to make it look like it was her decision to leave. Edward muttered inarticulately. I doubted I'd seen the last of them.

Mr. Giaccobi never took eye nor aim off of them as they exited the café. Vicky strode with her wide shoulders straight and her nose in the air, as if she weren't being run off by a ninety-year-old man who stood five foot two and weighed a buck and a half after a heavy dinner.

Edward stopped in the doorway, turned, and pointed a finger at me. A shot cracked next to my ear and Edward disappeared.

Giaccobi kept the pistol pointed at the doorway, as if hoping Edward would reappear.

"Assholes," he said. "I was afraid he might have a gun."

I reached for the pistol gingerly, the smell of burnt gunpowder tickling my nostrils. His hands shook a little.

"You sure this is a good idea, Mr. G? They do know where to find you if they come back."

Someone bigger and stronger, which meant pretty much anyone else, could have taken the revolver away and shot him with it.

"Bullies," he said. "They're harmless."

"I'd hate to have to find a new coffee bar."

He grinned and dropped the pistol into my open hand. It was lighter than it looked.

"Starter gun. I used to run the track meets at the junior high."

"Still."

"Don't worry about me. I'm in this city longer than any set of gangsters and I'll be here when they're gone."

I got the sense he was trying to tell me something without saying it out loud—maybe that he was connected?—but my hand hurt too much to concentrate.

"Well. Thanks for stepping into it."

He nodded.

"We're neighbors, isn't that so? It's what neighbors do. What about another coffee for you?"

I shook my head, thanked him again, and stepped out cautiously onto Holbrook. I wouldn't have been surprised if Viktoriya and her World Wide Wrestling brother were waiting outside. But the sidewalk was empty and I walked back down Mercy Street in a gray swirling damp that matched my mood too well. Burton was deep into something, none of it good.

# 11

Tuesday night in a bar can go one of two ways. Either you get people trying to extend the weekend or you're dead because the weekenders peaked on Monday Night Football or something else. The only time I booked a musical act on Tuesday nights was when I had a volunteer or I was auditioning.

Tonight, the audition brought along a medium-sized crowd of friends and family. The guitar player styled himself after Joe Pass, one of the old-timers I'd loved since I discovered him as a teenager. This young man called himself José Blanco, despite being about as Hispanic as a Fluffernutter. He would have been as fine a player if he called himself Joey White. But I was past the point of trying to tell a twenty-something *artiste* anything he didn't already know.

He'd done a creditable job on an up-tempo "How High the Moon" but really cut it loose on "Satin Doll", enough to generate enthusiastic applause when he finished. He called the break and walked between the tables to the bar.

"What do you think, Mr. Darrow?"

I gave him credit for his manners and for asking straight out.

"Very nice. I might have a slot for you in a couple of weeks. Friday night."

He frowned. I guessed what he was thinking.

"Friday night is actually better than Saturdays," I said. "Most of the name acts that come to town, the ones who play Sculler's and Ryle's? They book for Saturday nights. This way, you're not competing with them."

He was a serious-looking kid, playing up a resemblance to Dave

52

Brubeck with the dark suit, black-rimmed glasses, and pompadour. I hoped the emulation didn't extend to dabbling in heroin. He still didn't like the idea of not being the headliner but he didn't argue.

"How about a Sazerac, then?"

I grinned. Kid was old-school all the way.

"Haven't had an order for one of those in a long time," I said. "Let me see if I remember how to make one."

\* \* \* \* \*

Marina walked out of the kitchen in the middle of José's second set, with everyone settled in nicely with their drinks, and most of them actually listening to the music. He held an audience as well as he played. I had a find.

She handed me her cell.

"Call for you."

"On your phone?"

She shrugged and returned to the kitchen.

"This is Elder."

"I'm going to assume you're behind the bar in full public view. So don't say my name. All right?"

Burton. In a paranoid state of mind.

"Didn't I just talk to you? How's everything up at the . . ."

"Don't say it."

I rolled my eyes. This phase didn't surface too often but when it did? Everyone was suspect: the department, his snitches, random people on the street. Even me, I supposed.

"What can I do for you?"

"You haven't lent the house we were talking about to anyone else?"

"No one but you."

The place had sat unused since Thomas had died. Or maybe years before. I didn't know if he'd spent any time up there.

"OK," he said. "Then this is a lot more complicated that I thought it was. I'll talk to you."

He cut the connection without another word. If it had been my phone, I might have thrown it up against the wall.

53

I went back into the kitchen and handed Marina back her phone. She raised her eyebrows and I knew she'd recognized the voice. I shook my head.

"Nothing new."

"You ever feel like you're being used?" she said.

The thought surprised me.

"Not until recently," I said. "I still owe him plenty."

She turned her head away.

"Doesn't his tab expire after a while?"

From out front came cheers and whistles, José making it to the end of his set without offending any of the jazz purists. Time to go sell more drinks.

I settled in behind the bar and thought about what Marina had said. How much did I really still owe him? And what had he found in New Hampshire? Signs someone else had been using the house? We'd had problems with kids breaking into camps up on the lake, using them as refuge for all the things they couldn't get away with at home.

José pushed through to be first at the bar.

"That was some good Sazerac," he said. "How about another?"

I grabbed down the rye and the precious bottle of Peychaud's Bitters I'd smuggled north the last time I was in New Orleans.

"Coming up. And look. Let's confirm this gig. Two weeks from Friday. Three sets."

Joey's thin young face lit up like it was his birthday. When was the last time I'd felt that joyous and unfettered a reaction to something?

"That's great, man. Really. I'm glad you dug what I'm doing. In fact, make it a double."

He held out a twenty but I waved him off. He stuffed it in the tip jar instead. Classy. I liked the kid and I liked the music but neither of those things diminished my worries about what Burton was into up there in New Hampshire, all on his own.

# 12

The Esposito was empty as a confessional on Wednesday morning. Marina was leaning on the front bar reading *The Pilot*, Boston's Catholic newspaper. She blushed when she saw me recognize it.

"Carmen takes it," She said. "She likes to talk about the articles."

She noticed my hand, a shade or two lighter than a boiled lobster claw.

"What the . . . what happened to you?"

"Little accident."

I didn't want her to think that telling Viktoriya how to find me had caused the injury. And there was no benefit to telling her that gangster types were looking for Burton.

I did walk out back to my office and retrieve the unlicensed Raven MP-25 Burton had given me during the Alison Somers thing. Viktoriya and Edward had been over-bold in trying that in a deserted café. Coming at me in the Esposito would raise their risk but I'd be prepared if they did.

Marina took my hand and turned it over to inspect the skin, blistered and puffy.

"You put ice on this, didn't you?"

"That's not what you do?"

She ran water in the bar sink and wet a couple clean rags.

"Cold compresses." She set my hand flat on the bar and draped a cool wet cloth over it. "Let me see if I have any lotion."

My eyes prickled with tears suddenly, that there were people who cared what happened to me. It hadn't always been that way.

She returned with a half-gallon jug, reading the label on the back.

"This has aloe vera. It should help." She looked at me oddly. "What?"

"Nothing."

She lifted the cloth, patted my hand dry, and skimmed on some of the lotion. The cooling was instant, the pain receding.

"Better leave that out here," I said. "Thanks."

She ducked her head, suddenly shy, and took the newspaper back into the kitchen. And the Esposito moved on into an almost normal day. And night.

\* \* \* \* \*

I decided to tell Marina about Thomas's bequest while we were cashing out at the end of the night. Receipts and tips were above average for a midweek night and that put me in a good mood. That and the fact that my hand was now only throbbing intermittently.

Marina sat on the other side of the bar with a Shirley Temple and a pile of crumpled bills and silver she was sorting into piles. She was distracted and didn't seem to notice we'd doubled her normal take of tips, something that only happened three or four times a year.

"We need to talk," I said. "About Carmen?"

She straightened up from the piles of quarters, dimes, and nickels. I was always surprised to find pennies in the tip jar, especially since I made a point of rounding off all my prices to even dollar amounts. People dumping their pocket change, I suppose. Tacky.

"She's fine," Marina said. "I'm sorry I had to take off on you in the middle of the day like that. She was fussing with one of the caregivers. It shouldn't happen again."

She didn't sound so sure.

"It's not going to have to," I said.

She gave me a hard look.

"You going to fire me?"

"No. Jesus."

What I didn't want to do was tell her about the money in a way that would make her feel condescended to. We'd been employer and employee for so long I wasn't sure how to acknowledge a different kind of relationship without damaging it. And I wanted her to stay at the Esposito, even though I knew money changed everything.

"Carmen needs a place she can be safe, yes? Where you don't have to worry about her?"

Marina stared at me. My stomach hurt. I cursed my father for leaving it to me to tell her about the bequest. It was his own damn ego that kept him from doing it himself. Any overt act of philanthropy would have contradicted his sense of himself as someone working behind the scenes. The truth was that all of Thomas's actions and attitudes around money had been a mystery to me. I suspected his heavy hand from the grave was a last lesson to try and improve me, but what I was supposed to learn from it escaped me.

"There's some money to help with that," I said.

"What are you saying?"

One of the advantages of sobriety, I'd learned, was that I was no longer afraid to look like a fool, having been there while I was drunk many times.

"Thomas . . ."

"Stop right there." She straightened her spine as if I'd cursed out loud. "I don't want to hear another word."

Surprised, I scooped up my half of the tips and dropped them in the drawer by the register. I'd sort the bills and change later.

"Why? It was part of his will. He wanted to make sure Carmen was taken care of."

"She is being taken care of," Marina said.

"He loved your mother. Both my parents did. They were crushed when she decided to leave."

Marina's face was rigid as marble, her complexion pale enough to highlight the dark scatter of moles at the back of her jaw. I'd seen her angry, but not like this.

"You don't know why she left?"

Her teeth clenched. I shook my head.

"The story I heard was that Carmen worried you were getting in with a sketchy crowd in junior high. That she wanted to be there when you got home from school."

Marina puffed out air, a scoff.

"What, then?"

She shook her head.

"She never said, exactly. But it wasn't that. I never got in trouble in school." She smoothed out a wad of singles. "Can you change these for fives and tens, please? I'll keep the quarters for the laundromat."

I opened the register and exchanged the bills, started to count out the bank for tomorrow.

"So if she quit for a different reason? What was it?"

She tucked the bills in her purse, slipped off the stool, and reached for her jacket.

"If your father was alive, you could ask him. I really don't know. What I do know is that if Carmen thought the money was coming from him, she'd probably burn it."

All my old stories about how happy we'd been in the house on Louisburg Square were rocked. I'd have to fulfill the commitment one way or another—I was that much of my father's son—but I might have to find another way to do it.

"I would like to know the story," I said.

She zipped up the dark blue windbreaker and nodded.

"So would I. All I know is that when he tried to help us ten years ago? When all that real estate business in Hyde Park came up and we thought we'd be evicted. She almost blew the roof off the house telling him she didn't want his help. And we were a whole lot worse off than we are now."

She started for the stairs.

"Really? And you have no idea why?"

"That's what I said. Though if I had to guess, it was your father she was mad at. Carmen was devastated when your mom died."

She took the stairs two at a time, as if she were escaping. The street door hissed closed behind her.

I shut off the lights, except the bulb behind the back bar, and frowned. The bequest business would have to wait, then, until I figured out how to pass it on. She wouldn't believe me if I gave

Marina that big a raise and it sounded like Marina wouldn't lie to her mother about the money anyway.

I would have to get creative, not my forte, and right now, I was exhausted. I closed up the bar and went home to bed.

# 13

I don't normally indulge in nostalgia, mainly because I can't always remember enough of my past to make that worthwhile. The long swaths of my twenties and thirties lost to the heavy drinking meant there were more blank spots in my memory than not. And I doubted they would ever fill themselves again. Sometimes when I thought about it, I convinced myself it was better that I didn't remember everything I'd gotten myself up to in those long dark years.

Buying the Esposito had been a line in the sand, the place where I was either going to sober up enough to have a life or drink myself further into oblivion, peace, then death. So far, it was working out as planned, though there were many days when my sobriety felt as if I were dancing across a length of fishing line stretched between two skyscrapers wearing nothing but a Speedo. As always, when I opened the place up on Thursday morning, I wondered if this was going to be the day I fell.

Now that I'd discouraged the habitual drunks, my morning business was slow. Ten o'clock in the morning was too early for lunch. Opening early was more of a service to myself, a way to occupy me. Most of my business would come tonight, as the early-weekend types started in.

I spread the *Globe* on the bar in front of me, moderately optimistic about the article that said a grassroots movement to save *Eric in the Evening* had sprung up. If any sense remained in the local universe, the overseers of public radio in Boston would listen.

The bar was calm and quiet and you'd think that might make it more likely I'd drink. But this month I was educating myself on bass players, playing a long set on the sound system and wondering how I'd ever missed Charlie Haden. And the trios most of them played in was the perfect empty-bar dim-light soundtrack.

Then I turned back the front page and saw the headline inside: *Antoine Bousquet Missing.* Bousquet was free on bail, primarily because of Burton's thrashing, but yesterday he'd failed to show up for a strategy meeting with his lawyers. I booted up the laptop to see if the local news sites had any updated information and found a video.

After suffering through the commercial for pickup trucks, I turned up the sound on the newsman with the fake tan and the one cocked eye who stood on the brick plaza in front of the Suffolk County Courthouse.

"This morning at eight A.M.," he intoned into a bulbous microphone. "Antoine Bousquet, under indictment for the murders of two young women, left his office at Boston Landing, picked up his Audi RS6 Avant at the parking garage across the street, and drove off into nothingness."

I appreciated his specificity of detail and his dramatic sense, right up to the word "nothingness." He had little future in television if he insisted on complicated narratives, though his attempt at storytelling did obscure the truth that he had very few facts. And what was the news camera doing at the courthouse if the story started at Boston Landing?

According to the rest of it, when Bousquet failed to show, his chief lawyer called the designer's former mistress, one Viktoriya Lin, who immediately called the local precinct. Despite law enforcement protocol that said a person wasn't considered missing until forty-eight hours had passed, a politically aware assistant chief recognized Bousquet's name and instituted a regional search for the Audi extending north into New Hampshire and south to Providence. The high-end vehicle had been found in the New Hampshire State Liquor Store parking lot in Portsmouth Circle, with no sign of Bousquet himself.

I shut down the video, wondering idly if Viktoriya's visit to Mr. Giaccobi's café had anything to do with Bousquet's disappearance.

Had she known he was missing and wanted Burton to locate him for her?

Even if Burton hadn't been within miles of Boston, he was going to catch hell for this. In any bureaucracy, shit oozes downhill and he stood all by himself at the bottom. Though he was in New Hampshire, the family cottage was on the other side of the state. There was no phone and chances of getting Burton to answer his cell were slim to none. He'd probably hear about Bousquet going missing eventually, but no one was going to like the fact that Burton had been in New Hampshire at the same time. I just hoped he was going to be able to prove what he'd been doing when his colleagues came looking.

# 14

At the end of a very slow night, I set the alarm, locked up, and tested the door handle from outside. Burton thought I was crazy to install a hardened security door from the company that supplied the State Department in Washington, but when I started out, the South End was a lot rougher place than it was now. I'd had to do something after the night someone dumped a murdered guitar player on the stage of the Esposito.

I felt his presence long before I reached the back end of the alley. As I rounded the corner of the brick building and turned toward the loading dock where I parked the Cougar, out of sight of the street, I saw the bulky outline of a body sitting up on the hood of the car, backlit by the feeble yellow bulb over the emergency exit.

"Burton?"

"My question exactly, boyo. Where on earth is that young fella keeping himself these days? Would you know?"

Mickey Barksdale calling Burton a youngster was Irish storyteller hyperbole. The two of them had grown up in Charlestown together, back at the time when the aftereffects of urban renewal and forced bussing were wrecking the city and the elevated train tracks were coming down. They'd attended the same grade school and junior high, but when high school loomed, Mickey's disdain for academic pursuits bent him off in the quasi-criminal directions available to young Boston boys in the era: picking up numbers slips, shoplifting cigarettes for resale on the corners, retrieving batting-practice balls from the net at Fenway and forging the ballplayers' signatures to sell to the rubes. Maintaining the relationship was a dangerous dance for

Burton now, the two of them unquestionably on different sides of the law.

"Ah, Jesus, Mick. Did you have to scare the shit out of me? You could have come inside and had a drink. I run an equal-opportunity shebeen, you know."

If I'd thought using the old Irish term for a bar would soften him up, I was mistaken. He slid down of the Cougar's hood, the sound of the studs on his jeans scraping across the paint job making me wince. He stepped up to me, so close I could smell clove toothpaste on his breath.

"You of all people ought to know, Mr. Darrow, that I'm not much of a drinker. Much against the stereotype, I might add. Which presents the possibility you are mocking me."

My knees trembled in a minor way. Unlike some of the more physically imposing and louder characters I ran into in my bar, Mickey was a genuine hardass. My offer to buy him a drink in the Esposito was strictly *pro forma*—the last person I wanted as a customer now that the bucket of blood was a decent night spot was a certifiably half-mad, brutal, and well-known gangster boss. On the other hand, you couldn't roll over for him or he'd sink his teeth in your neck.

"I call it a bistro now, Mickey. Not a bar. You can have a nice meal, drink an Arnold Palmer. No offense intended."

"I'll keep it in mind. Not too foofy, is it? Maybe the missus would enjoy a night out."

I sincerely hoped not.

Under the pale yellow light, Mickey's sclera looked diseased as he stared at me for another too-long moment. The night deposit bag under my arm was the least of my worries. If he'd wanted to rob me, he would have sent a minion. Maybe being a friend of Burton's gave me some faint protection.

"You're evading my question. Truly?" He trilled the "r." "You have no idea where our friend has gotten himself to?"

"I don't." I could have told him and banked a favor with Mickey but not without talking to Burton first. "I haven't seen him in days. You know he was suspended?"

Mickey nodded, staring out into the dark.

"I'm sure he'll turn up," I said.

"I share your optimism."

He reached for my face and I thought he was going to pat my cheek in some Godfather move. Instead, he pinched the lobe of my ear between his thumb and forefinger with a steady, not heavy, pressure.

"We both know you two are close as brothers. I would purely hate to find out you knew where he was all this time and did not feel compelled to share that information with me."

I stepped back, pulling free. Sometimes my desire to go along gets the better of my pride but if I'd learned anything from dealing with assholes in the Esposito, it was that if you let someone step on your toe, sooner or later they'd stomp your whole foot.

"Mickey. Cut the crap, OK? You know he's in trouble at work. He's probably taking a little down time."

Mickey stepped back, the clove tide receding.

"In trouble from associating with me?"

I shook my head.

"More likely all this other shit going on."

"The Bousquet thing?" He mangled the pronunciation but it was affectation. He'd done three years at Bunker Hill Community College. "A flea fart in a hurricane. What he did, arresting that bastard? There's a half dozen places in the Town he could drink all night for free. One of the girls had family there."

"A Chinese family in Charlestown?"

"City's changed, Elder. You spend too much time reading the *Globe*."

He leaned in, a whiff of something meaty behind the clove smell, lamb, maybe.

"And you needn't be jealous of my interest, either," he said.

"Because you and Burton are friends?"

"Friends is overstating a tad. But I do know you upper-crust types like to dance on the edge of the darkness sometimes, don't you? Though you never seem to fall in."

That dug at me. Was that why Burton and I were friends? Because I liked to dabble at the edge of the criminal world?

"Mickey. Burton drinks here. That's mainly how we're acquainted. It doesn't go too much deeper than that."

He grinned, incisors yellow in the light.

"Sure enough. I'm not implying anything untoward, you understand. Just that you're like a lot of people who like a peek into the void without suffering the consequences."

I leaned over and unlocked the front door of the Cougar, tossed the vinyl deposit bag inside.

"Whatever you're smoking, Mickey? Put me down for a pound."

His back went rigid and I thought I might have pushed too hard. But Mickey was Burton's row to hoe, not mine. I trusted that while Burton might veer off the official path occasionally, he'd never cross over into illegal acts.

"Just tell the man I'm looking for him, the next time you come across him. Can you do that for me? I have some things he needs to know."

I slid in under the steering wheel and keyed the ignition.

"You're standing at the end of a long line of people who want to talk to the man, Mick."

He slapped the hood.

"And I know you'll do your best to bring me to the front. Won't you, Elder?"

I slammed the door and put the car in gear. Mickey stayed standing in the middle of the alley, not giving me room to turn around, so I had to reverse my way back up the alley out to Mercy Street.

"Asshole," I said, but well under my breath.

That was one man I didn't care if I ever saw again.

# 15

I walked up the granite stairs to my apartment building on Commonwealth Avenue and pulled the street door shut behind me. The latch was still loose. I climbed as quietly as I could so as not to wake Mrs. Rinaldi on the ground floor. My relationship with Susan Voisine hadn't worked out and she'd given up the lease on the second floor apartment and moved back to Oregon after her father died. I hadn't gotten around to clearing the place out and repainting yet. Every time I walked inside, I noticed a trace of her perfume. I wasn't carrying a torch for her, though. Maybe a lit match.

Mrs. Rinaldi had stayed loyal to the building, even after the work she did for the Boston Opera Company created a national demand for the delicate miniature sets she constructed. The companies' carpenters used them to build full-sized performance sets. With the ridiculous money she was being paid (her words, not mine), I was worried she'd want to move somewhere more upscale but she'd assured me she had no interest in changing her address at this late date. In a slightly ominous phrase, she'd told me she intended to stay "for the duration."

My hand ached dully and the blisters on the back of my wrist were puffy. I queued up a set of Charlie Haden-Pat Metheny duets on the iPod and boiled some water for herb tea, thinking about Mickey's accusation. If anything, he was more likely to be jealous of my relationship with Burton than the other way around. For all the history and background they shared, they could never be friends while Burton was on the force. Any relationship they had was of mutual utility, each using the other where convenient and possible.

I sat at my desk, sipping tea and writing checks for my personal bills, and made a note to call Thomas's attorney—mine, temporarily—to find out the actual date the trust for Carmen went into effect. He'd probably ask about the plans for my inheritance, too, as if I had any. All I knew right now was that it could change everything and I didn't want to face that yet. Part of me wished he'd donated everything to charity. I wouldn't have cared.

What I feared was not any explicit conditions attached to the money, since I would have known about them by now. But I sensed that my father would have expected me to take certain actions with it that I had to infer. One of the reasons I'd done so poorly working for other people was that I hated anyone telling me what to do, even if they were right.

I finished the tea, the dregs cold and bitter, and thought I might have unwound enough to go to bed. The longer my sobriety went, the better I'd been sleeping, and though that wasn't enough of a reason on its own to stay dry, it added weight to that side of the scale.

When the phone rang, I would have let it go, except that I saw it was Kathleen.

"Hey. How are you?" I said.

I was pleased she'd called. I'd been leaving the next move up to her.

"Not too well." Her voice was rough with tension. "I have someone here who thinks he knows you."

I stood up, heart thumping.

"What do you mean?"

"I'm holding a gun on someone whose only English seems to be your name. Doesn't have anything else to say."

I had the terrible thought that Mickey had found another way to intimidate me.

"What's his name?"

"His name?" Her voice flew up an octave. "I don't know his fucking name, Elder. Why don't I shoot him in the leg and see if he'll tell me?"

She seemed to be exaggerating her hysteria to keep her prisoner under control. The combination of a gun and a tone at the fine edge of madness ought to do it.

"Maybe you could ask him?" I said.

"Jesus Christ."

She barked at someone in the background. If it wasn't one of Mickey's thugs, could it be Burton? No. That made no sense. She came back on the line.

"All he'll say is 'Anatoly.' And 'Elder Darrow, Elder Darrow.'"

"Anatoly. He's Russian." Last thing I would have expected. I shifted the phone to my other ear. "Seriously?"

"Appears to be."

"And he won't say what he's doing there?"

"Elder," she said. "The only English words I've heard him say are 'shit' and your name. Are you going to come over here and see what this is all about? Or should I just give him your address. He's here because he thought you would be. Did we sleep together and I didn't even notice?"

If I had to guess, the question of that ever happening had been tabled forever. I didn't suggest calling the police, since she hadn't yet. This could have something to do with Burton.

"I don't know your address, Kathleen."

"I'm on Fayette. Number 30."

"Fifteen minutes. Try not to shoot him until I get there."

She laughed, as if she'd been considering whether to do that very thing.

"Then I'd never find out what the fuck he was doing here, would I? And I am a very curious woman."

Sleep would have to wait. It did intrigue me that her first reaction had been to call me and not the Cambridge police. That bespoke a lawless streak that might make for some interesting conversations along the way. That was assuming she didn't dump me because some Russian gangster came looking for me in her bedroom.

\* \* \* \* \*

I pulled up to the curb in front of her house, what looked like a two-decker on a tree-lined street that connected Broadway and Cambridge Streets. To the left of the house, two cars were parked in a gravel turnout, a C-class Mercedes and a Chevy Volt attached to a charging station on the side of the house.

Of course. Cambridge, granola. Electric cars.

The porch was on the long side of the house, perpendicular to the street. The storm door was open wide, as if its hinges were sprung, and I wondered if the Russian had done that. The steel entry door was unlocked. I pushed it in and rapped on the frame.

"Kathleen?"

"Second floor."

Her voice descended from the top of a broad wooden staircase, maybe four feet wide. What looked like a two-apartment house from outside was actually one dwelling. Either her father had been a more successful quasi-criminal than she wanted to admit or she had some serious money of her own. This was a two million dollar property. Easily.

I climbed up out of the foyer toward the light at the top of the steep stairs, aware that I was not armed. I had to hope she was equipped enough for both of us.

The horseshoe hallway at the top reminded me of the hotel balcony in an old Western, a mahogany handrail running along the rim. Five doors, four of them shut. Through the open one, I saw a high-posted bed with a gauzy white canopy, very Out of Africa. Several thick candles burned with the scents of vanilla and cinnamon.

And on the floor outside this door sat a despondent young man in a greasy black Levi jacket and black jeans, motorcycle boots. He was sitting on his hands.

"Great way to restrain him," I said.

She must have had some military or police training. You don't dream up a tactic like that on your own.

From one hand dangled a cheap silvered automatic; in the other, more securely, she held a Series 70 Colt Competition, which I recognized because Burton used one for target shooting. She shrugged at me minutely.

"Lift up your head, Sergei." She nudged him with a bare foot.

"Anatoly. My name is Anatoly."

Sulking, he was so overmatched I almost felt sorry for him. Whoever had given him this assignment hadn't researched Kathleen very well.

Anatoly was thin as a light pole, his black hair buzzed so short the scalp ghosted through. A gold nugget lodged in his right earlobe and his face was translucent and hairless. He might have been as old as twenty. Or not.

"Now you can tell Mr. Darrow what you're doing here," she said.

His head snapped up at the sound of my name.

"Elder Darrow?"

Based on what she'd said on the phone, I'd expected cartoon Russian, Boris and Natasha, but the accent was pure Chelsea. Massachusetts, not England.

"What do you want with me?" I said. "And what are you doing here?"

"They said you were fucking her."

Kathleen looked at me with a mean glee, then slapped the back of his head.

"You have a mother and you talk about women like that?"

He looked confused, as if he didn't understand the connection.

"So," I said. "Who, what, when, where, why?"

Now Anatoly looked more befuddled. Was he intellectually challenged, or whatever we were calling it these days?

"Can I stand up?"

I looked at Kathleen—it was her house. She handed me the cheap automatic and stepped back along the handrail away from us. But Anatoly seemed too whipped to try anything.

"Up," I said. "Now tell me why you're here."

His eyes were shiny with unshed tears, reinforcing my sense he wasn't operating at full power. Whoever had sent him had to know he was a weak link.

"They told me to come and bring you back. To talk to them."

71

"'Them?'"

"The men?" Anatoly said.

Kathleen frowned and pointed to the side of her head. She'd come to the same conclusion I had. The wires weren't all connected.

"And how were you supposed to do that, Anatoly?"

I spoke to him as if he were a tourist from a foreign country who spoke no English. Either these Russians didn't have a very deep bench or they were discounting my intelligence. Anatoly was no Putin.

He looked down at his hands, then back at Kathleen, obviously more frightened of her than he was of me.

"I can go in my pockets?"

She waved the Colt.

"Carefully," I said.

With exaggerated slowness, he reached two fingers into an outside pocket of the Levi jacket and produced an envelope, sealed, with my name on the outside.

I tore it open, slid out five crisp one-hundred dollar bills, and read the laser-printed message.

"Mr. Darrow. If you please. We would like to consult with you about your friend Daniel Burton and his issues with Antoine Bousquet. Please accept this token payment for your time and attention."

I folded the money and slipped it into my pocket. Apparently the entire city was looking for Burton. No wonder he'd decided to disappear for a bit.

"Please do not say no to this." Anatoly was interpreting my headshake. "I will be in very big trouble."

"Why not just slip this in the mail slot?" I looked at Kathleen. "He actually broke into the house?"

She nodded.

"Caught him picking the locks on the front door."

"My instructions," Anatoly mumbled. "If you're not here, place it on her pillow."

"Intimidation factor," she said. "Like the Godfather?" She raised the pistol and Anatoly cowered. "Clearly I've never met these jamokes."

"Didn't exactly go as planned, did it." I grabbed Anatoly by the

72

lapels, my fingers slipping on the fabric. "Go home now. Tell 'them' you talked to me and I have no idea where Burton is. And in the future? Someone wants to talk to me? Use the telephone. Or come to the bar. You know my bar?"

He shook his head like a cow in the slaughter chute. I gave him a card with the name and address.

"And you, or anyone else, bothers Ms. Crawford again? You can see she knows how to take care of herself. She might shoot you the next time."

Anatoly's eyes rolled white and before either of us could move, he dove head-first over the railing. The thud of his body landing on the lowest stair shook the house.

I looked over. His head sat at an impossible angle to his shoulders.

"Oh shit," Kathleen said. "Not again."

\* \* \* \* \*

"Again?"

She ignored me, stepped back into the bedroom, and called 911. While she waited on hold, she stood calm as a pond, as if a home invasion that ended with an intruder dead on the stairs was no big deal. My knees were wobbling.

She smiled at me, her eyes bright with excitement, and I wondered who, besides a bank teller, she really was.

The operator must have come on.

"30 Fayette Street," Kathleen said. "No need for sirens."

She left the line open the way the operators ask you to and balanced the handset on top of the bannister.

"Third time this year I've had a break-in." She shot me a sideways look, as if testing my curiosity. "Something about the neighborhood. Or the house? First fatality, though."

I was wondering whether any of her father's criminal cohorts could be alive but the sound of boots clattering on the stairs outside stopped that. They stepped into the foyer and halted at the bottom. We looked over the handrail at a uniformed officer, hand on his weapon, who looked down at Anatoly's body, then up at us.

"Everyone safe up there, Kathleen?"

If she was on a first name basis with the Cambridge cops, it put her one up on me.

"Fine, Larry. We're good."

He ascended one step and prodded the body with the toe of his boot, which even I knew was poor crime scene procedure. Not that I intended to say anything about it to a man with a gun.

"Didn't have to shoot this one, huh?" he said.

She snorted.

I watched out the clerestory window as the street slowly choked up with plain cars, squad cars. Then the big white pop-up van from the Medical Examiner's office lumbered in and climbed over the curb onto the lawn.

Kathleen and I remained on the upstairs landing while the two attendants packed Anatoly's slack body into a bag and carried him out the front door, the stiff plastic rasping against the screen door. I didn't hear any gallows humor or smart-ass remarks, another way life doesn't imitate TV.

A barrel of a man, five-eight and sleek in an expensive slate-gray hopsack suit said something to the young woman who'd inspected the body—the medical examiner, I assumed—then walked up the safe-passage area marked by tape on the stairs. In size and shape, he made me think of Biggs, the BPD IA guy, and I wondered if Burton knew him.

"Ms. Crawford," he said. "We meet again."

She extended her hand but he didn't shake it.

"Need to test for GSR," he said apologetically.

"Didn't fire a shot, Lieutenant Steere."

"Procedure. You know that." He turned to me. "And you are?"

"Elder Darrow. Friend of Kathleen's."

"ID, please."

She and I had agreed it would be simpler not to mention that Anatoly was looking for me here. I'd stuffed the letter and envelope from the Russians into my back pocket.

Steere gave me a quick dubious look from bloodshot eyes as he handed back my driver's license and I wondered if he recognized my name. People at Boston PD knew it, first from all the calls I'd made to clear the hookers and drug dealers from the old Esposito and later, from my encounter with Ricky Maldonado. I didn't want to think I had a reputation across the river, too.

Steere beckoned to a technician, who climbed the stairs and swabbed Kathleen's hands and mine.

"Same story, more or less?" Steere said to Kathleen.

Somewhere along the way, the two handguns had disappeared. Kathleen shrugged.

"I woke up hearing someone trying to pick the locks on the front door. Same as last time. He got inside and was up on the landing when I came out of my bedroom. I must have startled him because he tripped over the bannister and fell down the stairs."

Steer watched her as if they were playing poker.

"You didn't help him along? Give him a little shove? It would still be self-defense."

She shook her head.

"If he hadn't fallen over on his own, I would have shot him. As you know."

Steere turned to me.

"And how did you happen to be here?"

"That's a little personal, don't you think?" Kathleen said.

Steere looked irked.

"You ought to know how this works by now, Kathleen, Let's have Mr. Darrow answer for himself."

Keeping myself out of this also meant no one would connect it with Burton, who might need the protection.

"Pretty much what she said," I told Steere. "I came out of the bedroom behind her and he was down there on the stairs."

She frowned, as if disapproving my embellishment.

"OK." Steere sighed. "Leave your contact information with the officer at the door. We'll be in touch about a statement in the morning."

In my limited experience with Burton, an investigator took everyone in and got statements immediately, while the stories were fresh. That made me wonder about the relationship between Steere and Kathleen. I wouldn't have left if she didn't seem so much calmer than I felt.

"Thanks." I looked at her. "I'll call."

She raised her chin.

I threaded Steere's careful path down the stairs, trying to ignore the splotch of blood on the hardwood.

It took me the better part of half an hour to extricate the Cougar from in between all the police vehicles and it was coming on five-thirty by the time I parked in front of my building. Any adrenaline generated by the confrontation with Anatoly was long since burned away. I felt achy and nauseous. Kathleen's composure made me curious, but tomorrow—make that today—was going to be miserable if I didn't get at least a couple hours sleep.

# 16

About two-thirty on Saturday afternoon, my ass was dragging when a familiar man in a familiar good suit walked down the stairs into the bar, his heels ringing hard on the steel risers. He strolled down to the empty end of the bar where I was running some numbers on a calculator and trying to figure out why I wasn't making more money. I'd recognized the raspberry stripe in the fabric and wondered why the Professional Standards cops seemed to dress so much more nicely than, say, Burton.

"Mr. Riggs?" I knew his name but I didn't want him to know I'd been thinking about him and Murray at all.

"Biggs," he said, in a tobacco-scratchy voice. "Detective Biggs, that is. I'm impressed you got that close."

"I never forget a good suit. And contrary to popular opinion, I've cut down significantly on the number of police visits to my bar in the last couple years. I can actually remember all the officers who come in."

I tried to be cool but my gut was gnarled up. Bousquet was still missing and so was Burton. They wouldn't be cops unless they were trying to see if there was a connection.

"Came to present you with an opportunity."

When I didn't respond, he raised his dark caterpillar eyebrows.

"This is a bar," I said. "Can I get you something? Or are you on duty?"

"Draft. Bass."

I drew him a pint and set it on a coaster, waiting in front of him until he reached into his wallet and laid a ten on the bar. After

Murray's pointed questions about Burton paying for his drinks, I wasn't offering anyone a freebie.

"My partner," he said.

"Mr. Murray."

"Oh, you remember his name?" He leaned forward. "This is unofficial, all right? Two guys talking in a bar. My day off."

"If you say so."

He sipped the ale and smiled.

"First one of the day is always the best, isn't it? Except you don't partake any longer, do you? Have to say I'm sorry for you."

It would take more than that to irk me.

"Your partner?" I said.

"Detective Murray has something of a hard-on for your friend. He's convinced the man is guilty. Of something."

"Aren't we all?" I said. "Let me ask you something. Are you two seriously investigating whether he's moonlighting?"

Biggs quit pretending he didn't love his beer and drained half the glass.

"I'm not saying he would manufacture evidence. But your friend's gone completely off the radar. Nine, ten days now."

"I still don't know where he is." I repeated myself. "I don't know how this works. If he's on suspension, does he have to report in?"

Biggs held up pink meaty palms. They looked soft, paperwork hands.

"I don't know why you're covering for him, what you owe him. All right? All I'm saying is, when he comes in, tell him to ask for me directly. I'll give him a fair shake. The fact that he's missing, along with this other missing person? It doesn't look good."

He was talking about Bousquet, of course. Just what worried me. And I realized I didn't really have an answer for why I was looking out for Burton.

Biggs was calm and convincing but every cop I'd ever met, Burton included, was a professional-grade liar when the situation required. Biggs wouldn't know it, but I corrected for that.

"If I see him, I'll pass on the message. It's unlikely, though."

Biggs stiffened like a pointer.

"Unlikely you'll see him? Or unlikely you'll pass on my message."

"You must think I'm an idiot," I said. "Antoine Bousquet goes missing and no one can find him. Now you're looking for Burton. I'd have to be a dotard not to make the connection."

Biggs didn't like it but I didn't like being treated like his dumb cousin Bumpo, either. More than once, Burton had moaned to me about his peers' tendency to start with a hypothesis and fit the evidence to it, rather than let the facts lead to a solution. True enough, if most murders were impulse crimes, passion or greed, the obvious solution was probably the correct one. That wasn't always the case.

Biggs drained his glass.

"The questions have to be asked, Darrow. I'm not out to get him but I get that you have no reason to believe me. I'm trying to keep him from being steamrolled. Confidentially? Murray isn't even interested in this Antoine Bousquet bullshit. He did what he did and it's done. Screwing him over for that would only make us look like assholes. We need to do this by the book."

Do what? I wanted to ask him but I didn't really want the answer. Biggs seemed sincere but my previous declaration on world-class liars stood. Maybe he and Murray took turns being the bad cop.

"Here it is, Biggs. One last time. I haven't seen Burton. I don't expect to see him. And I do not know where he is. I will take what you said under advisement and pass it on if I see him. Which I do not expect to do."

Biggs shook his head and pushed himself upright. I expected one more try but he'd given up.

"All I can ask," he said. "Thanks for the beer."

He left the change from the ten on the bar. I didn't remind him it was there.

79

# 17

This Saturday night turned out the way I liked the bar business best, busy enough to keep my feet moving without any danger of falling into the weeds. The music was a compilation I'd made of female singers: Lady Day, Dinah Shore, Ella, and Carmen, but my memory kept flickering back to Alison Somers, the young singer, my one-time lover, who'd died almost exactly a year ago now. The memory was not as painful as it had been, though it left me with a skim of sadness. Waste of a life, waste of a talent.

For the first time in a while, I was hopeful about the bar and my place in it. Winter was always my difficult season—my mother and father both had died in winter—and I'd spent a good part of my January doldrums this year wondering if I was going to be wedded to the Esposito for the rest of my life. The money from my father's estate scared me. In a month or so, I would have to decide how those millions would change my life.

The phone under the bar rang, startling me as it always did. I don't think I got a landline call more than once a month.

"Esposito."

"Your pal and mine, Mr. Elder Darrow."

"Burton. What the hell is going on?"

All my frustration—being braced by the police, assaulted in a coffee shop by the Chinese mistress of a missing murderer, threatened by Mickey Barksdale and some unknown Russians—was ready to spew.

"Be cool, Elder. It's not impossible someone's listening in. Or at least keeping an eye on you."

"Seriously? Because that sounds a little paranoid to me. Why don't you let all these people know where you are so they'll stop bothering me?"

"Crab all you want," he said. "I do appreciate your catching the crap for me. But I have some very good reasons for not being down in the city right now."

"And those would be?"

He ignored my question.

"You want the rundown on everyone who's after your sorry ass?" I said.

"If I have to."

"A Russian thug who broke his neck in a swan dive. Your favorite Chinese hooker, who thinks you work for her. And your old pal Mickey Barksdale. In addition, of course, to your brothers in blue."

"Which ones? The Professional Standards guys?"

"Murray and Biggs."

"Shit."

"You know them."

"They're fucking bulldogs. And Murray hates me. Is it about Bousquet?"

"That's what's weird. They seem to be more worried about whether you're moonlighting."

"So there was no corruption complaint."

Odd question to ask.

"Apparently not. Not that you'd have anything to worry about on that score, am I right?"

More silence.

"I told you," he said. "I'm trying to keep you out of it. Remember what happened with the Quincy boys."

Burton and I had met when the son of a Boston politician had murdered a guitar player and left him on the stage of the Esposito. By the end of that, I'd been beaten, tied up, and shot at.

"Appreciate the concern," I said. "But it's a little late."

"I'm following up on something to do with that moron I punched out. But it looks like it's bigger than a couple of young women getting killed."

"You mean . . ."

81

"No names on the radio, please."

"Are you crazy? Or just stupid." My frustration boiled. "Are you trying to get yourself canned?"

"I know. Never going to make Detective of the Month, am I? But if I can break this, I'll be fine."

I would have asked him why he wasn't doing this officially, through channels, but I knew the answer. He was too impatient to wait to be reinstated and because he thought he'd screwed things up, it was up to him to fix them.

"You know Bousquet has disappeared, right?"

The silence went on so long he might have hung up.

"Fuck me. You're serious."

"Serious as a midnight door knock. Don't you read the newspapers? Three days ago now."

"My aching ass. But that isn't why Murray and Biggs are after me? They don't think I disappeared the man?"

"Don't think so. But your guess is as good as mine."

"Those two usually run a very close game."

A lighter clicked—was he smoking? The background music penetrated my consciousness, heavy country.

"You're in a bar?"

Burton snorted.

"Didn't know I'd taken a loyalty oath." He exhaled. "I still have to get this done. Professional Standards gets ahold of me, I'm not going to have room to move."

"You don't think it makes sense to come in and talk to them? Biggs, at least, acts like he doesn't want to fuck you over."

"You've never seen these guys operate. Believe me, neither of them understands the possibilities of mercy. By the book, all the way."

I loosened my grip on the phone.

"That's the sound of ice cracking under your feet," I said.

"You think I don't know that? One more fuck-up and I'm down the chute. Unless I can get this done."

He sounded depressed. I could feel the pull of despair even over the phone.

"What's important enough to risk all this? You've nailed Bousquet for the murders."

"No names," he said. "I can't talk about it right now. But if I make it happen, all will be forgiven. Or most of it."

That seemed optimistic. I changed topics.

"You know Giaccobi's café? Down the block from me?"

"What about it?"

I told him the story about Giaccobi running Viktoriya Lin and her brother off, thinking it might lighten his mood. Instead, his voice got darker.

"Shit. I'm sorry," he said. "She is not someone you want to fuck around with."

"I think she wants something from you, Burton. Does she blame you for arresting her sweetie?"

"She was the one who brought in the evidence that tipped the case," he said.

"Then maybe she wants to thank you."

"Not fucking likely. I am pretty sure arresting Bousquet saved his life, though. When her cousin disappeared, she was ready to put a hit on him. The two women who died were beaten, a caution to the rest of the people working for him. They did not die a pretty death."

"If there is such a thing."

"Look, I said I was sorry. I know you don't have a horse in this race."

"Can I do anything?" Not sure why I was offering but it seemed like the right thing to do.

"There's a big difference between the off-the-cuff stuff we did last year—which I admit you handled adequately—and a police investigation involving high-level international gangsters. Icky Ricky was not a guy who struck fear in people's hearts."

"If you say so. Though it appears I'm already linked to it."

"I'll make sure you get disconnected. There's no reason for you to get tied up in this."

Except that I still felt I owed him, for Alison, for the help with Timmy McGuire.

"Burton. Talk to Biggs. Find out what they're cranked up about.

At least cover your ass on that score. If nothing else, save your job."

He snorted again.

"You have no idea how the bureaucracy works, do you? Once they settle on a story, all the effort goes into propping it up. Not looking for alternative explanations. If I can break this one case, no one's going to want to fuck with me."

"Your mouth to God's ear," I said. "Just don't make things worse."

"They let Bousquet out on bail, Elder. If he has half a brain, he's cleaning up his messes, including Viktoriya's cousin. You want me to let him get away with that to satisfy some bullshit complaint about moonlighting?"

I sighed my frustration. No sense of self-preservation.

"Call me if you need anything. Short of money or weapons."

He laughed.

"Appreciate it. Hey, if this doesn't work out, it might be time for me to move on anyway. The shit is definitely going to hit the fan here, and soon."

And with that pregnant announcement, he cut the connection without a goodbye.

I hung up the phone and walked back into the kitchen, my head loose on my neck, as if I were drunk.

"That was Burton."

"So?" Marina didn't look up from chopping onions.

"He's all tangled up in something again. Has he been talking to you about any of this?"

Her eyes were red and wet.

"We don't talk that much anymore," she said. "But I'm not surprised. The man's a trouble magnet. And he needs you to help him."

That had been my thought, though without any encouragement from Burton. I turned without saying anything and walked back out. I thought I was trying to help him.

\* \* \* \* \*

Later on, not quite closing time but close, Marina came out front, wiping her hands.

"Love this kind of night," she said. "Not like some of those crazy Saturdays we used to have."

It was a sort of apology—she knew I worried about Burton. This time, though, I'd accepted there was nothing I could do. He would do what he thought was right and nothing I said was going to change that.

"Yep. That amount of business is right on the edge of what we can handle ourselves. Just the two of us, I mean."

At least five or six nights a month over the last half year, we wound up working at top speed for seven or eight hours at a time. I'd resisted hiring more help but if I did, I might be able to pay more attention to improving the music situation, maybe bringing in some better players. And in a month or so, I'd have the capital to do that. The building's owner was after me to take over the street-level space next door, currently a hydroponic gardening store he was convinced was selling pot.

"I know," she said. "Up or out, right?"

I'd queued up three long sets of Keith Jarrett concerts—Paris, Vienna, and Stockholm—so I didn't have to think about the music for a while.

Marina squirted herself a glass of cola from the soda gun and closed her eyes, leaning against the back bar.

"You and Carmen getting on all right?"

"She's up and down. We're going to have to decide on the assisted living thing pretty soon." Her voice cracked. "Couple months, maybe. It's getting to be too much."

For her to complain, it must have been. I thought I'd try again.

"Got another call from Thomas's lawyer. He's pretty eager to close up the estate before the end of the month. Can you talk to her about it?"

"If it were up to me?" she said. "I'd grab the money. I know she's going to need it eventually. And these places—you have any idea what they cost?"

"Could she forget why she doesn't want it? If we wait, I mean."

"What if you talk to her. Face to face. Maybe she'll tell you what the problem is. Even on a good day, she dances all around it with me."

It wasn't my favorite idea, but if it helped?

"When?" I said.

"You'd do that?"

"You two are my family," I said. "But it needs to happen soon. This is taking up too much space."

"Are you going to sell the bar?" she asked suddenly. "When you get your money?"

"It's not my current intention. They tell you not to make life-changing decisions too fast when you come into money."

Notwithstanding the fact that I'd known for almost two years I was getting it. She put her empty glass in the dishwasher.

"Come for brunch. Next Sunday. She's usually better in the mornings." She started back to the kitchen to clean up. "I'm always going to try and do what she wants, you know. But if I have to make the decision? I will."

I hoped she had the medical papers and power of attorney to back that up. If she was willing, then all I had to do was convince her.

"Eleven. I'll stop at Three Fat Cats and pick up some pastry. Does she still like those raspberry crème horns?"

She looked startled that I would remember.

"Eleven. And don't eat too much ahead of time or she'll be insulted. I know she's going to want to cook."

# 18

I didn't hear anything else from Burton over the weekend, which didn't mean I didn't worry. Marina had been right when she said I needed to help him—it had been our friendship that caused him to color outside the lines on at least one occasion. He'd always managed to jeopardize his job on his own but I'd been part of that too.

I needed to talk to him face to face, preferably without alerting any of the cast of thousands who wanted to talk to him so badly. I didn't want to close the Esposito for any length of time in case that gave it away—I didn't know who might be watching.

So I worked as if it were a normal Monday, hoping anyone watching would be lulled by the routine. After I closed up, I grabbed a bottle of No-Doz from the junk drawer and slipped it into my jacket pocket.

Marina and I walked up the stairs together. She looked worn, as if she hadn't been sleeping well.

"You need a ride home?"

"Carmen's visiting her sister," she said. "We're staying over. She lives like three blocks from here."

"You're sure? It's no strain."

She shoved her hand down into the shoulder bag and pulled out a shiny black leather sap. The puffiness around her eye from last week was gone, leaving only a fading bruise.

I laughed.

"A gift from the Dan Burton School of Self-Defense?"

Under the dim street light, I watched her face crumple and wished I hadn't said his name. They might not be involved any longer but I knew she worried about him.

"You haven't heard anything from him either?" I said.

She shook her head. I was tempted to tell her where I was going but if anyone came looking for Burton while I was gone, I wanted her to be convincingly innocent.

"See you tomorrow, then. I might be a little late. Give Carmen my best."

I yanked on the steel door to be sure it was latched and watched her walk off up Mercy Street. The route to Carmen's sister's place would be pretty well lit and the night was cold enough that the usual knuckleheads wouldn't be out looking for trouble. And she could take care of herself. Still, as I walked down the alley to the Cougar, I felt a pinch of guilt.

I filled up at the gas station on East Berkeley Street and jumped on 93. City traffic was light at this hour and lightened even more as I drove up through the northern suburbs. Once I was into New Hampshire, the trees and underbrush crowded in on both sides of the road and in the rhythm of all night-time long-distance driving, my mind rambled over what I knew and didn't know.

Antoine Bousquet was missing but that could be by choice. The fallout from his arrest had made him radioactive. The good-immigrant narrative—Bousquet arriving on America's teeming shores with nothing in his pockets, building a multimillion dollar business from a single sewing machine and a dusty storefront, employing other immigrants, paying lots of taxes—had been in short supply in the country's recent political climate, even here in ultraliberal Massachusetts.

So when it came out that this paragon of civic virtue, attuned enough to the Boston zeitgeist to have seats behind the dugout at Fenway and in a box at the Pops, was enslaving the immigrants he brought in to work for him, the media darling became a stinking turd with the neck-snapping suddenness of a lover betrayed. The murder charge had been the frosting on the cupcake.

Some voices—the big-mouthed Marty Laird, also killer of jazz radio in Boston, among them—floated tepid apologia about how local unemployment rates forced Bousquet to import his help illegally, and that providing them housing, even at exorbitant rates, was a kindness in the city's brutal rental market. These were mostly the token local conservatives, though, and except for Laird, not much listened to.

In Concord, New Hampshire, I jumped over onto Interstate 89 and headed north toward the lake, the trees and greenery closing in the farther north I drove. The only traffic I saw was a Ben and Jerry's truck on its way to Vermont.

The fact that the city's insiders had turned on Bousquet surprised me not at all. I'd seen from the inside how power in the city moved. My father's bank—my family's, I should say—had been in continuous operation as a supplier of capital since right after the Revolution. Capital, for the most part, to those who didn't already need it.

Boston's behind-the-scenes wealth was billionaires driving rusted-out thirty-year-old Volvos and resoling their shoes instead of buying new ones. This was inherited money, without respect for working for wages or even building a business from scratch. None of my parents' relatives or their peers would have lusted after a job with the cops or the fire department. Or even in the State House.

I curved off the highway at the Route 11 exit, no headlights in my rearview, and wended up the two-lane road past gas stations and convenience stores and a lumber yard before taking the turn up the thin country lane running alongside the shore of the lake. I doused the headlights but left my parking lights on so I could see the rutted dirt road that led to the house.

On Cape Cod, what someone called a cottage could be anything from a five hundred square foot shack to a twelve thousand square foot mansion in Osterville. In New Hampshire, a more self-consciously egalitarian population built modest camps on the lakes, though the big lake out to the west did have its share of McMansions. One of the things that attracted my parents to this smaller lake was that they were less likely to run into someone from their social stratum in Boston. Which made a real vacation more likely.

The Darrow cottage was a square bungalow with about twenty yards of sand beach in front of it. I parked on the road's verge, beyond the mouth of the gravel driveway so I didn't block in

Burton's Ford pickup parked next to the house. The tailgate was up and the tiedowns for his motorcycle neatly coiled and secured, which suggested he was out riding. But at three in the morning?

Lumps of dirty frozen snow remained on the ground and the cold gravel squeaked underfoot as I walked along the drive to the front of the house. The back door, the one visible from the road, was always boarded up for the winter—protection against mischief from cruising delinquents—but the storm door and steel inner door on the front side were only bolted. The prevailing winds off the lake glanced off the house's face, keeping that side free of snow.

I wished there had been recent snow, though, so I could see footprints. No lights shone inside and the trash barrel was empty, though if Burton had been hiding, he might not have wanted to leave traces of his presence. I didn't think he'd come up here to hide, though. He must have had bolt holes in the city if he wanted to drop out of sight.

Security lights in the upper corners of the second story lit up as I rounded the corner. Or rather, one of them did; the other was dark. My boots crunched over broken glass. Had someone shot the light out? Or taken it out with a rock? But why only one?

I picked up a shard of glass, coated with frost. It had been here a while. Still, my stomach twisted as I stepped in closer to the shadow of the eaves.

I walked around the front of the house and climbed the stairs to the porch that in sunny weather provided a shaded place to drink, read a book, watch the sailboats. I stood still and let my breathing slow until the frigid wind started to sneak in between the buttons of my barn coat. There was no evidence anywhere in the neighborhood that anyone was awake, even if they were in residence.

Both doors were locked, as they should have been, but my keys turned easily. I smelled the distinctive fishy odor of WD-40.

I shut the doors behind me. The heat stayed at 45 degrees all winter so the pipes wouldn't freeze and as I followed the hallway past the staircase to the second floor, the old furnace rumbled into life. I was shivering but I withstood the urge to turn up the thermostat. If Burton wasn't here, I wasn't staying.

"Dan?" I had to force myself to speak louder than a whisper. "Burton? You here?"

The great room, as my mother had called it, occupied one whole side of the ground floor. It conjured memories of rainy summer days in the window seat, reading a book, watching the placid lake out the front bay windows. Sheltered in a bowl of trees, the lake rarely showed more movement than riffles.

At the far end of the room sat the long table with the glass top and chairs of unfinished wood where we ate our informal breakfasts and lunches. A formal dining room occupied the other side of the house, where my mother insisted on staging dinner every night with china and silver and linen.

One of the chairs was missing, leaving a hole like an extracted tooth in the mouth of the table. As I swept the flashlight around, I saw where it had gone.

Planted in front of the center window, it faced out at the lake, as if to give its occupant a view. Strips of gray tape dangled from the legs and struts, cut ends down where someone's ankles had been fastened and then up around the slats of the chair back. The cutaway slab of layers of tape stuck to the top of the chair made no sense until I mated the cut ends into a crude horse collar.

My foot slipped and when I looked down, I was standing in a spread pool of dark, almost black liquid, shining like oil against the wood of the floor. The red tinge said someone had lost a significant amount of blood here recently. My throat stuck and I coughed to clear it.

Stepping back, I wiped off the bottom of my shoe with a handkerchief. If this turned out to be a crime scene, I didn't want to disturb things anymore than I had.

I pulled out one of the innocent chairs from the table and sat down, as much in need of a drink as I'd been in a year. The blood might have been Burton's but I was more inclined, because of the scene, to think it had something to do with Antoine Bousquet going missing. For an instant, I wondered if I could have misjudged Burton that badly, that he was capable of torture, then shook my head. He wasn't that evil. But even if he hadn't done it, someone was going to suspect him.

I'd left my phone out in the Cougar. As I stood up to go out and

91

call this in, the furnace clicked off. In the silence came a faint squeal of metal on metal. As I stepped out into the front hall, I caught a flash of light out in the driveway. The pickup's starter ground, the motor roared, and as I ran out onto the porch and looked around the corner of the house, the tail lights of Burton's truck disappeared up the lake road.

Heading back down the highway to Boston, I had one of the most difficult conversations I'd ever had with myself about whether to get involved. The odds were good that Antoine Bousquet had been taped to that chair in my family's cottage. And I had no other evidence other than my intuition that it hadn't been Burton who tortured him, that someone other than Burton had driven his truck away. But I couldn't pretend I didn't have some responsibility here and if I didn't report it, some of the guilt might slop over onto me.

I got off the highway in Concord, stopped at an Irving station, and used the payphone to call in an anonymous tip to the local police about a break-in at the lake. It was close to dawn and I'd be back at my apartment by the time they investigated. It might take them a while to connect it to events in Boston or they might not link it up at all. I hoped I'd talk to Burton again before that happened.

One bit of luck came my way when I got back into the city, an empty double parking space ten feet from the entrance to my building. I backed in, tucking the Cougar in tight to a Mercedes SUV, leaving a full space for some other late night driver. Had to keep my parking karma going.

I locked the car and started up the sidewalk, staggering a bit with fatigue. Upstairs, I turned off the phone, wishing I could trust my addictive nature enough to take a sleeping pill. I planned to stay asleep for as long as I could manage.

# 19

Marty Laird had been a radio voice around the city for at least twenty years, with a reputation as a cross between a conservative Larry King and a screaming sports jock. In a recent attempt to claw itself into relevance in the cable/internet world, a local alternative TV station set him up with a talk show where he could pontificate on local politics and government. The little I'd heard said he wasn't good at anything more complicated than talking over the top of the people he was interviewing. Last month, the *Phoenix* had printed a snippy article that said he tracked his own minutes of air time versus his guests and pitched a fit if he didn't come out ahead.

About which I wouldn't have given a rat's ass except two of my regulars always skipped out of work early on Tuesday afternoons to sink a martini and dissect Laird's show. It was the only time the Esposito's TV showed anything but sports.

Dana Odom was a fourth-year associate at Bynum and Martin, a boutique law firm down in the financial district. Christine O'Hair, who still had to convince people from Southie she wasn't related to Madeline Murray O'Hair, was an executive at a biotech startup in Kendall Square. They were the kind of people I liked as customers: quick, intelligent, well-mannered. Both of them reminded me of Kathleen that way. Good company for a slow afternoon.

"He only did that Locks for Love thing because he was going bald anyway." Christine bit into an olive savagely. "Mark my words. He starts shaving his head all the time any day."

Even though I had prep work to do, I found myself leaning on the bar and listening to the wit crackle. On the screen, Laird was cheering a story about an Iranian day laborer in Quincy who was about to be deported for accumulating four DUIs.

"Old Farad would have had a better chance if he lived in Cambridge," Dana said. "Sanctuary city. Though I do not know what these INS morons are thinking. If they'd deported all the unpapered Irish and Italians a hundred years ago, half this city would never have been built."

Cambridge reminded me—I hadn't heard from Kathleen since Anatoly's self-induced face plant on her stairs. I had to call her or she might think I'd been frightened off.

"What? What did he say?" Dana cried. "Turn it up."

I punched the remote. Laird's whiskey-frog voice rose from the speakers.

". . . absolutely disgraceful they haven't fired this rogue cop. He's been on and off suspension half a dozen times for various acts of malfeasance and some in the know say he was involved in the disappearance of one Antoine Bousquet. Bousquet, faithful watchers will recall, was the alleged mastermind of that heinous plot down in Chinatown to provide jobs and housing for immigrants, as well as pay beaucoup taxes to the Commonwealth."

He pronounced it "bo-coop," pretending he was a rube.

"Fucker," Christine said. "He's talking about Burton, isn't he?"

Her defense of Burton didn't surprise me. She had a small crush on him—a thing for the darker types—and I'd watched her watch him when he was down in his black hole. I was surprised Laird would take on the BPD so directly: there were rumors he was connected to some non-Mickey Barksdale criminal fringe elements in the city.

"More than likely," I said. "Though I think it's bullshit that anyone in the department thinks Burton made Bousquet disappear. They'd have arrested him, if they believed that."

Though the memory of the blood and the duct tape and Burton's pickup in the driveway gnawed at my certainty. If it hadn't been him, who?

"Doesn't look good for him, though. Optics, I mean."

Dana didn't practice criminal law but she'd talked us through the legal implications of the Charles Stuart case one night, making a strong case for the way appearances and inferences can divert the course of justice. She was right, and the physical evidence on the floor of the New Hampshire house would only add weight to an argument for Burton's guilt. Not for the first time, I wondered if I were putting myself at risk here.

"Where is Burton anyway?" Christine said. "We haven't seen much of him lately."

"Busy, I guess. Or laying low." I looked back at the screen. "What's the ding-dong raving about now?"

"Antoine Bousquet was a visionary for this city." Laird slapped his hand on the desk in a gesture that probably blew the ears of every sound person on the set out. "Sure, he cut some corners, maybe cheated on his taxes, worked people hard, but isn't that just an extension of the attitudes that make this country great? Nothing comes easy, folks, and if there's a better lesson to teach the poor and unwashed who come onto our shores, I don't know what . . ."

I pointed the remote and muted him.

"Sorry, guys. Just can't do it tonight."

Christine tipped up the last few drops of gin and set down the glass ultra-carefully on the bar. I had to watch out for her—two was her upper limit and she usually left half of the second drink behind. She owl-eyed me.

"You think Burton would go out with me, Elder? Or does he have that class-conscious thing all those good-looking boys from Charlestown have?"

"Whoa, lady." Dana slipped off her stool and grabbed Chris's arm. "You're done for the day, darling. You weren't planning to go back to work, I hope?"

Christine's eyes, blue as the sea, focused on me.

"Seriously, Elder. What would he say?"

Like any good bartender, I steered to the middle of the road. I wasn't even sure where the edges were anymore.

"You'd have to ask him, Christine. I have no idea. Not to mention it would be none of my business."

Dana pinched her thumb and forefinger together and drew them across her mouth, a request.

I nodded. No need for me to repeat any of this. Or remind Christine of it, next time I saw her.

\* \* \* \* \*

After my two TV critics shuffled up the stairs and out, Marina appeared from the kitchen. Laird's oversized head bobbed silently on the tube and I wondered why he'd picked this exact moment to tee off on Burton. Because anyone in the city with a platform like his had an agenda. Given his reputation, I would have bet his defense of Bousquet had something to do with money.

"God, he's a jerk," she said.

"You know him?"

I forgot sometimes that though my family had been a big deal in the city for a long time, Marina and Carmen had lived here for decades too, Marina almost as long as I had.

She set a pad of paper on the bar, knelt, and opened the cupboards to inventory the napkins, stir sticks, all the rest of the odds and ends, reminding me once more how much I relied on her. She gave me an odd sideways look.

"Maybe you don't remember. He was an investor in that real estate group that wanted to raze our block in Hyde Park and put up a medical complex?"

It had happened about ten years ago. My father told me the story before he died. Before Marina and Carmen moved to the South End, they'd lived in a bungalow in Hyde Park that Carmen's father bought after emigrating to the U. S. after World War II, when the country encouraged that sort of thing. The neighborhood was a short dead-end street of maybe half a dozen houses close to Cleary Square, all older homes. Its proximity to the MBTA and a lack of medical services closer than Roslindale or Mattapan attracted a loose collaboration of doctors who moonlighted as real-estate tycoons.

No one had been terribly concerned about displacing a handful of elderly homeowners with paid-off mortgages until one of the white-haired holdouts turned out to be the great-aunt of the Middlesex County District Attorney. The building got built regardless, of course, but the owners of the torn-down houses got very good prices and full help relocating. Marty Laird had been the PR face of the project, reassuring the owners on TV that progress was inevitable and they should be proud to be part of it. He'd told them everything but "lie back and enjoy it."

"I forgot he was their mouthpiece," I said. "What a crappy deal that was."

Marina stood up and jotted a couple items on her pad.

"Not that crappy, by the time we were done. Carmen took enough away to buy our building here. And Laird almost blew it completely for the developers, trying to pressure those old folks, telling them how much happier they'd be in those cheesy condos they were trying to put them into, all while he was living in a twenty-room house in Dover. These were people who'd lived through the Depression and World War II. Man slithers instead of walking."

"Amazing what some people will do for a buck."

She shot me a sharp look.

"Spoken like a man who never missed a mortgage payment."

I didn't react to that. I might always have had enough money but I'd lacked some other things.

"Burton's in real trouble this time, isn't he?"

"I've seen him in worse," I said. "He's pretty nimble."

"He's supposed to be on suspension. But I know he's working on something else." She picked up a rag and polished the bar.

I knew that much, if not what it was, but I didn't know if she was supposed to know.

"What makes you say that?"

"I'm not stupid, Elder. He hasn't been around here, for one thing. This place was like a second home."

Part of why he'd stayed away was to avoid her. She had to know that.

"I don't know what he's been up to. You do know that when he gets his teeth in something, he doesn't let go."

I shut off the TV. Sirius XM's jazz station was playing Blossom Dearie's "Everything I Have." I still hadn't called Kathleen.

Marina picked up the pad.

97

"I'm going to need a couple days off next week."

"You sure you need to do this? I talked to her about brunch on the phone. She seemed perfectly fine to me."

"Try living with her." Marina swallowed. "She's pretty good at hiding it, but she's been doing some of those things they warn you about: leaving the stove on, putting her keys in the freezer. Getting physical with the caregivers."

"You hired a caregiver."

I felt guilty for trying to tell her things weren't that bad.

"Just the last couple weeks." She shook her head. "I found a placement over in Milton: little suites, a secure floor so she doesn't wander, when it gets that bad. It's clean. And the people seem nice."

Her voice tremored. If she'd been the kind of person who'd take a hug, I would have offered one.

"Have you tried to talk to her again?"

"About the money. She says she doesn't want it." Marina shook her head slowly. "We have enough. Probably."

"It comes to her by law, Marina. If she turns it down? It just goes back to me. And I won't need it. How much does that place in Milton cost?"

"Carmen has long term care insurance," she said stubbornly. "And there's still equity from the house in Hyde Park."

"Look. Thomas obviously wanted to do something for your mother." I couldn't believe we were still arguing over this.

"Clearly."

Her sarcasm perplexed me.

"And you don't know why she's turning it down?"

"It's not my story to tell. Maybe she'll tell you Sunday."

It sounded like Marina did know. All the fencing had tired me out.

"So brunch is still on?"

"Far as I know."

She retreated to the kitchen.

The upstairs door swung open and a party of five descended the stairs. It was five-thirty and my workday was getting started. I swapped out the Blossom Dearie—an acquired taste—and put on some straight-ahead piano music.

As I refilled the mixes, cut more fruit, dispensed the drinks, I wondered what had caused this friction between my father and Carmen. She'd been a family member as much as a cook and a housekeeper and though I wasn't so numb I didn't understand the relative balance of power, I'd never sensed any tension. What else could Thomas's bequest possibly represent than gratitude for her long service?

As the first wave of customers took off coats and pushed tables together, I was glad that it looked to be a busy night. I had too much on my mind and not enough facts to think with.

Edgar Izbicki, a technical writer with a software company in Cambridge, knocked his knuckles on the bar.

"Champagne, my good fellow." The accent was phony but I would have known he wasn't British anyway—he tipped. "Looks like our little venture on the Charles is getting bought out. Those bloody stock options might be worth something yet."

"Very nice, Edgar. So I can assume you'll be drinking the Dom Perignon today?"

I kept a couple expensive bottles for just this kind of situation.

He gulped and looked at his credit card, as if interrogating it. Then he nodded bravely.

"Absolutely, my good man. Let us have the good stuff, for once in our wretched lives."

I rang it up before he came to his senses, unwound the wire, and popped the cork with a quiet little fart. I set out a tray and four flutes, then tossed a bag of almonds on the tray.

"Nuts are on the house, Edgar. Enjoy."

# 20

When the pounding on my apartment door started the next morning, I was out of bed but still foggy. The digital clock in the kitchen read only seven-thirty. Usually I slept until nine or so but last night I hadn't been able to fall asleep, to the point I considered running down to the all-night packie and buying a couple nips of Scotch to help out. Fortunately, I'd waited that stupid impulse out.

The coffee hadn't even finished dripping through the filter. I walked out to the foyer and opened the front door without looking through the peephole first, a mistake even in this relatively civilized part of the city.

The door flew inward and rapped me hard in the knee. I yelped, stumbled back, and Viktoriya Lin shoved her way into my apartment.

Rubbing my kneecap, I slammed the door behind her and locked it. Mrs. Rinaldi must have left the downstairs door open again. At least Viktoriya wasn't traveling with her nasty brother today.

"Good morning to you too." I pointed at a kitchen chair. "If you came to shoot me, be my guest. If not, sit your ass down while I get some caffeine into my blood stream."

Her look would have given me toxic shock if it had hit my system, but at that hour, I was numb and befuddled. Though if Edward had been with her, I might have been more polite. Or lying on the floor listening to my ribs cracking. The skin was sloughing off where the blisters were receding, my hand in a different kind of pain.

"Go ahead." She flounced into a chair. "Drink your fucking coffee. And then you can explain to me how you're going to take over my project from Daniel Burton."

I wasn't quite awake enough to parse that. She wanted me to what? I moved slowly, taking a mug down from the shelf, watching the coffee drip the rest of the way through the filter until the timer buzzed. I poured my own and dropped an ice cube in it, raised a second mug in her direction, to be polite.

She turned up her retroussé nose but favored me with a small nod, as if she didn't expect it to be worth the effort but was trying to be polite.

"You have some almond milk?" she said.

I brought out the quart of skim that had sat in the refrigerator for a couple weeks now and plunked it on the table in front of her, sat down, and swallowed as much coffee as I could without burning my throat.

"Why are you here?"

She sniffed at the open carton and made a face.

"I have not been able to locate your friend Mr. Burton. Still."

This was getting tiresome.

"And I still do not know where he is."

"Did he tell you what he was helping me with?"

Vicky was modulating her natural aggression, which meant she thought she could get something out of me. I shook my head, finished my first cup, poured another.

"My sister," she said. "Also a seamstress in the shops of Antoine Bousquet. She has been missing."

"Burton was looking for her?"

"I couldn't do it myself while Antoine was in my picture. I was afraid . . ."

Bousquet had been five-nine and weighed about one-sixty. Viktoriya was taller and more solid, not a delicate Asian flower— there was something of the Steppes in her lineage. She wouldn't have had anything to fear from him physically.

"That she'd been killed too?"

She nodded.

"You know Burton. He doesn't take advice."

Her perfume, an herbal blend, was subtle but there was a lot of it and it tickled my nose.

"Not so you'd notice. Did he make any progress finding her?"

At least now I knew why the Professional Standards cops were looking into the moonlighting thing.

Vicky's expression darkened, reminding me she was someone who liked living in a storm. Her control over all that energy and rage was tenuous.

Fat heavy tears started down her cheeks, but the attempt to seem pathetic was, well, pathetic.

"He disappeared. I think he did find her but he told me he couldn't help me anymore. Something about his job." She flipped a hand, dismissing him. "So now it's up to you."

"To help you find your sister."

"Daniel, he told me what a good friend you were. That you would help."

I shook my head. He never would have tied me to the tracks like that.

"He's a square peg in a round hole, for sure. But he wouldn't have volunteered me."

The slang confused her.

"He is a wonderful lover, though. And I feel responsible for getting him in trouble with his job. The Holland."

"Dutch," I said. "You got him in Dutch, Viktoriya."

"Vicky. Please."

"I'm a bartender, Vicky. Not any kind of investigator."

Aside from the comment about Burton's prowess in the sack, which I could have done without, nothing she said was making sense. This was a woman who'd lived on her looks and her wits since her breasts had shown. She could find better help than me.

"But you are very close to him. I know. You have helped him in his investigations before. You know how he thinks."

Burton must have been running his mouth, if she knew all this. Or she'd misinterpreted a few pages of Google results. Then I remembered Burton had said he was looking for her cousin. Not a sister. My bullshit meter redlined.

She reached across the table and took one of my hands, her soft and warm and limp.

"But Kuan-Yin is still missing. And Burton has stopped searching for her." Her luminous gray eyes widened, pools of need and regret, and a deep breath shuddered the black Spandex of her top. "I am still very worry for her."

Her command of the language seemed to slip a little more with each sentence, no doubt a ploy. But she was about as helpless as a cab driver on the Southeast Expressway at five o'clock on Friday.

"I don't know what to tell you, Vicky. I'm sorry your sister is missing but I can't help you. Have you tried the police? Officially, I mean?"

"Pah. They think all Chinese girls are hookers, all good-looking foreign girls. That we only get what we deserve."

I stood up, hoping to usher her out.

"If I hear from Burton of course I'll tell you." I was lying—I hadn't forgotten or forgiven Edward's little trick with the tea. "It's pretty unlikely, though. I'm trying to stay away from police and other people not involved in my business."

She made no move for the door.

"Maybe it would be polite for us to have some more coffee? And I could explain to you?"

"I have to leave in a few minutes," I said. "I'm already late for an engagement."

"At the early morning? With your Miss Kathleen, perhaps?"

The casual name-dropping had an opposite effect from what she wanted: it pissed me off.

"Don't mistake me for someone you can push around, Viktoriya. Or you will be surprised."

She slapped both hands down on the table like a drunk making a point of argument, her nice-girl veneer shattered.

"That is what I mean," she crowed. "I knew you were tough enough to help me. And smart enough."

I shook my head.

"I run a bar, Vicky. Six long days and nights a week. I don't do what Burton does and I don't want anything to do with you or Antoine Bousquet. Find someone else to bully."

"You won't help your good friend out?"

103

Such a good friend that I didn't know where he was or what he was doing.

"Help *you*, you mean. I don't know you. And after meeting your brother? I don't trust either one of you. So leave. Please."

She stood up finally, her full lips working with anger.

"Such a good friend you are." She sneered. "I will be sure to tell your good friend Daniel how helpful you were not willing to be."

She slammed my front door so hard as she left that it popped open again. I listened to her pound down the stairs and out the front door, then I closed and bolted the apartment door. If nothing else, at least I was awake, and wondering how Burton had gotten involved with her. Viktoriya wasn't his style at all.

# 21

When Burton said the shit was going to hit the fan, he was off by a couple of days. I think he'd expected something to happen sooner than Thursday afternoon. After a pretty heavy lunch rush, I was sitting at the bar with a glass of ginger ale and a chicken salad sandwich. My sleeping patterns had been ruined by the last week and I wondered if an herbal sleep remedy would do any good without engaging my addictive nature. At least my hand had stopped hurting, the raw weepy patches crusted over and drying out.

Full of my own worries, I hadn't checked the news this morning. I ate half the sandwich, then shook the paper out of its yellow plastic bag and lost the rest of my appetite. The front page headline screamed in seventy-two point type:

### Antoine Bousquet Slaughtered in Chinatown

"Shit."

The writer had tried to pump up the story but the article was long on background and short on facts. Burton's punch-out of Bousquet was mentioned prominently but the reporter must have bumped up against deadline because the only new information was that Bousquet's body, throat slit side to side, had been found under the awning of the Lo Fang Grocery Market off of Kneeland Street in Chinatown. The body was swaddled so convincingly in old blankets that the beat cop assumed it was a homeless person trying to survive a cold night, until morning came around and the bundle hadn't moved.

The rest was a compilation of rehashed skimpy detail and coy enthusiasm, unspecified signs of torture and a "double *coup de grace*" in the forehead. Literal overkill. I refolded the newspaper and shoved it under the bar. The TV would have nothing new until evening.

A pocket of acid formed in my stomach and tried to crawl back up my throat. Burton was going to be ground zero for this, everyone's obvious suspect. If and when the New Hampshire cops connected the bloody scene in my cottage—I was certain now that the blood would turn out to be Bousquet's—to the case down here, Burton's travels to New Hampshire would look suspect as hell. I would have called to warn him if I thought he'd pick up but it might be smarter not to make contact. He'd hear soon enough.

Unfortunately, there were people in the news business in the city who knew Burton and I were friends. They were making some of the same connections I had and the bar phone started ringing. I shut it off and set the system to drop to voice mail. The mailbox filled up in half an hour.

Feeling like a very old man, I prepped the bar for tonight. Even the bright bop of Oscar Peterson did nothing for my mood, nor did five or six cups of coffee do anything but make my mouth feel like I'd been licking a steel pipe. I sat on a stool and tried to come up with anything I knew that might help keep Burton for being blamed for Bousquet's murder.

Because as clearly as I knew he was not a killer, no one outside the department would know about all the people who'd been looking for him this week, people who might have a stake in a disappearing Bousquet: Vicky and Edward, the mysterious Russians who'd sent Anatoly to Kathleen's house, even perhaps Mickey Barksdale.

"Elder." Marina walked in, down the stairs, and dropped her clanking shopping bags on the counter. "You heard?"

I nodded.

"You know he didn't do it," she said, shucking her coat.

The swift and unconditional vote of confidence didn't surprise me at all. Even though the two of them were not dating anymore (which I'm sure had something to do with Burton sleeping with Viktoriya), Marina was loyal.

But the court of public opinion, abetted by the print and TV reporters following the story, would have him convicted for the sake of their ratings. He had little political capital left in the BPD, either, too independent, too willing to chase a wild hare. This might be the time the nail sticking out got hammered down.

"I know that," I said. "Did you talk to him since yesterday?"

"He came by the house last night."

That surprised me. It was encouraging. Burton always tried to solve everything himself, but if he was talking to Marina, someone who believed in him, he might survive this better. Because if he became a serious suspect in Bousquet's murder, the bar for finding the actual murderer would be high. His brethren in Homicide, already inclined to believe he was a loose cannon, would have to be convinced to look in another direction.

"Did he. What did he say?"

She blushed.

"He gave me some money for Carmen. And told me not to believe what I heard about him." She shook her head angrily. "I never do."

She poured herself tomato juice from the cooler under the bar and washed down a handful of vitamins.

"They're going to try and blame it on him, aren't they?"

"I don't know," I said. "They will have to prove it and I can't believe there's any proof. The man's been a homicide cop for eighteen years, for goodness' sake. He must know a hundred ways to kill someone without getting caught."

I wasn't naïve enough to think it wouldn't fuck up his work and his life if someone in the department believed he'd killed Bousquet, even if he was never convicted. Careers were always getting screwed up by rumor and innuendo.

"You need to help him," she said.

"You said that before. What the hell can I do?"

She rinsed out the glass and slotted it in the dishwasher, picked up her vitamin bottles, and started for the kitchen.

"I don't know," she said. "But you helped him out before. I know you can do it again."

I cleared the voice mail box of multiple requests for comment from the *Globe*, the *Herald*, two radio stations that still thought of themselves as news sources, and one long bloviating demand from Marty Laird to call him as soon as possible unless I wanted him to go on the air with the facts he had. I took a maximum dose of satisfaction from deleting that one.

# 22

The next day, I forgot it was Friday until the Esposito's upstairs door opened around six and José Blanco/Joey White started to lug his Fender Frontman amp down the stairs. He pushed it up onto the small triangular stage, waved at me once, then trotted back up the stairs, presumably to get his axe. I envied him his excitement and the state of his knees.

It was early but we had a massive TGIF vibe going on. While I was grateful from a business perspective, I was still distracting myself with trying to knit the connections between Viktoriya Lin, her missing sister/cousin, Burton, and Antoine Bousquet. Marty Laird was in there too, since there was no obvious reason for him to abuse Burton on TV. I'd considered researching Laird's background, but as soon as I got my laptop set up on the bar, the night started going. I was pouring beer and wine as fast as I could and mixing up the odd Cosmo for someone who was still taking drinking advice from *Seventeen* magazine. I did have time to jot myself a reminder note on the back of a deposit slip.

Joey slid one end of the hard-shell guitar case onto the stage next to the amp and started for the bar. A red-headed woman in a flannel shirt and camo cargo shorts said something that made him grin and he tossed her an answer that raised a raucous laugh in return.

He was a good-looking kid, which was almost as big a deal these days as how well you played. I kept hearing musicians talk about "building the brand," which sounded to me like PR bullshit. You couldn't get famous just by pimping yourself.

Tall and slim, he'd cut his hair, which was short, bristly, brushed

109

straight back, and held down with a discreet amount of product. He was dressed for a night on the town: black linen trousers, a slate blue T-shirt under a short-sleeved gray bowling shirt. Oddly enough, considering his generation, he sported no tattoos.

His walk was smooth and his enthusiasm blindsided me with a deep stab of regret for all the time I'd wasted, all the potential washed down my throat by the years of drinking. He stuck his hand over the bar. I shook it. His orange-rimmed spectacles had red earpieces, a combination that should have been ridiculous but looked hip on him. His eyes were espresso brown.

"Mr. Darrow. Very pleased to be here."

He seemed a touch hyper. First night nerves?

"You're straight," I said. "Correct?"

He eyed me.

"We discussing my level of intoxication? Or my preferences?"

"The former. I don't allow illegal substances in my establishment."

Even minor ones, anymore. The situation where Timmy McGuire's dead body wound up on the stage of the Esposito started out with him and Jacquie smoking pot in the walk-in.

He spread his hands out over the bar to show me steady fingers.

"Nothing more potent than a little wine with my dinner. I'm only here for the music—I don't like to let anything get in the way of the playing."

"Just so you know."

He tipped a couple fingers to an imaginary cap.

"Aye, aye, capitaine." He smirked. "Too bad you weren't asking the other question."

That sat in the air for a moment, until I smiled and shook my head.

"Heterosexual," I said. "Aggressively so."

"Anyway. Couple big glasses of club soda? Keep my throat lubed?"

"You're not planning on singing, I hope." He hadn't auditioned for that and it wasn't part of our deal.

"Not after watching that YouTube of George Benson making an ass out of himself. You ever heard me in the shower, you'd know better than to ask. It gets dry under the lights."

"OK." I filled a plastic pitcher halfway with ice.

"One more thing?" He sounded tentative. I braced myself for a renegotiation of the pay scale.

"What's that?"

He smoothed out a piece of notebook paper on the bar.

"Go over the set list with me? You know your clientele better than I do. I want to hit them head-on."

Nothing he could have asked would have tickled me more, though I detected a certain amount of ass-kissing. I filled the pitcher, threw in a handful of lemon slices, and passed him a pint glass. Then I looked at the list.

"Milt Jackson?" I frowned. "You're going to play *Bag's Groove* on the guitar?"

Joey picked up the pitcher and glass and headed for the stage.

"Read the rest," he said. "Tell me what you think."

\* \* \* \* \*

Of course the whole thing was a head-fake. Joey barely followed the list, though he was fingering his way through a creditable version of the Milt Jackson classic when the street door opened and someone slipped inside.

The lights were too low for me to see who it was but he or she had the class to wait until Joey finished the number and the applause rose. He still had five or six numbers until the set break, so I was relaxing against the back bar until I saw it was Kathleen walking down the stairs. The sight of her gave me a shot of adrenaline. I'd forgotten to call her, so she must have decided to grasp the situation herself.

She skirted behind the crowd—as I always did on music nights, I'd pushed all the tables and chairs together up near the stage—and stepped to the far end of the bar where I stood. Joey swung into Grant Green's version of "Jean de Fleur".

"Hey." I damped down how glad I was to see her—I didn't want her to think I was assuming anything. I'd left her a phone message after the night Anatoly died, reminding her about Joey's performance, but I hadn't heard anything back. "Didn't know if you were going to make it."

111

"I never turn down a chance for a drink and some music." She looked up at Joey, hunched over his frets. "Is he good? I don't think I know enough about jazz to tell."

"Think of it like wine." I cringed. It sounded pretentious. "You like it, it's good. You don't like it, it isn't. Unless the musician is plain incompetent and this one is not."

In the low light, her eyes shaded more toward lavender than blue, though it might have been the reflection of the purple linen jacket she wore over a white silk top and black pants. Her hair was piled in one of those messy arrangements that looked as if it took no time to create and probably took hours. Her tiny gold earrings were shaped like oyster shells and her scent, citrus with a sharper element like rosemary underneath, set me dizzy.

"Any chance of a drink?" she said. "Or is the bar just for show?"

Joey finished the tune. I raised my voice over the applause.

"Red wine? Beer? Whiskey?"

"Is tequila an option?"

"As long as you're not slamming it."

She gave me a mock-disappointed look.

"Haven't been to Spring Break in years. How about a Juan Collins?"

I grinned.

"You should meet my guitar player. He calls himself José."

She tossed her head. A couple of graying strands slipped loose from the barrette.

"He doesn't look Spanish."

"My point exactly."

When I returned with the glass and set it in front of her, she nodded her thanks. Hefting the large purse, she locked eyes with me.

"Just so you know? I brought my toothbrush with me."

\* \* \* \* \*

It was a job getting the last of the crowd out the door. Joey White had made some new friends and thought that playing in my bar gave him after-hours privileges. We cleared that misunderstanding up fast. I'd had too much trouble with the ABCC and the cops early on to take any chances with that.

Still, it was nearly two AM when we finally climbed into the Cougar and started for my apartment. Her scent filled the interior of the car as I navigated the nearly-empty streets.

"I do love the late-night city," she said. "Peace and quiet. Opportunity."

That seemed like an odd comment but I didn't ask what she meant. We drove the rest of the way to my apartment through the light and the dark of the night city without talking.

The benefit of age and experience is the setting of expectation. Neither of us expected the smooth sleek body of a twenty year old or all those heightened reactions, the frantic striving. And I was grateful to be sober, to feel, as we stood there in the living room and I kissed her for the first time, that we brought each other our full histories and our knowledge, that the love we made would be a thoughtful construction of attention and pleasure.

In the aftermath, she lay on her back in the moonlight flooding the lower half of the bed. As always at that slightly sad moment, I found myself storing up images of her pale pearl body, her curves and dips, the sounds and scents of our lovemaking against the time when all I would have would be memories. Though my rational side knew nothing lasted, I hoped the only time I would need those memories was when I was old and in a wheelchair in the old folks' home. I knew I could leap too easily but at the moment, I was already half in love with her.

"I'm glad I met you," she said.

She sat up on the end of the bed and looked out the window glass at the bottom of the shade, her back curved like a snowy hill.

"That sounds a little elegiac," I said.

"No."

She lay down on her side, her dark-tipped breasts an offering. I touched her nipple.

"Just trying to be grateful for what I have," she said. "In the moment, for the moment, whatever that means."

I made a noncommittal sound, not sure if we were talking philosophy or diving into relationship talk already.

"Gratitude," she said. "Being thankful when you have something to be thankful for. Not always looking forward to the next thing."

"Philosophy wasn't my strongest subject." I rolled up onto my side, into her body's warmth. All I wanted was all of my skin touching all of her skin.

We kissed. She ran a finger across my eyebrow.

"I'm in for whatever you decide." My throat was dry. "Temporary or not. But right now I'd say I'm leaning toward something other than talk."

She reached down and touched me.

"So you are, darling. Not leaning at all, in fact. Lead on, my friend. Lead on."

# 23

I slept the sleep of the thoroughly fucked-out and when I woke up, Kathleen was gone. I must have felt comfortable enough with her not to wake up when she got out of bed. She left me hot coffee in the steel carafe and a note quoting the Leonard Cohen line about the crack being where the light comes in. I wandered around the kitchen making toast and grinning like the village idiot.

Dawdling over my toast and coffee a little longer than usual, I checked the New Hampshire papers online for any mention of mysterious break-ins or violence in the house at Pleasant Lake. No matter how I tweaked the search terms, nothing showed, but that didn't keep me from worrying. The local cops might be keeping things quiet until they connected with Boston.

It had been Burton's truck fleeing the driveway but I didn't believe he'd been driving it. Nor did I believe he was cold-blooded enough to tape someone up to a chair and torture him. He was too direct for that kind of calculated violence—he was more likely to punch someone out. But I still worried how he was going to explain where he'd been and what he was doing between the time Bousquet went missing and the time his body was found.

I set my mug and plate in the sink, grabbed my keys and a sheepskin jacket. Spring had sprung all the way back to winter and though no rain or snow was forecast, the morning looked cold. I'd opened the apartment door to leave when the phone rang.

"Mr. Darrow?"

Mrs. Rinaldi, my downstairs tenant. I still hadn't replaced the light bulb in the foyer and Mrs. R. was particular about my meeting my landlord obligations. Life had been simpler before she found out I owned the building.

"Good morning, Mrs. R."

"Would you stop down to my apartment, please? There's something I need you to see."

Not the light bulb, then. A cockroach? Mildew on the shower stall?

"Of course. I was just on my way in to work. I'll be down in a minute."

I slipped into my coat, locked the door, and walked down to the ground floor, wondering how many more years Mrs. Rinaldi had left in her string. She'd celebrated her eighty-sixth birthday last year and though her work with the opera sets gave her something to occupy her time, I had to wonder how much longer that frail body would hold up.

All of which only reminded me of Carmen and how I was going to resolve that problem.

I stepped in through Mrs. Rinaldi's open door and into the kitchen, where Burton sat on one of the dinette chairs.

He looked better than he had, healed from the cuts and bruises I'd seen on him last time. The high color in his face could have been the result of enough sleep or a couple quick pops—it was after ten in the morning and he never stood much on ceremony. What was most remarkable was that he was wearing full uniform.

A china cup of coffee steamed on the table beside him, but he was staring at the floor, elbows on his knees. He barely acknowledged me.

"Elder."

Mrs. Rinaldi, thin and brittle as a sculpture of bird bones, sat down at the table next to him. It irked me that he'd dragged her into this, though I knew she didn't sleep much and was often lonely for company. She'd laid out coffee cake and plates and forks.

"Looking pretty sharp there, Dan. You couldn't make it all the way up to the third floor?"

"Last time I looked, you were having company. I didn't think you'd appreciate the interruption."

116

Which meant he'd been here most of the night. He raised his head and flushed. He must have been embarrassed about inconveniencing Mrs. Rinaldi.

"So what brings you back into town? Staying for a while?"

The sarcasm rolled off.

"Disciplinary hearing."

"Hence the monkey suit."

"Uniform of the day."

"On a Saturday."

"I'm trying to do what they tell me."

"Any idea what they'll do to you?"

"Worst case, foot patrol."

Our unesteemed mayor gave great lip service to the idea of "community policing," the practice of having officers patrol and work in neighborhoods, both to increase visibility and build relationships. As practiced by midlevel brass, though, it became a gulag for officers who wouldn't get with the program, whatever that month's program was. None of the amateur sociologists evaluating the effort saw it but the residents reacted poorly to having officers assigned to their neighborhoods as punishment. Surprise, surprise.

And if there was anyone who didn't work well within a program, it was Burton. If he did wind up on foot patrol, it wasn't going to be in one of the nicer neighborhoods.

"I might quit, if they do that," he said. "Except I'd probably forfeit my pension and Sharon would sue the shit out of me."

Mrs. Rinaldi tutted and picked up a long knife to cut the coffee cake. I doubted what we were talking about evinced more than a slight interest in her. She'd been hoping for a nice Saturday morning over coffee and cake.

"So why am I here?" I said. "Sounds like your day's all planned out."

"Need your help. There are things I can't do right now. Whether they bust me or not, I'm under eyes, clocking in and out."

"If I can."

Mrs. Rinaldi had started to pour me a cup of coffee.

"I have to get to the bar," I said. "You want to walk with me?"

She shook a finger at me, her watery blue eyes sparking.

"Don't you treat me like some crazy old lady, Elder Darrow. Are you forgetting some of the things I've been through with you?"

"I have not forgotten. But I really need to get down there and open up. No use owning a business if it isn't open."

She laid a couple slices of the coffee cake on a paper plate and covered it with plastic wrap.

"Take this with you. You boys drink enough but I don't ever see you eat anything."

She hawkeyed Burton, knowing I'd been sober for a while. He got up and went out the door. I accepted the plate.

"Ouch on his behalf," I said. "But thanks. I'll come back later and tell you all the dirt, if you want."

She raised a gnarled hand as if to slap me.

"Get out of here, you."

Out on the sidewalk, Burton was adjusting all the paraphernalia on his belt. He probably hadn't been in uniform, except for funerals, for a decade. It must have felt strange.

"Walk or ride?" I said. "It's not too cold."

"Ride," he said. "I'll be walking plenty if they bust me back to foot patrol."

We strolled up the block to where I'd parked the Cougar, Burton creaking and jingling. I decided not to say anything about it. The Mercedes SUV sat about an inch off my rear bumper and an old white panel van hemmed me in in front.

We climbed in and I started the car, reversed hard into the SUV, smiling at the crunch of plastic. Obviously not one of the more expensive models. I forced myself enough room to get the Cougar out of the parking space without doing it again.

"What do you think I'm going to be able to do for you?" I said. "I'm certainly not going to chase that Kuan-Yin woman for you."

He frowned, then nodded.

"Vicky tried to sign you up?"

"She did. I told her I was just a simple bartender." I headed east on Commonwealth Ave.

"Just like I'm a simple cop," he said. "Simple-minded, maybe."

Burton stared out the windshield as we rolled along in traffic.

"Last couple weeks. Since they put me on suspension? I've been working on something else."

No real surprise there, except that maybe I was going to get the full story.

"Chasing Antoine Bousquet? Or stalking him to make sure he didn't kill anyone else."

"Not exactly." He half-turned in the bucket seat. "You know what we arrested him for."

"Having two of his illegal immigrant seamstresses beaten to death."

"With an emphasis on the illegal immigrants. Both of them were Chinese nationals. They came to the city with a story about being smuggled in to work in his sweat shops. Specifically. Later on, he turned them out. As hookers."

"So he's connected," I said. "Not too surprising. But let me guess— your bosses were happy with the case against him. They wanted you on to the next thing."

"And with him dead? It begs the question even more of putting resources on it. As far as they care, it's solved. But Bousquet was the tip of this. And Viktoriya's cousin—I take it you met Vicky."

"I should say so. And her thug brother." I turned right onto Mass. Ave. "She makes an impression. She was very complimentary about you, though."

He said nothing but the tips of his ears turned pink.

"The cousin," he said. "Kuan-Yin?"

"She said sister."

"Whatever. She was also working in one of the sweat shops."

I sped up to beat the yellow light and turn onto Tremont.

"She knew the victims?"

"She might have been another one. No one's seen her."

"And Vicky was paying you to find her? In something besides trade, I hope."

I turned into the alley off Mercy Street and drove back toward the loading dock, glass and other trash crunching under the tires. I saw syringes back here all the time. This neighborhood wasn't ever going to be pure.

Burton climbed out of the car and nodded at me over the tattered vinyl top.

"The only thing I'm reasonably sure of is that Bousquet didn't have her killed because she disappeared after he was arrested. Though there is evidence he turned her out, too. Pulled her out of the sewing room for other work."

"Maybe she didn't like the idea and ran."

"Not to the police. I would have heard."

He followed me out of the alley and around the corner to the Esposito's door. The lock was open and we walked in, down the stairs.

Marina's eyebrows climbed when she saw him, first because he was there, second because he was in uniform. The air felt heavy.

"Very nice," she said. "You should get dressed up more often."

He blinked, stunned to silence.

I turned on the coffee pot first thing. Burton took a stool.

"You want a drink?"

I said it quietly, though Marina was rattling pans in the kitchen.

"Better not. My hearing's at noon."

"So what do you need me to do? Though I will say, if it involves Vicky's baby brother? I'm out. That is one scary child."

"Strictly research," he said. "I don't have the time right now and you're much better at that Google shit than I am anyway. Plus you have sources I can't touch."

He was talking about my family's connections, through the bank and our history in the city. They were only provisionally mine with Thomas gone, but they still had value.

"Sure. Who, what, when, where, why?"

"Give me some coffee. I might as well be caffeinated for this meeting."

He was hesitating, either because he didn't want to involve me—too late—or he wasn't sure how to ask. I pushed a china mug across the bar.

"Viktoriya?" I said. "You want background on her?"

"Marty Laird."

"Cable TV's answer to political porn? Anything special you want to know?"

"I don't want to point you in a particular direction," Burton said. "Whatever you can find out, his business connections particularly."

Was this payback for Laird roasting him on the air? Or did he think Laird was guilty of something?

"You did know he was trashing you on his show the other night?" Burton perked up.

"Really. Anything relevant? Or the usual innuendo and bullshit."

"Rogue cop, poor misunderstood Antoine Bousquet, doing so much for the city, couldn't possibly have a reason to murder anyone."

"So. Nothing new."

"You sound like you expected more."

"My pickup." The topic change was a wrench. "It got stolen from a parking lot in Laconia."

"You were riding?"

He nodded.

"Planning meeting for Bike Week."

"When?"

"A week ago today."

"Last seen in the driveway of the family cottage, leaving fast."

He raised an eyebrow.

"Ballsy," he said. "So you were there. Along with a puddle of blood and evidence someone had been taped to a chair?"

That rocked me.

"How'd you know that?"

"I heard about it," he said. "It might look like someone's trying to set me up."

"For Bousquet? Shit. Here we go again."

"Oh," Burton said, getting down off the stool and staring at me. "We've been going for a while. You want to watch yourself, Elder. Or you'll get dragged down into this too."

"Really," I said. "I hadn't thought of that."

# 24

Burton left for his hearing, not showing a bit of nerves. I was probably more worried about the outcome than he was. If he had to go back into uniform and work regular shifts in another part of the city, I'd never see him. Helping him out by researching Marty Laird was the least I could do, though it was going to take time I didn't have tonight.

I didn't have to do it myself, I realized. I had money, or the promise of it, which meant I could afford to hire someone to do the work for me. A professional would probably do a more thorough job more quickly than I could cobble something together.

Though it was eleven on a Saturday morning, Daniel Markham, my father's personal attorney and temporarily mine, would be in his office. He was a divorced, childless, seven-day-a-week workaholic, with no interests outside the law. I pulled the old leather address book out of the junk drawer and thumbed through to the M's.

"Elder Darrow. How are you, son? And what can I do for you?"

I imagined a stop watch clicking on and a sweep hand recording the minutes like a taxi meter ringing up the fare. Daniel Markham didn't clear his throat for free.

"Daniel, didn't you have a researcher on staff a while back?"

"Not on staff." He corrected me immediately, no doubt concerned the IRS was monitoring his calls and might find him liable for payroll taxes. "Strictly an independent contractor. Why? Was there something you needed done?"

His voice carried the faint desperate suspicion I might snatch away the remnants of my father's legal affairs from his firm. Once the bequests were disbursed, he wouldn't have anymore Darrow business to conduct. The Esposito didn't generate enough legal work to hold a boutique law firm on retainer. His nervousness made me glad all over again that my livelihood did not depend on sucking up to the rich and powerful.

"Small job of research. Very small. Not important enough to take up your time." I couldn't resist a jab. "Or pay your rates."

"Ha. Ha."

Markham was one of the most humorless people I'd ever met and that covered a lot of ground. He would have preferred to engage the researcher on my behalf and add on a commission for himself, but there was no polite way for him to refuse me the name.

"Rasmussen Carter."

I remembered the name as soon as he said it.

"And would you have his number handy?"

Markham actually harrumphed. I had to remind myself he was my age, not seventy. He played very old.

"Usually I'd have Deirdre here to do this."

"I know you can do it, Daniel."

The line went dead. I rolled my eyes. What evolution was doing to us was frightening. Humans in the twenty-second century were all going to have enormous asses from sitting down all day and enormous thumbs from texting.

The clatter as he fumbled the phone off his desktop made me wince. Our workplaces were very different too, his seventeenth floor interior office and my subterranean bar. One of the sweet surprises of owning the Esposito had been finding out that I liked people, even listening to them complain. I could never sit alone in an office and listen to the sound of my own brain spinning.

"Rasmussen Carter." Markham cleared his throat as if to deliver an oracle, then rattled off the number at speed.

"Would you repeat that, please?"

He sighed, then slow-spoke each digit.

"Thank you." I started to say goodbye.

"Another issue we should discuss. While I have you."

The sweep hand on the stop watch made another slow circuit.

123

"What's that, Daniel?"

"This bequest of your father's to Mrs. Antonelli? We need to schedule the handoff soon. And your own disbursement, of course, depends on the successful closing of hers."

"News to me. Why is that?"

"You have the residual. I can't calculate the final value before she inherits." He sounded bored, explaining the obvious.

I'd been counting on a little extra time to convince Carmen.

"Technically," he said. "We have until May 31st. But I'm on vacation in April and I have a case before the Supreme Judicial Court that will consume most of March. It would be to everyone's advantage if we took care of this sooner rather than later."

To Markham's advantage, certainly.

"I'll talk to Carmen and Marina, get something scheduled." I hope my concern didn't come across. I didn't need to give him an excuse to generate more billable hours. "I'll get back to you this week."

"Very well, Elder. That's all I had."

"And I. Thank you."

My answer was the click of a severed connection, reminding me that Markham's time, at least, was money.

I immediately dialed the number he'd given me for Rasmussen Carter, but only got a voice mail message. The voice was male but high and effeminate, which didn't give me a lot of confidence.

"This is Elder Darrow, a client of Attorney Markham's. I'd like to speak to you as soon as possible about a research project."

I left him the bar number as well as my cell and hung up. Time to get to work: Saturday, the night of the week that had to make up for all the rest.

\* \* \* \* \*

We had a decent night but I let Marina close the kitchen early and go home. Serious late-night drinkers, if they thought about food at all, didn't eat until two or three, long after we closed. For them, there were the all-night diners, or Dunkin' Donuts.

By twelve-thirty, I was down to four couples and a group of six or seven female tourists doing their best to taste-test every one of the craft beers I sold. They were moderately rowdy, in the way a group got when they thought they were drinking in a place a step below their usual quality. I didn't know whether to laugh or be insulted.

The street door creaked open between a couple of Brubeck numbers and I set a small can of WD-40 on the bar by the register to remind me to lubricate it on the way out.

A thin mixed-race man, Afro-Caribbean if I had to guess, bounced down the stairs on the balls of his feet and drifted across the floor toward the bar. One of the tourist ladies said something under her breath that cracked the rest of them up. The man's stride broke but that was his only reaction.

"You'd be Mr. Darrow," he said.

He rocked from one foot to the other at the bar, as if he had too much energy to sit. His face was smooth, to the brown side of hazel, and a single diamond punctuated his left ear lobe. He lowered his sunglasses to show eyes that were almost colorless in both pupil and iris. His cropped curly hair was an improbable black with golden highlights and it shone with pomade. My mother would have called him a lounge lizard, complete with the tight emerald shirt and black pleated pants.

My first thought was that someone else was now looking for Burton. He didn't appear ready to order a drink.

"What can I get you?" I said.

He looked at me as if I knew why he was here.

"Go ahead and take care of your customer," he said. "I'll wait."

The woman who'd commented on his descent of the stairs stood at the other end of the bar. I nodded at him and walked down to draw another brace of drafts from the beer taps. She was thirtyish, a bright blonde with her hair cut in last decade's asymmetrical hedgehog style, a touch too fleshy for the tight khaki capris and zipped-up Patagonia vest. She'd had enough beer to be staring at me and I hoped she wasn't about to say something drunk.

I adjusted the tab and walked back up the bar. She headed to her table, her attention on my visitor now and I half-expected her to pull a pratfall. The amusement on his face was mild and we shared a smile. I got the impression he was used to that kind of attention.

"Ginger ale?" he said. "I'm not much of a drinker."

"Interesting reason to walk into a bar." I nodded at the glass. "To not drink."

He smiled in a tight way, picked up the can of WD-40, and looked at the label. His eyes twitched once every forty or fifty seconds.

"You called me about a research project? I would have thought Markham described me."

"You're Carter?"

"Rasmussen Carter, at your service." He looked around the bar. "Though I guess you must know something about service."

It seemed like an odd thing to say, until I realized he was nervous.

"Odd time of day to be doing business," I said.

He also seemed like a strange choice for the straitlaced Markham, which meant he was good.

"My eyes bother me," he said. "Ocular albinism. Bright lights hurt." He dropped his dark glasses down. "Even these ones."

"OK. Let me tell you what I'm looking for."

Rasmussen pulled out a small leather-bound notebook and a fountain pen, uncapped it, and touched the nib to the page to be sure ink was flowing.

"Go."

"You know who Marty Laird is?"

"The TV guy? Big mouth, bigger ego?"

I looked at him.

"You've had contact with him."

He frowned.

"I'm a friend of Eric Jackson's," he said. "And I'm pretty sure he's behind what's going on there. Don't know what a man could have against a little jazz music on the radio."

Already I liked him.

"I need a deep dive on him. Financial and business. Any dealings he's had with Antoine Bousquet. Or a Boston Homicide cop named Daniel Burton."

"Homicide. Isn't he a friend of yours?"

"OK," I said. "You can Google. I hope there's more."

He pinched his lips together.

"Is there any potential for physical danger? Because I know Bousquet was killed. And there are rumors about organized crime being involved."

"Rumors." Was he talking about Mickey Barksdale? Or something else?

"I heard some Russians might have an interest."

Anatoly came to mind.

"I don't anticipate anything. All I want is research. I assume you don't interview most people directly."

He took off the sunglasses to stare at me. Like anyone with a prominent physical characteristic, he'd figured out ways to use it. But the colorless eyes were less disturbing now that I knew what caused them.

"I do use a lot of secondary sources," he said. "I find people tend to lie to you in person a lot of the time. But I'll tell you what, Mr. Darrow."

"Elder, please."

"I'll tell you what, Elder. I won't advise you how to mix a martini if you don't tell me how to do my work."

Fair enough, though his client manner could use a little work.

"There are unpredictable people involved," I said. "But I'm unaware of any connection to organized crime."

Carter showed flawless white teeth.

"Who of us is that reliable, yes? I'll begin in the morning. Assuming you're willing to pay me a retainer. Cash, if possible."

"How much?"

He named a figure almost too low to be reasonable. I counted bills out of the cash drawer and passed them over.

As we'd talked, most of the beer tourists had left the bar. The woman who'd ordered the last round sidled up to Carter, accompanied by a tall witchy woman with long purple hair and one eye off plumb. The first woman handed me a messy pile of cash.

"Wondered if you know of any after-hours places in the neighborhood." She spoke directly to Carter. "Mirabelle and I would like to buy you a drink."

He folded the bills and buttoned them into the pocket of his slick green shirt.

The purple-haired woman nodded, baring shiny sharp teeth. It was all I could do not to laugh. If I'd turned the Esposito into a place where patrons picked each other up, my work here was done.

I expected Carter to brush her off, but he asked me for a piece of paper and a pen, wrote something, folded it, and passed it to her.

"Ask for Gaetano," he said. "Perhaps I'll see you later but right now I'm conducting some business."

Neither woman seemed put off by his bluntness. They hip-switched away and up the stairs. I smiled and pointed to his glass.

"Refill?"

"Thank you, no." He tapped his breast pocket, where the money lay. "I'll get back to you in a day or so. I don't anticipate any difficulty in finding out what you want to know."

He jogged up the stairs as if weightless and I wondered how he could be so sure. I didn't know exactly what Burton was looking for or what he hoped to find out. Or whether it was going to help him keep his job. I feared that if the department put him back in uniform, he wouldn't last long.

# 25

Whatever information he wanted on Marty Laird couldn't have been too critical. Burton didn't contact me for the rest of Saturday night or Sunday morning. He still had access to the New Hampshire house, so he might have gone back up there. The fact that no one from law enforcement had contacted me about a break-in made me wonder if the local cops were conspiring with the BPD to keep the whole thing quiet for now.

My windshield wipers squeaked as I turned onto the little side street off of Shawmut Ave. in front of Carmen's building. I parked the Cougar in a taxi zone half a block down from their front door. I didn't think anyone would care on a Sunday morning.

Locking the car, I grabbed the bag of pastries from Mastucci's in the North End—Three Fat Cats had closed up shop and moved to Portland, Maine—and picked my way along the sidewalk. It hadn't rained or snowed or sleeted for days and the sun was trying hard to break through the cloud cover this morning, but the concrete bore a rough skim of salt and sand that crunched underfoot. The stairs to the building, a rare two-decker, were swept clean.

The dark green door held the remains of a Christmas wreath, a tarnished gold ball hanging from the rusty brown branches by a twist of wire. I pushed the buzzer and an immediate click unlatched the front door.

Marina stood on the second floor landing, frowning down at me.

"You're late," she said. "Carmen's losing her mind."

I didn't ask her if she meant literally, held up the paper bag so she saw the logo.

129

"They were late opening up. And there was a line."

"Come on." She disappeared into the apartment, leaving the door ajar.

I climbed the creaking wooden stairs, wondering about the provenance of this building, a vintage old brick lady in the midst of all the new condominium construction. Most of the old buildings like this that remained were triple-deckers. And how had the two of them afforded this, the Hyde Park settlement notwithstanding? Even before the downtown building boom, this would have been a million-dollar building.

"*Tesoro!*"

Marina had convinced me her mother was frail, both from age and her health problems, but the old woman practically ran across the floor with her arms wide, nearly knocking me over. I set the bag on the table and folded her into a hug, letting her pat my back and squeeze me around the ribs, exclaiming how skinny I was. She didn't seem to have lost her physical strength, at least.

Her eyes were teary and I felt guilty I hadn't managed to get here to see her sooner. She had known me since my age amounted to single digits and had treasured me long before my addictions got the better of me.

"Finally, you come to see an old woman," she said. "You must think I'm getting ready to die."

"Mother!" Marina said.

The push-pull of the mother figure came back to me like a set of old habits. Her complaints were part of her way of love.

"You know how busy we always are at the bar," I said.

"Nice one." Marina spoke under her breath, standing at the stove spreading grated cheese over the top of a cast iron pan full of eggs. She bent and slid it under the broiler. "Way to spread the guilt around. You want coffee?"

"Of course." I rarely turned down coffee.

I sat at the kitchen table before Carmen could tell me to and looked her over. She was still taller than Marina at five-seven, despite the age stoop in her shoulders. Her gray hair was freshly permed—Saturday was hairdresser day—and her color seemed healthy enough, her eyes clear and her attention bright and sharp.

"My Marina," she said. "She says you want to talk to me about something."

I looked across the kitchen but Marina wouldn't meet my look.

"Wouldn't you rather wait until after we ate?"

"Not if it's important," Carmen said. "Business, we get that out of the way and then enjoy ourselves. I made you some gravy to take home for later, too."

I wrapped both hands around the coffee mug and leaned my elbows on the table. Now was as good a time as any.

"OK. You know when Thomas died, he left quite a bit of money."

She started when she heard my father's name, nodded, then reached to take my hand.

"I told Marina I don't want any of your money. You should do something good with it." She grinned, her original equipment teeth crooked and yellow. "Pay my daughter better."

"It isn't all my money, Carmen."

She frowned.

"He left it to you, didn't he?"

"Not all of it. Some of it he left to you specifically."

She straightened up as if someone had poked her in the back.

"He did. Thomas? This isn't you being nice?"

"When he wrote the will, he put that money aside for you. Like a pension, I guess."

Carmen dropped my hand like a hot rock and stood up. She disappeared into the living room, trailing a sob.

Marina opened the oven door to check the frittata.

"What did you say to her? That wasn't unhappy crying."

"And what makes you so sure of that?"

Marina glared.

"Maybe because she's my mother? And because I think she's waited a long time for your father to acknowledge her?"

"For what?"

I was developing a notion what she might be talking about. It bothered me less than intrigued me that my buttoned-up and emotionally-restricted father might have dallied, as they'd say in his social stratum, with a younger Carmen. My mother was never the warmest woman in the world and she distanced herself progressively as her depression worsened. I wouldn't argue cause and effect necessarily but I couldn't find it in myself to fault Thomas. Despite his effort to always appear cold and rational, I'd had glimpses before he died of how human he could be.

"There's actually a little more to it." She shook off the potholders. "She told me the whole story. Finally. He was the reason she stopped working for your family."

I'd gotten that part. I nodded.

"There's one other small fact," she said. "It appears you and I might be related."

A wave of unreality washed over me.

" 'Appears.' What does that mean?"

She chewed her lower lip, half embarrassed, half proud.

"Seems Mom used to get around a little bit."

"Really." Any calm I was showing was artificial. Marina and I might be siblings? Or half-siblings, however that worked? I was surprised and concerned. I found it easier to imagine Thomas philandering than siring children out of wedlock.

Marina was placid, considering the bomb she'd dropped. She'd had time to get used to the idea, I guess.

"I don't have any evidence to believe her," she said. "Or disbelieve."

She slipped on the oven mitts again, pulled the pan out of the oven, the crust of the eggs puffed up over the edge.

"Doesn't change anything, really." Her flat look was a challenge. "Does it?"

"Our personal relationship? Or professional?"

"Either."

"Does this mean she'll accept the money? Now that she knows it was his wish?"

She shrugged, cutting the cooled frittata into pieces like a pie. She slid pieces onto three separate plates and called something in Italian into the next room.

"Makes it more possible," she said. "I think all she wanted was your father to acknowledge her somehow."

Carmen returned, drying her eyes with a tissue. She wouldn't look at me.

"Let's eat," Marina said.

I tried to keep up the small talk, since Carmen clearly didn't want to talk about Thomas or money. The idea Marina and I might be related got too big for me to shove aside, though, and neither of them protested when I said I had to leave, only minutes after we'd finished eating.

"See you at the bar tomorrow morning?" I said to Marina on the way out.

My last view of her was a nod and a forlorn smile. I shut the door quietly and walked down the stairs.

# 26

All through Sunday afternoon, I brooded about what I'd learned about my father and Carmen, but nothing I thought helped me sleep that night and I was still groggy when I keyed open the Esposito's door and stumbled down the stairs. I was an hour or so later than usual and I expected to find Marina tapping her foot outside the door. She wasn't there and I hoped she wasn't answering my question from yesterday this way.

At least I didn't have to do Burton's research for him. Rasmussen Carter would do a better job than I could and it was my chance to help Burton somehow. He'd covered for me when Cy Nance and I had to rescue Alison Somers and then he'd helped me work through her murder a few months later. I'd been supercargo on both those journeys, though, and it felt good to contribute actively.

Marina still hadn't shown by eleven-thirty, when normally she'd have everything prepped and ready for lunch. It was Monday, though, not the day most people ate out, but I called her at home anyway. I hoped she hadn't been so freaked out by Carmen's revelations that she couldn't work here anymore.

"Carmen? Elder Darrow. Is Marina home?"

"Elder! How nice to hear from you. How have you been?"

As if we hadn't had brunch together yesterday. And early in the day was supposed to be the best time for people with memory problems, those faculties diminishing the closer a person got to nightfall. Sometimes I even felt that loss of focus at the end of the day.

"I'm fine, Carmen. Sorry I couldn't stay later yesterday."

She made a tentative sound, not sure what I meant.

"So, is Marina home?"

"No, she went to work a couple hours ago. She's not there?" Her voice rose in worry.

"What time did she leave?"

"Regular."

"Maybe she stopped off to buy me a doughnut."

"That's it." She was relieved. "Sometimes she'll do an errand for me on the way to work."

"She'll be here soon, then. Sorry if I upset you."

"She's her own woman, that one." Carmen laughed. "She thinks I don't know all the things she gets up to. With that policeman? Sometimes she acts like I'm senile."

Any thought I'd had of asking more questions about her and Thomas fled.

"I should think not," I said. "You're as sharp to me as you ever were."

"You're a lovely boy, Elder. But I have to go now—my program's coming on."

And then she hung up on me.

Twelve o'clock came. Twelve-thirty. No one ordered lunch, unless you included a city street repair crew that drank theirs in the nutritious form of Guinness.

At one o'clock, I walked into the kitchen and shut down the grill and fryer. Assuming she made it back for the dinner rush, they'd reheat in time. She must have been paying me back for yesterday somehow. The only thing I could be sure of was that it wasn't Carmen holding her back.

Burton burst in the door about three-thirty and ran down the stairs two at a time.

"Where's Marina?" he said as he jogged to the bar, red-faced, panting.

"Not in yet. Why?"

He inhaled and exhaled like a distance runner, trying to tame his heart rate.

"You talk to her today?"

I shook my head. He pointed at the soda gun. My hand shook as I filled a glass. His panic was contagious, even if I didn't know the source.

He drank half a glass of club soda, then dialed his cell phone and put it on speaker. When the disembodied voice prompted him, he entered his voicemail password.

"Mr. Burton." The voice was tantalizingly familiar, more the accent than the words. The speech had a mechanical cadence, as if it were words being read by someone unfamiliar with the rhythms of English.

"You have made yourself very difficult to locate. Perhaps knowing we can detain your lady friend Ms. Antonelli at any time will encourage you to speak with us. Please call the following number at your earliest convenience."

Then the voice chanted an unfamiliar area code and number.

"He didn't say they had taken her," I said. "He said they could."

"Suzy fucking sunshine. Then where is she?"

He glanced at the kitchen door as if she might be hiding. My gut tightened.

"I told you. She hasn't come in yet." I refilled his glass, not wanting to attract more attention from the sleepy afternoon crowd than we had. No one came to a bar at this time of day because they were looking for something interesting to happen.

"What is it that everyone in the known world is so fucking hot to talk to you about, Burton?"

"If only I knew."

I thought he did and that crumbled some of the trust I had in him. Maybe he was so deep he felt he had to protect me and Marina, though if someone had taken her, it hadn't worked very well. But his worry was infecting me. Whether Marina was safe was a more important conversation right now than his transgressions.

"Where were you a week ago?" I said.

"You probably don't want to know," he said. "If the wrong person asks."

I felt that like a blow. Had he been in the camp, torturing Bousquet?

"Then why was your truck in the driveway of my house?"

"I told you once already. It was stolen. I told you, it was a setup. You want to tell me why any of this matters, if Marina's in trouble?"

He was avoiding something.

"No doubt you weren't there, all right. But when the local cops up there make the connection to me, they're going to talk to Boston, right? Shouldn't you be in ahead of that?"

"No connection," he insisted. "You're the only one who knew I was staying there."

Was he asking me to lie for him now? Omission or commission?

"Along with whoever stole your truck. And tortured Bousquet."

"Not established it was his blood." Burton crushed ice between his teeth. "They can connect me up all they want. I wasn't there. I was out making sure more people didn't die."

He might have been overdramatizing, but he was right. If Marina was in trouble, we had to fix that first. I untied my apron, cut off Miles Davis in the middle of "Bye Bye Birdie," and started to cash out the register.

"What are you doing?" he said.

"Shutting down so we can get out of here and find her." I zipped the cash into a bank pouch, which made me think briefly of Kathleen.

Burton shook his head, shucked out of his raincoat, and draped it over a stool. He was in civilian clothes and I realized I hadn't asked him how the hearing had come out.

"Relax," he said. "They're coming to me. Make me a sour while I'm waiting."

"Waiting for what? The Good Fairy to rescue her?"

"Relax," he said, louder. "I made the call. I'll talk to whoever it is and that will take care of it."

"You trust whoever it is not to do anything to her?"

"First." He bounced a fingertip off the bar. "I'm certain this is just a threat. No one has been picked up, abducted, or otherwise endangered. If they were actually holding her, they would have made a point of saying so. They'd expect me to ask for proof. They know I've surfaced."

"And who might 'they' be?"

He shook his head.

"Better you don't get involved. Suffice to say it's yet another group of clowns worried about Antoine Bousquet corking off."

"Which I'm still assuming you had nothing to do with."

Burton's eyes darkened like a storm, as they always did when he got angry. His fists closed and his shoulders pushed up under his cheap sport coat. He took a series of breaths, like a long jumper preparing to take off.

"Are you going to make me a drink? Or do I come around there and mix it myself?"

I took a stemmed glass down from the overhead rack and slowly, deliberately, inspected it against the light for dishwasher spots. He hadn't responded to my comment, though that was likely simple anger that I might not believe he was innocent.

I free-poured the whiskey into an aluminum shaker—house brand, since he wouldn't taste the difference—doused it with mix from a plastic container, and added a dash of egg white. Capped the shaker, shook it, poured through the strainer into a stemmed glass.

"You really think Marina is safe?"

"Didn't say that." He sipped the cocktail, leaving a faint line of foam on his upper lip that he wiped away with a finger. "But I don't believe anyone is detaining her."

Then, as if his certainty had conjured her, the street door opened and Marina stepped in, letting the door sigh shut behind her. She started downstairs, burdened with two stuffed grocery bags.

"As I said." Burton waved his hands like a magician.

"Where the hell have you been?" I called.

Burton walked to the bottom of the stairs and relieved her of the bags. She removed her coat, her face as pale as paper except for the dark under her eyes.

"I left you a note on the door," she said. "I went to the farmer's market. The one in Somerville. Then the train got stuck coming back."

Burton resettled on his stool, daring me with a look to give anything away.

I helped carry the groceries back into the kitchen, flipped on the lights, reignited the grill and fryer. She stayed out front, saying something in a low voice to Burton.

"Everything all right?" she said when I came back out front.

Burton barely controlled his grin. His phone jiggled in the polished surface of the bar, then peeped with an incoming message. He looked at it and sobered up.

I stared at him as Marina went out to the kitchen.

"What?" he said.

"Shouldn't you have backup?"

He rolled his neck.

"I'm only going as far as your back alley," he said. "Crack the door if you want to listen in. Call the precinct if it gets too crazy."

"OK. I have the pistol."

"Suit yourself," he said. "Just don't blame me if you get dragged into something you didn't want a piece of."

As if he didn't realize I was already in deep, at least in terms of worrying about him.

# 27

Burton climbed the stairs toward street level with all the enthusiasm of a man walking up to the gallows. The threat to Marina was the only thing that could have made him confront this directly. He didn't want her dragged into this just because she knew him.

I unpacked the night deposit bag again, replaced the money in the register, turned the music back on, and picked out a medley of ragtime piano. Fats Waller swung into "Ain't Misbehavin'" as I stepped back into the kitchen.

Marina was staring at the clock on the wall.

"Can you keep an eye out front for me?" I said. "I need to do a couple things in the office."

No sense worrying her that something violent might be happening out in the alley. She glared at me, her reverie smashed.

"I have a lot to do here, Elder. That darn train made me late."

"Fifteen minutes. And I'll chop the onions for you."

She hated that chore because it made her cry. She sighed, plucked the big cleaver out of the rack, and slapped it down on the cutting board.

I grabbed it and walked down the hallway past the walk-in cooler to my office and the emergency exit. I gathered that Burton did want me to witness whatever was going on, though he seemed indifferent about whether I got involved. Was he trying to protect me again? Or punishing himself?

The exit door was heavy steel, insulated and fireproof. It opened from the inside by pushing on a panic bar. I applied pressure slowly until the mechanism disengaged with a tiny click and pushed the door open a couple of inches. Cold air flowed in, but no one who wasn't actually looking at the door would notice the small gap.

My timing was right. The three of them, Burton and two men in long black topcoats, rounded the corner of the building and walked deeper into the alley. As soon as they were out of sight of the street, the taller and broader of the two shoved Burton up against my Cougar, breaking off one of the side mirrors. The tinkling crack as it hit the pavement made me shake my head. It took forever to find parts for these old cars and I usually wound up paying a ridiculous price over the Internet to some teenage car geek in the Midwest.

"You do know I'm a Boston police officer?" Burton straightened up off the car, wincing as he rubbed his right kidney.

The thug wound up to hit him again, but the older man put up his hand. His voice was rough in a way that sounded like he had a case of dysphonia, a speech disorder that made your voice sound like it's being filtered through iron filings. One of my father's assistants at the bank had had the condition.

"I also know your department doesn't love you very much. You're not exactly the . . ." He turned to the younger man and spit out a mouthful of what I assumed was Russian. It sounded like he was gargling carpet tacks.

"Fair-haired boy," the younger man said, ready with his shovel-paws if further physical persuasion was necessary.

"Just so," the old man said.

"Dmitri." So Burton knew them. "We've been over this already. I don't know what happened to Bousquet. I didn't kill your stooge. I was too invested in convicting him for killing those two women."

Dmitri clapped slowly.

"Well said, Detective. But I would expect nothing less than nobility, given your reputation. You forget that I witnessed how deeply you abhorred Mr. Bousquet when you arrested him. I cannot believe you would let him live, out of jail."

Burton shifted to the right, out of my line of sight.

"I wasn't the one who granted him bail. And I lost my temper that day. Not my mind. If I'd known where he was, I'd have put him back behind bars. He'd be alive."

141

"Mr. Bousquet was an integral part of a business development project I'm working on. I needed his input on some ideas but now that has been denied me. If you were not responsible for his death? To whom would I speak?"

"Not a clue. I was taken off the case."

"I noticed you've had some time off from your employment as well," Dmitri said. "New Hampshire is quite lovely at this time of year. It reminds me of my home."

"New Jersey?" the younger thug said, surprised.

All three of them had moved back into my line of sight. Dmitri nodded at his muscle, who drove a sharp jab into Burton's unprotected midsection. Burton offloaded the whiskey sour and whatever he'd had for breakfast, Dmitri dancing back on his shiny black loafers to avoid the splatter.

"Not quite so hard the next time, Ermolai," Dmitri said. "He needs to be able to talk. For now, at least."

Burton glanced at the door, clocking the gap. Was that a signal?

"Dmitri." He coughed and spit a gob of phlegm next to the Russian's shoes. "Even if I were the most corrupt cop in Boston, which I'm not, I wouldn't help you. I don't love that your pal was murdered anymore than you do, but only because I wanted his ass in prison. I couldn't care less about your business problems."

"You might sometime care more than you think," Dmitri said. "But I won't quibble with you. All I require is that you keep me informed as to the progress of the investigation into who killed him. My good friend Antoine."

Burton shook his head. Why was he being so stubborn? He could easily agree with Dmitri, then not deliver.

Dmitri clucked and nodded at Ermolai again. I shoved the back door wide.

"That's enough," I said.

Ermolai looked at the meat cleaver in my hand and started to laugh. Dmitri displayed a thin feral smile. Burton took three long steps toward me, away from the Russians.

"And who would be your skinny protector, Detective Burton? Is this your personal bartender come to the rescue?"

Ermolai unzipped his topcoat, folded back the skirt, and showed an ugly long-barreled revolver in a shoulder holster. My sphincter tightened and my knees ached like they'd been injected with ice water.

"I called the police."

Dmitri's smile widened to show his teeth, a ruin of decay.

"I believe Mr. Burton actually is the police, is he not?" He shook his head at Ermolai, who closed his coat. "But I take your meaning. This is not a matter that can be discussed intelligently among people who are not friends. Am I not correct, Mr. Burton?"

Dmitri stepped in and punched Burton in the gut, doubling him over. Burton whooped for air as Ermolai drew back his leg, intending to punt Burton into tomorrow.

"Enough!"

I ran out into the alley and waved the knife at Ermolai, startling him enough that he lost his balance and had to stagger back to the brick wall. The fire door slammed shut behind me.

Dmitri held up his hands and backed away until Ermolai's bulk shielded him.

"No need for further theatrics, Mr. Darrow." He registered my surprise. "Of course I know who you are. Don't you also subscribe to the theory that the friend of my enemy is also my enemy?"

He trained his pale gray eyes—lake ice in winter—on me. His thin black hair was lacquered straight back, pale scalp showing between the strands.

"Though I admire your loyalty to such a difficult friend. I have not forgotten about Anatoly, by the way. We do owe you something for that." He exposed those wrecked teeth. "Ermolai and Anatoly grew up in the same orphanage. They were like brothers."

The sound of a siren pierced the tableau. I hadn't called the police in case it jammed Burton up further, so it must have been an ambulance. Or a cop car headed elsewhere.

Dmitri shrugged, his indifference scarier than rage.

"Let us depart, Ermolai. I believe we have communicated the message we came to say."

He loomed over Burton, who was still cradling his rib cage.

143

"I expect your help and your cooperation, Detective. You've only experienced one of the levers I can pull."

Ermie looked disappointed they were leaving. He looked at the knife in my hand again, then touched the butt of his pistol. Dmitri pushed him toward the corner of the building then turned back, afflicted by the common bully's desire to have the last word.

"The *погреб* will appreciate the cooperation, too." The Russian word sounded something like "bowl-kick." "Which may be of some value to you professionally."

"Fuck you, your scabies-infected mother, and your oozing dog of a sister," Burton said under his breath as the two Russians disappeared up the alley.

I helped Burton over to the wall where he could lean. Trying to straighten up made him cough. He spit. No blood, though the wince shook his torso.

"Ribs." He glanced at the cleaver. "That's what Ermolai thought was so funny. You bringing a knife to a gunfight? You are a unit."

"You're welcome," I said.

"No, really. Thank you."

He coughed again, his voice fading out like a distant radio station. He slid down the wall until he lay on the trash-strewn ground. The fire door clanked open behind me, a scraping sound meaning that someone more thoughtful than I'd been was blocking it open.

"Daniel!"

Marina ran out and grabbed his left arm.

"Get him off the ground," she said.

I took the other arm gingerly.

"Carefully. I think his ribs are broken."

She gave me a familiar my-boss-is-a-dope look and we raised his body until his eyes fluttered open and he helped take some of his own weight. He groaned when he couldn't straighten all the way up, then rolled his neck as if it were stiff.

"I'm fine." He pushed our hands away and took a deep breath, groaned.

"Inside," Marina said. "And you are going to the emergency room. I don't care how macho you think you are."

He shook his head, suppressed another moan.

"I'm fine. There's nothing they can do for broken ribs but tape them. I have ace bandages at home."

"Cut the crap, Burton," I said. "A broken rib can put a hole in your lung. Do what the woman says."

I knew he wouldn't do it for me. I nodded to Marina.

"Let's get him into the car. I'll drive him."

I picked up the Cougar's smashed mirror and weighed it in my hand.

"Seven years' bad luck," I said.

"Fucking people," Burton said.

I wasn't sure if he was talking about the Russians or us.

# 28

I went with Burton to the ER at Mass General and got him checked in but there were a couple of stabbings and a suspected heart attack ahead of him. He promised me he would stay long enough for X-rays, though he couldn't find a comfortable way to sit in the plastic chair. He was certain all he needed was some painkillers and a tape job but his face was gray as a pigeon.

"Dmitri and his pal are just the tip of the berg," he said as I stood up to leave. "Shit's really going to hit the fan in a couple of days."

I left the Cougar in the loading zone in front of my apartment so I could collect some supplies from my storage unit in the basement. Of course there was a ticket on the windshield when I came out again. I tossed the armfuls of paper towels, toilet paper, and cleaning fluids into the back seat and climbed into the driver's seat, fuming.

Ramming the shifter in and out of gear as I sped back to the bar, I slammed the car around the corner of Mercy Street, then down the alley into the back. As I jogged up to the Esposito's front door, my breath spumed white vapor as if I were breathing smoke. My head throbbed with an anger too large to be caused by a traffic ticket.

The wipers on a plain gold Taurus—steel wheels, black wall tires, four antennas—flicked on and cleared mist from its windshield, revealing two men inside. I ignored them and started for the Esposito's door.

The passengers' side door of the car opened and my old pal Detective Murray stepped out, careful not to rub his suit against the dirty skin of the car they were blocking in.

Today's three-piece was brown, too. He must have thought the color flattered his skin tone. He smiled as he stepped between the parked cars and up onto the sidewalk. I turned with the door open.

"Detective. Good morning. If your partner can find a legal place to park, I'd offer you a cup of coffee."

My chest was still tight with that anger and Murray stone-faced my invitation. He was shorter than me by several inches, which pleased me for some reason.

"Burton," he said. "Absolutely imperative we speak with him."

I closed my eyes and sighed, believably, I hoped.

"I didn't know where he was the first few times you asked and I don't know now. When he gets cleared for duty? If he's still working for the BPD then? You probably won't have a hard time finding him."

Murray thinned his lips.

"We know he's back in the city. He called in sick but he's not at home."

A prophetic call, given where he was at the moment.

"You did lend him your place, didn't you? Could he be there?"

Time slowed. I wasn't going to insist on talking to a lawyer because that would imply too much, but I wasn't going to give Murray the store, either.

"All my apartments are leased right now."

Murray was looking for a reason to boil—I probably shouldn't have pushed so hard.

"Not that house. The property in New Hampshire."

"Oh, my father's place. Yes, he asked to borrow it for a few nights, couple weeks ago. I got the feeling he wanted to get away for a while."

Murray's eyebrow twitched, which meant he was going to tell me a lie or he already had.

"We had a call from local law enforcement up there. About a break-in? Have they been in touch with you?"

I hoped my surprise looked genuine.

"No. Shit. I hope there wasn't any damage. The local kids break in sometimes, looking for booze. Or a place to get laid."

Murray's smile twisted to one side.

"Minor damage only. But blood on the floor and some other evidence that someone had been restrained there. Maybe tortured."

Pretending this was all news was a strain. The engine on the Taurus revved as if Biggs was antsy.

"That doesn't sound good," I said.

"We're waiting for the full DNA. But the blood type is the same as Antoine Bousquet's."

"The sweat shop guy? The one who just got killed?"

Murray didn't look impressed by my innocent surprise. I had to be careful not to overplay.

"The one your friend Burton beat the shit out of a couple weeks back."

"In full view of the TV cameras. You don't think Burton would be stupid enough to go after him again?"

"It's possible. Does it surprise you to know he missed work yesterday?"

'I'm not his keeper, Murray. Look, think what you want about him, but he's a good cop."

"Which is why he's working on the side for Bousquet's girl-friend?"

"I wouldn't know anything about that."

He spread his hands out in the air like a conductor. I'd said it too fast.

"Of course not."

"I'll tell you this much. We started out investigating him for moonlighting, possibly misusing his authority. Serious enough, but not likely to get him more than a hard slap. Now all of a sudden he's connected to a murder? If you really don't know how to reach him, OK. But he's going to have to answer."

My hope Burton would slide through this unscathed was melting like ice in a cup of hot tea.

"I will carry the message, if he happens to come by." I stared at Murray, looking for that tell. "He may go his own way, Murray. But he's loyal. To the job. To doing things the right way."

"Let's hope they're the same thing."

"What's that supposed to mean?"

"Nothing."

The horn sounded and he raised his hand at the car.

"I believe what you're saying," he said. "We want this to have a safe and peaceful conclusion."

I might have believed him if his eyebrow wasn't jumping. Why "safe?" Was he implying someone in the department was out to get Burton? Because who better to sandbag a cop than another cop? Neither Biggs nor Murray was a trustworthy advocate.

Murray grabbed my wrist. I froze.

"No one on our side is playing games, Mr. Darrow. Burton needs to protect himself. Forces are at work that we have no control over—he could be in jeopardy."

No eyebrow tic this time. I stared at him.

"If I put my hand on you like that," I said. "You'd arrest me for battery."

Anger darkened his face almost black. He released my wrist.

"You're a smart guy, Elder. But if there's one thing my father taught me? No one likes a smartass."

# 29

I'd left Kathleen a bunch of phone messages since Friday night, none of them returned, and I hoped that didn't mean she was backing away. One night with a woman rarely put me in the frame of mind I was about her, and it wasn't only lust. She was easy to talk to and there were depths to her that intrigued me. I only hoped she wasn't having second thoughts, after Anatoly's death and all the extralegal excitement around the bar, to convince her that dropping me was the better part of valor. She was the first woman since Susan Voisine who'd intrigued me enough to let my guard down, and if I'd seen the last of her, it was going to hurt.

Lunch had been slow, as usual on Tuesdays, and the speakers were pushing out the Pandora station I defaulted to when I didn't feel like managing the music. For some reason, the algorithm picked a Doc Severinsen version of "*Kansas City Blues*," the brass too happy and tinny, the trumpets too brash for an empty bar. I turned it off and tried to enjoy the smells of roasting garlic and tomatoes from the kitchen.

I noticed the thin manila envelope leaning against the cash register that hadn't been there earlier. Probably my tax forms; it was close enough to March that I expected to hear from my accountant. I slipped it in the junk drawer and walked out back.

Cold air flowed up the hallway from the open exit door.

"Are you smoking back here again?"

Marina stared through the steam from a boiling pot.

"I need some way to fight the stress that isn't yelling at my mother. That OK with you? You see the envelope?"

"Dominic came by?"

150

Dominic Panatelli, my CPA, always delivered the papers in person, a security fetish of his. She shook her head.

"Some kid, fourteen or fifteen. Acne, greasy hair, fake leather jacket."

Sounded like Anatoly. Was it another of Dmitri's minions?

"He say anything?"

"She. Not a word. Knocked her knuckles on the bar to get my attention, pointed at the envelope, and left."

I couldn't feel good about this. Dominic never used a messenger.

Out front, I slit the envelope open with a paring knife, wondering if I should worry about fingerprints. I shook out a single sheet of photo paper, which landed face down on the bar. A terrible sense of foreboding made me crave the cold comfort of a glass of Scotch. Tiny angular script down in the lower left corner read: Love, Anatoly.

Turning the photo over sent an icicle through my chest.

"Marina!"

The picture showed Burton from the neck up, his face the pale and faintly shadowed shade of death, eyes closed and his sandy hair mussed to the wrong side. Most definitive was the charred black hole above his left eye and the spreading black pool underneath his head. The image was grisly, even in black and white.

"Jesus Christ." Stinking of old cigarettes. Marina put her hands up to her mouth, sobbed, then whirled and headed for the rest room. The door shut but could not block the sound of her retching. My own gorge rose.

I slipped the photo back into the envelope and tucked it away. Clearly Burton had underestimated the Russians, and the fact that Dmitri had signed the photo meant he was unafraid of the consequences of killing a cop. Or at least prepared for the fallout. But what could Burton have done, in less than a day after the dust-up in the alley, to aggravate the situation?

My knees shook. I had to sit down. So. Burton was dead. The grief, I understood, would come later, after the shock wore off, but I was surprised by a sense of inevitability, that this was the logical culmination of his character and how he did his job. He'd taken some risks since I'd known him, on my behalf as well as his own, and had finally taken one too far.

I reached under the bar and pulled out the telephone, fished through the junk drawer for the card Biggs had given me. He and Murray could get the process started without my having to explain everything to a beat cop first. But before I could dial the number, the phone rang. I let it go to four before I answered it.

"Esposito. This is Elder."

"Mr. Darrow." Dmitri's voice, stones in a blender, was instantly recognizable. "Can I take it you have received my message?"

My vision went black, as if my brain had suddenly been starved of oxygen. A visceral anger clawed at me.

"Not an intelligent move, Dmitri." At least my voice was steady. "And not just because Burton was my friend. You can't possibly think killing a cop will get you what you want."

"It has been my experience that a bold move often shocks people into acting correctly. When someone doesn't do what I ask them, I need to demonstrate that there are consequences. Besides, your friend is under investigation, is he not? I doubt the pressure to find his killer will be too heavy to bear. Not that I know who might have done such a thing."

He was playing, in case my phone was tapped.

"I thought you needed him, to track the investigation."

"With Bousquet gone? It would have been convenient. But the message I send? Is much more important."

I sensed hand-waving, smoke and mirrors. Had Dmitri had Bousquet killed? And was now trying to confuse things?

"All the same," he said. "Ermolai would like to meet you again. As I said, he and Anatoly were like brothers."

"Anatoly jumped. No one pushed him down the stairs."

"Anatoly was what you call here, development. Do I have the word correct?"

"Disabled? Developmentally disabled?"

"Yes. Such a complicated way to say slow. But if he was frightened enough to do what he did? Whoever caused him that fear was responsible for his death."

Kathleen and me. I closed my eyes—did I have to warn her?

"I'm calling the police now, Dmitri. I can't imagine you are unknown to them." Christ, now I was talking like him. "I'm sure they'll be with you soon."

I started to hang up.

"Mr. Darrow," he growled. "Wouldn't you like to know what Ermolai has planned for you?"

"No. Goodbye."

"What about for your woman? This Kathleen Crawford?"

I had nothing to say to that, though I was already afraid they'd drag her in. But I knew I wasn't up to dealing with the Russian mob on my own. Or any mob, for that matter."

"Goodbye, Dmitri. I will come and watch your trial."

As I finally hung up, my legs started shaking again, as if I'd run a hundred miles. Marina leaned against the bar, wiping her mouth with a paper towel. Her skin had faded to a pale beige and she gulped for breath, though her eyes were dry.

She looked up at the ceiling as her breathing slowed down.

"We had things left to say," she said.

I nodded. It was exactly what I'd felt when my father died unexpectedly. Words unsaid, thoughts unshared, relationships left strained. The grief began to creep into my center, a glacier of nonfeeling that would suffocate all other feelings for a while.

"We need to inform the department," I said.

She straightened up and pulled herself together by will, her neck and back as straight as a telephone pole.

"Of course," she said.

# 30

A couple years back, I'd had to come to terms with the fact that I had a family of sorts and that I owed them as much as they owed me. Then Cy Nance betrayed me, Alison Somers and my father died, and Susan Voisine had left town. I thought then that Burton and Marina were my last remaining friends. Marina and I now had to work out what it meant if we were siblings. And Burton was gone and I had to decide for myself what I owed him in terms of vengeance.

For the next couple of days, life inside the Esposito returned to its normal character, though Marina and I were much subdued. We served drinks, we served lunch, we served dinners. We did not talk about Burton's death or whether we were related. There was no official notice of an investigation into Burton's death, though Biggs had come by and picked up the photo. We hadn't even heard if they'd found a body.

I pushed down my grief and the waiting by experimenting with new playlists, auditioning a couple student musicians from the Berklee School who were willing to play for the exposure, and hoped Marina and I didn't get dragged any deeper into this, either by Dmitri or anyone else. I'd left a phone message warning Kathleen, but I suspected she was staying away from me. I tried to concentrate on the simple life I'd been trying to create for myself: recovering alcoholic, bar owner, jazz lover. It seemed like that should be enough for one life.

By Friday afternoon, I felt as if the world had regained a normal rhythm and so I should have guessed something strange was going to happen. The Red Sox had started playing spring training games and I was hungry for that, both the sport and the weather it was mostly played in: sun, heat, and humidity. I'd lived in New England too long to bitch about the weather but the transition to spring felt excessively drawn out this year.

Five minutes after I had that thought, I wished the weather was all I had to worry about. The upstairs door opened and Viktoriya Lin stomped down the stairs, the hard heels of her knee-high red leather boots ringing on the metal. All three of the males hunched at the bar turned to look like birds on a wire, then straightened their shoulders.

"Where is that fucking Burton?" she barked, stalking across the linoleum. "I found her."

"Who?"

I modulated my voice, hoping to discourage any oversharing with my afternoon drinkers.

"Kuan-Yin, you fool! Who else would I be looking for? Give me something to drink."

I did not raise my elbows from the bar. In the light of Burton's death, I gave not one small shit about her problems.

Her eyes showed a buzzy antic energy.

"Why are you here, Vicky?"

Her wide mouth pulled inward. Maybe she didn't like the nickname as much as she'd said.

"Burton needs to come with me to retrieve her. This is what I paid him to do. I need a policeman to rescue her."

"She's being held against her will?" I said. "Then you do need a policeman, don't you?"

She heard something in my voice.

"Burton would already be leaving to help me. Where is he?"

"You haven't heard?"

"What?"

I felt the laser burn of her attention.

"He's gone, Viktoriya. He was killed. By the Russians."

She didn't ask which Russians, which said something. But unless she was a very good actress, she could not have faked the tears so quickly, no more than the abrupt loss of color and the slump onto a stool.

"He is dead?"

Usually what *killed* means, but I was no judge of how shock ought to affect people.

"As best we can tell. He hasn't been found."

She shook her head.

"This is not possible." She stared at the row of bottles. "I would like a drink, please. Vodka."

Her politeness showed how shaken she was. I reached for the Tito's bottle, not economizing under the circumstances.

"Not that shit from Texas," she said. "You must have something better."

I held up the Stoli bottle.

"Double," she said.

I poured, she slammed it. Tears rose in those glacial eyes. She nodded for a refill.

"You're sure about this, my friend Elder?"

"No *corpus delicti* yet, if that's what you mean. But I have no doubt."

She frowned, maybe at the foreign words, sipped her drink.

"Until I see the body?" she said. "I choose not to believe. He was a wonderful . . ."

"So you've said."

She finished the drink and stood up.

"Well. Since he is not here, you will help me. Rescue Kuan Yin."

"I will not. I'm not Burton and this is not my problem."

She reached into the pocket of her short leather jacket and laid a small flat automatic on the bar.

"I need someone to help me when I take her back. You don't have to do anything. Just look tough."

Was her pistol an offer or a threat? I cursed Burton for ever getting involved with her.

"Where is she? What happened?"

"She was in slavery, from Antoine. Like the other two. He made her out into a hooker."

I didn't see a choice if I wanted her to leave me alone. And maybe this was a way I could make up some of my feeling of debt to Burton.

"And you'll leave me alone, if I help you?"

She nodded. It might be worth the risk, too, if it kept her and Edward out of my life.

"Maybe later on," I said. "I have a bar to run."

She took out a silver-covered phone and tapped in a text.

"This will be taken care of. We need to go now."

Apparently the answer was right outside on Mercy Street. The door banged when it opened, which took considerable force, and Edward pounded down the stairs with all the grace and delicacy of a World Wide Wrestling actor. One of the beer drinkers at the far end of the bar slipped into his jacket. Edward glared at him as he stepped past and started up the stairs.

"No," I said. "That thug will not run my bar."

"Done deal," she said. "We leave now."

"No."

Edward tried to sidle his thick self in behind the bar. I held my ground. Vicky reached for the pistol. The other two customers got up and left, Edward grinning at them maniacally.

"All right," I said. "I will come. But your idiot brother is not in charge here."

He shoved his chest at me and growled. Vicky snapped at him.

"What, then? Kuan-Yin will not be there long."

"My cook will cover the bar. You two go upstairs. I'll meet you outside." I pointed at Edward. "You, especially. I don't want her frightened."

Vicky waved a hand at him and they moved.

Marina stepped out front as they exited at the top of the stairs. She must have heard the commotion because she was holding the big cleaver, the one I'd defended Burton in the alley with. Her eyes were wide and her hands vibrated with a desire to take someone or something on.

"Is she the one who poured tea on your hand?"

I didn't know how she knew that but it wasn't time to ask. All that

157

remained of those wounds was shiny new skin. I unpinned Biggs's card from the corkboard by the door and handed it to her.

"I need to do this," I said. "For Burton. But if I'm not back in a couple of hours? Call him."

"Bullshit you have to do it." She glared. "But take this with you."

She handed me the black leather sap Burton had given her, which made me tear up. I dropped it in my pocket.

"Just cover the front for me until I come back?" I said. "Feels like I need to do this."

She made her usual sour face, set the knife down, and grabbed my shoulders.

"Don't be stupid, Elder. We lost Burton. And you know he wouldn't want you hurt."

True enough, though at a deeper level, he might have expected me to try and avenge him, too. And if the tables were turned? I might want the same. Dmitri claimed credit but Viktoriya was part of the story somehow.

"Move your ass," Edward said as I emerged onto Mercy Street.

"First actual words I've heard you say." I brushed past him. "Enough of this bullshit. If we're going, let's go."

Viktoriya had stowed the gun but kept her hand in her jacket pocket. A dark wash of pessimism swept through me—what the hell did I think I was doing?

"If you're the brains and Edward's muscle, you could handle this yourselves. What do you need me for?"

Vicky watched the buildings flash past as we drove out to the end of Mercy Street and turned left, her lips a stark red against her colorless complexion.

"What's the one thing your friend Burton could bring?" she said.

"That he's a cop, of course. But I'm not."

She pooched out her lips.

"People know you and Burton have worked together. This person will assume you have an official connection."

"That's ridiculous."

"At worst, you'll have to say 'Stop, Police!' You can do that, can't you?"

"They'll have to be awful gullible."

"It's a kidnapping." She dug her nails into my thigh. "They're not going to fight back."

I sincerely hoped those weren't famous last words.

\* \* \* \* \*

It was four-twenty-seven by the clock outside the bank on Tremont Street when Edward pulled up in front of the Bee Stack and double-parked. The outdoor patio wasn't open for the season yet, though a couple die-hard smokers sat on the black wire chairs. Inside the bar, it was warm and raucous, with an early after-work crowd.

I envied the capital that had gone into the place, as well as the taste. The owners had left the old brick and pipes exposed but added an intricate art deco chandelier over the bar and a dozen cane-backed stools. The place mixed a sense of the upscale with the vibe of a neighborhood bar, something I could have coveted for the Esposito. The one TV was pointed off into a far corner, in a nook where only a table of four could see it.

Vicky led our small raiding party in that direction, Edward bringing up the rear, possibly to keep me from bolting. I was having second and third thoughts about my involvement in this, but if it got Vicky off my ass, it might be worth it. And I hadn't forgotten Burton's interest in Marty Laird, who was sitting in front of me.

The woman sitting at the small round table, assuming this was Kuan-Yin, looked about as Asian as pickled herring. She was delicate and very thin, blonde, blue-eyed, and pale as milk. As we walked up, she was laughing at something her tablemate was saying, but her laughter seemed tense, as if she were desperate to please him.

Marty was what made the scene surreal, though, sitting with a bottle of Veuve Clicquot and two flutes, watching himself on the bar's TV. In a night when a spring training game with the Pirates was playing, he must have bribed the bartender. Or maybe the Bee Stack didn't attract any sports fans. It must have been a taped rerun, which qualified in my mind as video masturbation.

"Kuan-Yin." Viktoriya sounded like a mother disappointed in a child. If there was a family resemblance, I wasn't seeing it. "I've been searching everywhere for you."

"Vicky." Kuan-Yin whined, an entitled child, never told No. "We went to Quebec City." She shivered. "Very cold."

"You were stolen from me," Vicky said. "By Antoine."

My doubts about the story she'd told me, and Burton, were growing.

Kuan-Yin touched Marty's arm. He was silent, focused on Edward.

When Vicky started to lift her from the chair, Kuan-Yin shook her off violently, knocking over the champagne glasses and spattering all of them. Marty started to rise.

"Hold on a minute here."

Edward reached around me and shoved Marty down into his chair.

"You'll come? Or I'll drag you," Vicky said.

Kuan-Yin held up her hands in surrender, picked up a pearl-encrusted clutch, and rose.

"I'll call you, sweetie, OK?" she said to Marty, who was staring at me now, as if my face was familiar.

"I know these two." He nodded at Vicky and Edward. "Who the fuck are you?"

Vicky nudged me, my cue to proclaim myself a cop. I wasn't that stupid. Besides, she was well in control.

"Enforcement arm." I gestured at the champagne left in the bottle, probably flat by now. "Enjoy."

Kuan-Yin pouted, partly I thought because Marty hadn't fought any harder for her. Vicky hustled her toward the door, Edward following.

Sliding into the front seat of the SUV, I finally clued in to what was going on. Viktoriya and Kuan-Yin were lip-locked in the back seat, four hands straying here and there. Pretty soon the windows would start to steam up.

I buckled my seat belt and turned to Edward.

"Drop me back at the bar, will you?"

He lifted his chin at the rear view mirror. I heard heavy breathing and the snap of elastic.

"Motel first," he said. "But I'll get you there."

Half an hour later, he dropped me outside the Esposito. Apparently Viktoriya and Kuan-Yin were well-known for their knock-down fights and makeup sex at the in-town hotels, so Edward had to take them all the way out to a Best Western on Alewife Brook Parkway. The only people they'd scare there were the traveling software engineers.

# 31

Back behind the bar, I relieved Marina and did my best to forget the bizarre afternoon. I craved my usual problems, late beer deliveries or a bounced check from one of the regulars.

It was slow enough that I had time to read the sports page between customers. The Sox had laid out a bundle of money for Edgar Renteria, who'd had a hell of a year in St. Louis, though the pundits—the sportswriters Ted Williams had called the "Knights of the Keyboard"—were already picking apart the trade, wondering if Renteria had the mental toughness to withstand the brutal Boston baseball climate without acknowledging that they were often the ones who made it so brutal.

Marina was strained, dark under the eyes.

"How's Carmen?" I said.

"And all the rest of it?"

"What do you want to do about it? Do you believe her?"

She shook her head.

"Honestly? I don't know what to believe. Saturday night, when she told me? She was clear, rational, right on point. She didn't want anything to do with the money because she thought you were giving it." Marina's look beseeched me to help make sense of it. "Could it be wishful thinking? That she had a crush on him? But if she was making it up, wouldn't she take the money to make it more believable?"

"We could take DNA tests?" I said.

She shook her head so quickly I could tell she'd already thought about it.

"Not on the tall tale of a half-crazy old lady. Even if she is my mother. That's not fair to either of us."

Not yet, was the way I took that.

"But you do think she'll take the money now?"

She nodded.

"At least that's where she was last night. Your father acknowledging her, finally. And me, I guess. If that's her view."

I was grateful in a perverse way that both of my parents had died before I had to worry about their mental acuity.

"I'll call Thomas's lawyer and schedule it, then. Let's get it done while she's still agreeable. We can hash the rest out later."

She'd gone distant and sad and I suspected she was looking forward to a time when Carmen would not be here and Marina would be alone. I wished I could reassure her that being without family was not insupportable, given time. But then we were missing Burton, too, though neither of us had spoken much about it.

"I'm not after your inheritance," she said.

"I know that."

I wished I'd been a better friend. She could have used support from a friend with Carmen, even if ultimately we're all alone with our losses.

She returned to her kitchen. I moved down the bar. There were still people to serve and there was music to play.

# 32

Emerging from the terrible years of my drinking, I was too familiar with depression, having lain down with the black dog many times. I always found the T-shirt from that restaurant on Martha's Vineyard amusing, because to me the black dog was not a fuzzy, warm, obedient, and friendly creature but a sly thief of joy, a sneaky bitch who bit when you weren't expecting it and held on with her jaws locked tight. You couldn't loosen the bite without losing some flesh.

My grief over Burton's death, as it finally washed in, was deeper and more debilitating than that, even. Instead of being able to blame the blackness on a chemical imbalance, I had a legitimate reason outside of myself to feel so dark. Burton and I hadn't known each other more than a couple of years, but we were connected in ways I never would have expected, especially considering our different histories in this city we both had been born in.

First and foremost, we both loved Boston, its peculiar politics, its ethnically diverse set of tensions, its goofy mix of Puritan ethic and liberal values. We shared an askance view of the world as well as an agreement that something like equity in that world was worth striving for. We believed in a balance, in other words, though his work probably did more to effect that than mine.

Before he died, I'd started to see the Esposito as an attempt to create a community, a place where all types could form an attachment to jazz music. But the loss of Burton quashed that desire. There were too many people in the city who now had one fewer witness against inequality, one fewer person committed to making things right. My personal sense of loss was nothing compared to that, even if I had so few friends I couldn't afford to lose one.

"Night, Elder," Marina said. "You closing up?"

She was nervous about leaving me alone in the bar. As long as the daily routines of business and work gave the skeleton to my days, I rarely thought about drinking anymore. Tonight, though, I was thinking about nothing else. The black dog was stirring, looking for an excuse to come out of its cage.

"Remind Carmen about seeing the lawyer next week."

She hesitated on the bottom step.

"Don't be stupid, Elder."

"Do my best."

The door shut with a metallic thud, like a cell closing. I listened to the silence for a minute or two before pulling over the iPad and scrolling through the playlists until I found a set I hadn't played in months, a collection of old-time blues. Too lugubrious for a drinking establishment but perfect for a wake.

And as Bobby Bland swung into the dirge-like rhythm of "St. James Infirmary," I pulled down the bottle of Macallan 18 from the very top shelf of the back bar, wiped off the dust, and set it down in front of me.

With the exquisite familiarity of a ritual I knew would kill me if I started practicing it again, I took down the Waterford crystal tumbler Alison Somers gave me before she moved to New York, rinsed it out with very hot water, and wiped it dry.

I walked around to the customer side of the bar and sat, while the horns welled up and Bland started singing, the gospel inflections clutching my heart in a fist. I wished and prayed for the music to obliterate my thinking, my guilt, and not at all successfully. Images of my friend Dan Burton—working, drinking, teasing with Marina—flowed out, leaving the largest part of me hollow.

I touched the crystal glass, cool now, and turned it over on the bar, ran my fingertip around the rim to produce an atonal squawk alongside the music.

"So dead," Bland sang. "So cold."

And yes, I pulled the cork out of that bottle and filled that glass

165

and held it up to the dim light that was left in the Esposito when only the back bar was lit. I tipped the whiskey back into my throat and felt the solo fire of blessed heat on my tongue and then the back of my throat and then on down into my stomach. I shuddered at the feeling of coming home, coming to life, that this was everything, and though I knew I was lost, I could not care anymore.

\* \* \* \* \*

And yet I was saved from myself, or at least from ruining myself all at once, by the opening of the street door. I wondered why I hadn't followed Marina up and locked it behind her. At first, I thought it might be her returning, divining what I was doing and coming to rescue me. But the voice from the shadows was rougher, darker, distinctly male. And very well-known.

"Darrow. Would you put your hands down flat on the bar, if you please."

What on earth did Mickey Barksdale think, that I might shoot him with the gun I wasn't holding? I supposed that was what it took to be a gangster, never dropping your guard.

"It's safe, Mickey. I'm a harmless fellow. Come down and have a drink."

My tongue felt too big for my mouth. When I looked at my glass, I saw I'd downed at least half a pint of whiskey like it was milk. When I spun my stool to face the stairs, I felt dizzy. My tolerance for alcohol was gone.

"Drowning your sorrows? I could use a bit of that my own self." He pointed at the bottle. "You sharing your tipple?"

Something in his smug tone—maybe his knowledge of my history—washed away my desire to drink more. For how long, who knew. It was odd to feel grateful to this violent thug for anything.

I reached across the bar, grabbed a shot glass, and shoved the bottle along the bar.

"Have at it." I pushed my own glass to one side.

"Had enough, have you?" Mickey sat down, leaving a stool between us.

"I thought you were a teetotaler."

"Only in public, boyo. Where it makes a difference. And wouldn't you say this is an appropriate occasion?"

He uncorked the Macallan, waved it grandly under his nose as if he were a wine lover, then poured to the glass's brim. He waved the bottle's mouth in my direction.

"You're certain, then?"

I hoped my glare told him he wasn't funny, though in his world an insult might pass as a joke.

"You heard, then," I said. "About Burton."

Mickey lowered his fleshy mouth to the brimming shot and sipped off the top quarter-inch. My need for the whiskey returned with the force of a punch in the face. If I'd been alone, I'd have had both hands on that bottle. Despair of being free of that urge shook me down to my feet.

"I did hear." Mickey seemed not to notice my struggle. "Though I must say, I find it hard to credit."

He slammed down the shot, exhaled like a horse, and poured himself another.

"That's a two hundred dollar bottle of Scotch, you know."

Mickey reached into the pocket of his black Dockers and pulled out a pale gray wallet with the pimples of some exotic skin— ostrich?—and laid two Benjamins on the bar.

"I do know, actually. Let me know when that runs out. But I didn't come here for a wake, Darrow."

The golden scent of the Macallan, richer than the smell of sun-warmed skin, made me think of chemical warfare, those biological weapons where a single molecule could kill you. Of course, the victims of those wouldn't welcome them with love.

"Then what, Mick?"

He narrowed his eyes, then sipped from the second shot with his stubby pinky extended.

"I'm feeling a bit taken advantage of. And I'm wondering if you could help me."

I couldn't think of anything I wanted less, either tonight or ever.

He met my look in the mirror behind the bar. The faint burn of my one drink had died into ash.

"And how do you think I can help you, Mickey? You—your group, that is—you're pretty much the only organized factor left in the city."

Mickey drank again.

"Daniel always said you had your way with words, Elder. You just managed to slander me without using the words criminal or mob. Well played."

I might have been frightened if there was anything left in the world that I feared at the moment.

"No," he said, before I could reply. "It's more the fear that I've been misled by a business associate. That my good nature has been taken advantage of."

"I find it hard to believe someone would try and screw you over, Mickey. So, again. What do you think I can do about it?"

"It's to do with an agreement I had with Antoine Bousquet and some of his cohorts. And because our mutual friend Dan is gone, I'd like for his name to stay clear of any stain."

Mickey had been connected to Bousquet? Was he confessing to the murder? If so, I couldn't see his play.

He lifted the glass and swallowed the rest of the Scotch. It pained me to see a beautiful drink not savored. I took a wild guess.

"And you're thinking I might have some law enforcement contact soon? You'd like me to whisper someone's name? It's been four days and they haven't even called."

"I would think you'd have a modicum of curiosity," he said to my reflection in the mirror. "Since the people who betrayed me are likely the engineers of our good friend's death. And responsible for police thinking Burton killed Antoine Bousquet."

It was the first I'd heard of that, though it made sense. Mickey clearly had some inside track in the department.

Needing to distance myself from the bottle, I walked around the bar, turned on the sound system, and played some early Brubeck and Desmond. I filled a glass with club soda, my usual weak defense against the urge, and stood on the duck boards across from Mickey.

"Tell me a story, then."

"In hypotheticals?" he said. "What would you say if I told you a certain organization that someone like me might be associated with exercises some control over the entry of undocumented individuals into our fair city?"

Of course. With so much of the country's service economy resting on the backs of illegal immigrants, Mickey would find a tight hold over such imports a lucrative thing. Though, truly, this had gone on in port cities like Boston, New York, Miami, forever. There was always a path, however ill-lit, for people finding their ways to this country's golden shores. Regardless of the political climate.

"You maintain that pipeline into the city?"

"Hypothetically." He eyed the whiskey as if contemplating one more, then shook his head. "But, hypothetically, suppose this. Suppose deserving lads and lassies, having paid their passage, instead of being welcomed into jobs and neighborhoods, were essentially enslaved? Put to work in sweat shops. Indentured. Abused. The women interfered with?"

It was hard for me to see Mickey as anyone's benefactor.

"So," I said. "Hypothetically, of course. This group was supplying workers for Antoine Bousquet's shops?"

"We were bringing people in," Mickey said, eschewing the hypothetical. "And Bousquet was fucking them over. Not acceptable."

Was I supposed to believe Mickey Barksdale had a Samaritan impulse in his tiny black heart?

"And making me look responsible. Which has led to a loss of interested clients for passage to our town. On top of which, Mr. Bousquet was in arrears on his financial obligations."

Much more believable than altruistic Mickey. But again I wondered if he were working himself up to a confession of murder.

"But the money isn't the main issue," he said.

"Oh." I managed a respectful tone, free of my disbelief. Mickey could lull you with his fancy language and quiet voice, then explode, volatile as a gas can in a match factory.

"You know your city's history, Elder, I'm sure. Built on the shoulders of immigrants. Am I right?"

"All the way back to Plymouth Rock. Legal and illegal both."

He refilled his shot glass, slid the bottle in my direction in case I'd changed my mind. I looked away.

"And the incomers," he said. "Always, but always, get shit on by the ones who came before."

I nodded.

"Brahmins on the Irish. Irish on the Italians. Italians on the Jews. Right down to the Asians and the Hispanics today. Nothing new there, Mickey. What's your point?"

He'd skated off so smoothly on this tangent, it felt polished by repetition.

"Even the blackies, am I right?"

Like many people in Boston, he was a touch too glib about race. But there was no point arguing with him.

"So?"

"My da' was a brickie," he said. "He built the Baker House."

One of the MIT dorms. I rolled my eyes, wishing I had a dollar for every blue-collar origin story I'd heard from a person with wealth. It was a favorite form of nostalgia.

"And all of that. The point?"

My interruption annoyed him enough to gulp another shot.

"Point is, me bucko, this hypothetical organization of which we speak was none too pleased to see its customers abused in that fashion. Puts a damper on prospective travelers, as I've alluded to."

Either he thought I was thick or that repeating his story gave it more force. Pretty sure I was not witnessing *ex post facto* guilt.

"What did you think was going to happen to them, Mickey? When they got here with no money and no prospects?"

His nostrils opened wide. His shoulders thickened. He wrapped his big hand around the empty glass and I feared momentarily for the future of my mirror. His bloodshot eyes braced me.

"Not slavery, Mr. Darrow. Certainly not that."

He reclaimed the bottle, holding it without pouring.

"You know Mr. Burton and I grew up in the same project."

I passed my own empty glass back and forth between my hands like a chess piece, the need for a drink starting to overwhelm my patience. I wished he would finish whatever he was trying to say and leave.

"Why tell me all this? What do you want?"

"Justice." He poured himself one more shot and regarded it without pleasure. "I am going to ruin these bastards who abused my privilege. Mr. Bousquet was punished before I could get to him—no, I didn't end the bastard—but others were involved. And I'm going to take something in return for the murder of my friend—no, I won't demean the memory that way. We were not friends. But I owed him as much as he owed me. And I will be compensated."

The rage was controlled, subterranean, but powerful.

"And you want me to help somehow."

Now he sipped the whiskey delicately, like a Beacon Hill lady with a glass of very dry sherry.

"Martin Laird," he said. "Thick as bricks with Mr. Bousquet. Financially as well as personally. Insofar as you could integrate his name into any conversations you might have, it would be appreciated."

"You heard me say the police haven't contacted me about Burton's death yet?"

"Puzzling." He nodded. "But they will, I'm sure. And you can speak."

"There is nothing I'd like better than to find out who killed Burton, Mickey." My throat closed up and I had to pause. Showing emotion in front of him might not be wise. "Whatever I do, it'll be within my limits. Respect for Burton, as much as anything."

"Understood." He blew out a booze-laden sigh. "Grand, in fact. I don't know what else will happen. But I will be in touch."

He corked the bottle, finished off his drink, and pushed the two bills toward me.

"Considering I've paid for it," he said. "I'll take the rest of this with me."

Nothing I could say wouldn't sound chintzy. It occurred to me it was an act of mercy toward me.

"Thanks, Mickey." I forced myself to say it, though he'd complicated things all over again. "We'll probably do a thing for Burton here one night. I'll let you know."

He held the bottle in the air as he ascended the stairs. The door shut behind him and I pushed away a sense of being bereft—there was another bottle out in the storeroom, though I didn't sell more than a shot of it a month. There was always another bottle.

But I left it there and sat down in the dimness to think, tapping my finger idly to Paul Desmond's melodic sax. Mickey had named Marty Laird as a partner in crime with Bousquet. Was it possible they'd fallen out, that Laird had killed Bousquet over money? Or women? There were the rumors of Bousquet turning out seamstresses as hookers.

Marty was one of those people who looked at the world as a garden that grew for him, that he was owed. I knew I had to correct for my prejudices, though—my family had always looked down on the overt strivers, people with too public a taste for wealth or fame or power. We preferred the discreetly greedy.

And was Dmitri involved in all this? He claimed credit for Burton's death but other than sheer vengefulness, why had he done it?

I needed to hear what Rasmussen Carter had found. It had been a week and I hadn't heard from him, despite his promise. Tomorrow, I told myself. I'd chase him down.

# 33

I heard nothing from anyone on Sunday and by Monday morning, depressed about the lack of response from the cops about Burton, I decided Kathleen must have dropped me too. I'd called any number of times and left messages, and yesterday, there hadn't even been a machine to talk to. When I tried again on Monday morning and still got no response, I decided to drop by and see her. If she didn't want to know who I was anymore, she could tell me in person.

"Running to the bank," I called to the kitchen.

No answer from Marina, who was probably lost in her own thought about Burton and her mother. No doubt Carmen's memories had thrown her a curve. And the DNA test was the only way to prove or disprove what Carmen was saying. I'd offered but Marina refused.

It was a raw morning, edging toward spring but not quite free of February's grip. I shivered in my canvas barn coat as I walked up the sidewalk and over to the bank branch. I nodded to the security guard as I walked in—the unemployment rate meant even the guards were young and fit these days, not the old retired cops who used to do the job.

A different face, young and black and wearing a loud pouf of Afro and big gold hoops in her ears, occupied Kathleen's usual window. I laid the night deposit bag on the counter.

"Good morning. Is Kathleen Crawford here today?"

The teller gave me a suspicious look as she unzipped the bag and pulled out the sheaf of bills and checks.

"I'm sorry, sir. I don't know anyone in the branch. I'm a temporary."

I did my best to smile past the attitude.

"Would you mind asking for me? She was very helpful the last time I was in. I wanted to thank her."

The young woman, Waranji according to her nameplate, paused in flicking through the bills to give me a dark look. She spoke quietly over her shoulder to an older woman supervising.

Thirtyish going on fifty, in a mauve pants suit and glasses on a gold chain around her neck, the woman frowned. Then she seemed to recognize me, though it wasn't mutual.

"Mr. Darrow." She stepped up beside Waranji, her brown bob so stiff with hairspray it barely moved. "Good morning. Can I help?"

I put the question down to bureaucratic habit, stepped on my temper, and read her name from the badge pinned to her nonexistent chest.

"Ms. Powers. I was asking for Kathleen. I didn't mean to create a stir." I returned Waranji's frown. "Just wanted to say hello."

"We don't usually discuss our employees." Powers bit her lower lip and her hair slipped slightly. I connected the wig with her thinness, the pallor, her brittle manner, and felt like an asshole. "I remember the two of you were . . . well."

She gave me an awkward wink that almost broke my heart.

"Friends," she said. "She's had to take some time off. I believe she said her father was quite ill."

Everything Kathleen had ever said to me indicated her father was long gone, but I couldn't argue the point here. However I wanted to sweeten the story, she'd slept with me the one time, then decided to leave town. Or at least avoid me. The most positive spin I could think of was that everything to do with the Russians, myself, Burton, and Bousquet, had driven her off. I felt as if I'd been plunged down a well, the depth of my sense of loss surprising me. We'd had possibilities, in my mind, at least.

"Was there anything else, Mr. Darrow?"

I shook my head and turned to leave, stepping past the short queue built up behind me. Waranji stepped back into the window and called my name.

"Your receipt, sir." She held out the empty vinyl bag and a slip of paper. "Have a good day."

She sounded not a whit more sympathetic than before, which only irritated me. Though her lack of customer service skills meant she would probably go far.

# 34

For unknown reasons—sunspots, state of the stock market, harmonic convergence—we were slammed on Monday night when Detective Biggs showed up. I was still waiting to hear from Rasmussen Carter, whose input I needed even more now that Mickey had dragged Marty Laird's name in. Carter might have information that the cops investigating Burton's death didn't have, assuming they ever got around to talking to me. Burton's death hadn't even made the papers.

It took me almost ten minutes to get free enough to head down to his end of the bar. As I did, Marina exited the kitchen carrying two chicken sandwiches and a bowl of soup. She nodded at Biggs.

"I called him," she said. "I'm tired of waiting to hear what they're doing about Burton."

I was glad she'd done it. They would have ignored me.

"Did he say anything?"

"No. But I get the feeling he's on Burton's side."

The most we could do for now was keep Burton from being blamed for things he couldn't defend himself against.

Biggs was moving his shoulders to the music coming from the stage, Joey Blanco noodling his Telecaster through "Surrey with the Fringe on Top."

I set a coaster in front of him.

"Bass?"

He rapped his finger on the bar beside a familiar envelope.

"I'd drink a beer, since I'm not working today."

I drew him a draft and set it on the coaster.

"Got a strange call today," he said.

"Yeah. Marina gets excited sometimes."

He took a long drink of beer, shook his head.

"Not that call. A different one."

My heart rate jumped. Mickey?

"From?"

"Unknown. The ubiquitous burner phone. But someone who wanted me to know Burton was involved in killing Antoine Bousquet. Pretty sure it wasn't you?"

"Nope."

So was Biggs representing the department's view? That Burton killed Bousquet and then killed himself, out of remorse, say? That would tie their package up neatly. If that was true, I wasn't going to share what Mickey had implied. Biggs and Murray didn't care about Burton anywhere near as much as Mickey and I did.

"Look, Darrow. This Professional Standards thing with Burton?"

A pair of young women at the far end of the bar held up glasses in mock dismay.

"Hold on."

As I mixed them fresh drinks—Sidecar for one, straight bourbon for the other—I struggled with how much to tell him. Maybe now the department would back off of Burton's minor misdeeds and focus more on the provable crimes that had been committed: illegal immigration, slavery, financial shenanigans (because money was always involved), and murder.

I delivered the drinks, adjusted their tab, and smiled back at the bourbon drinker's speculative look. She was in her thirties, a black-haired and blue-eyed Irish girl, sure she'd seen all there was to see already.

"Burton was many things," I said, returning to Biggs. He'd finished the beer but didn't order another. "But never crooked. Can we agree on that much?"

He pushed the empty glass at me.

"At this point? I'm in total agreement with you. I can't say the same for Murray, though. Someone's going to a lot of trouble to make Burton look guilty of things he couldn't have done and Murray's on board with it. You need to understand that if someone makes a complaint, we don't get to say 'Oh, he's a cop, we know he's all right.' If we do, everybody looks worse."

I mimed playing the tiny violin.

"So someone makes a bogus complaint and you go all Napoleonic Code on it? Guilty until proven innocent? I'm sure this isn't the first time you've run into someone trying to screw over a cop."

Biggs' face turned red and his voice rose. Two people raised their cellphones, ready to record.

"Which makes you as much a sheep as anyone," he said. "You think TV tells you what being a cop is like. I'm not here to debate my professional ethics. I'm trying to find out who's got it in for Burton badly enough to frame him for murder."

I took a breath.

"So you don't think he killed Bousquet."

Why were we even debating this, if Burton were dead?

"Caller said he'd seen Burton's truck in the driveway of a camp up in New Hampshire. Yours, I believe."

He caught my flinch.

"You didn't think we'd make the connection? Or find out Burton had been there? Just because the New Hampshire cops don't train with us doesn't make them rubes. And the blood on the floor?"

He nodded.

"Yep. Bousquet's, right down to the little swimmy things in his DNA."

I think he had DNA confused with sperm but I got the message. It wasn't a surprise.

"He didn't do it."

"Murray and I started out investigating whether Burton was misusing his police powers," Biggs said. "In a private investigation."

Looking for Kuan-Yin on Vicky's behalf. And while he was on suspension.

"And while we're doing that, some asshole he beat up while he was arresting him gets killed. You see why we need to talk to him."

"Wait. Didn't you get the photo I sent you? He's dead."

Biggs laughed and pushed the envelope toward me. Rage boiled up.

178

"You think this is funny?"

"Calm yourself and look at the picture. Really look."

I slid out the photo, feeling my heart bump at the mess of Burton's head. Biggs turned the picture around, took a pen out of his pocket, and pointed to an area of shadow around the bullet hole.

"See that?"

I shook my head.

"You have reading glasses?"

I found a pair of 3X in the junk drawer and handed them over. Biggs held the lens over the area he'd pointed. I barely saw the pixilation where two images had been joined electronically.

"You don't believe me, I'll let you talk to our tech guy. But he bet me a hundred bucks this picture's doctored."

Then I saw something I hadn't noticed on first look—that Burton's eyes still had light in them. I'd seen dead people and pictures of dead people and without exception, that light was missing, flat and gone.

"But why?"

Biggs shook his head.

"Take the pressure off himself for a while, maybe? We're not the only people in the city looking for him, I know. He convinces everyone he's dead, he buys some time?"

Burton wasn't that sly. And Dmitri had claimed to be responsible, which I hadn't told anyone.

"Too convoluted," I said. "He doesn't run from his troubles. Is someone else from the department looking for him? Besides you and Murray?"

"I can't discuss that."

Which meant it was possible. Maybe someone higher up the chain of command wanted Burton out of the picture.

"So," Biggs said. "What are you going to do?"

He slipped the photo into the envelope and handed it back.

"Not a damn thing," I said. "Really. I'm tired of getting dragged into these things when all I want to do is run my bar. Listen to some music."

Though I was suppressing my hope that he was right and Burton was alive. I wondered whether to drop Marty Laird's name into the mix but I thought I better hear from Rasmussen Carter before that.

Burton did a paradiddle with his fingers on the edge of the bar.

"And assuming Burton is alive and contacts you?"

I didn't have any compunction about lying to Biggs, but it had to sound believable.

"I talk to him, I'll do my best to convince him to come in. But to you, right? Not Murray and not downtown."

The brass would sacrifice Burton on the altar of public relations in a heartbeat.

Biggs nodded easily and I wondered what that said about his trust for Murray. Or maybe he was lying to me too.

"All I care about now, Darrow, really? Is who killed Antoine Bousquet."

Yep. He was lying.

"Seems pretty simple when you put it that way, doesn't it?" I checked the bar for customers needing drinks. The Sidecar drinker was gone but the bourbon was holding her glass up again, smile awry.

"Got to get to work," I said. "Thanks for coming in. And the photo thing."

"Sure. That's got to be a relief." Biggs stood. "That's how it can work, Elder. I help you, you help me."

\* \* \* \* \*

I was torn whether to tell Marina that Biggs and the police thought Burton was alive, at least until Burton resurfaced. Nor could I decide what benefit Dmitri thought he'd get out of phonying up a picture and claiming he'd killed Burton. He must have thought I was soft enough to scare. But away from what?

The bourbon drinker's name was Eileen and we chatted over the bar while Joey played some background music. I knew he'd come in on an off day to butter me up, still hoping for a Saturday night gig, but I hoped he didn't think he was getting paid.

"I like your place." She pointed to the iconic black and white photo of Dizzy Gillespie with his cheeks puffed out round as an orange.

"I'm a huge jazz fan myself. Only thing is, you can't smoke in bars anymore, right? I could murder a ciggie."

She seemed open to something beyond a couple drinks and conversation and I was still stung enough by Kathleen disappearing that I thought about acting on it. I beckoned her back behind the bar and pointed down the hallway past the kitchen.

"You can smoke out in the alley, if you want. Just tell my cook I said it was all right."

She ducked her head and thumped me on the shoulder as she passed. Her hair smelled of rosemary and lime and stale smoke.

"Back in a smoke," she said. "If you'll pour me a refill."

I filled her glass with Blanton's—she had good taste in bourbon—and thought some more about how I might get Burton to come in. He was deep into a mess and maybe Biggs was the cop to help straighten him out.

On the other hand, I had my own concerns: to mind my business, listen to music, maybe have a chat with an intelligent attractive woman.

Except that Eileen never returned. When I turned up the lights at last call, the bourbon still sat at her place untouched, her purse slung on the back of her stool.

I picked up the purse and stepped out back, where Marina scrubbed the grill with a pumice stone.

"Woman come back her to smoke a half an hour ago? Went out the back?"

"She didn't come back in?" Marina shrugged. "I'm not the traffic cop back here, Elder."

An ache started up in the base of my neck. I walked back into my office but everything looked fine, the piles of invoices and other paper on the desk untouched. I opened the purse, a cheap Coach knockoff in stiff pleather that didn't go with the elegant Eileen. Inside were some crumpled newspapers and a plastic DVD case, unlabeled.

I took the DVD, tossed the purse on the desk, and walked out front to close up. More fucking mysteries. I wanted to ignore this one, but as I climbed the stairs to lock the door, the plastic case weighed down my coat pocket.

# 35

As I turned the corner to the loading dock behind the building, I saw a shape in the passengers' seat of the cougar and my pulse accelerated. I hoped it was Burton, but when I opened the car door and the dome light came on, Rasmussen Carter was sitting there with a notebook in his lap, his opaque black sunglasses in place.

"This isn't such a nice neighborhood you don't need to lock your car," he said.

I was pretty sure I had, but the Cougar was old enough that you could slip the lock with a slim-jim too.

"Novel way to report to your clients."

He smiled.

"Night time is my time," he said. "We can do it here or at your home. Closer to my subway stop."

I got in and turned over the engine, not too happy about the mystery but interested in what he'd found out.

The bulb in the foyer of my building was still dark and I shook my head at my own laziness. Maybe it was time to hire a property management firm. And maybe once my inheritance came in, I'd move out to the suburbs, put in a vegetable garden.

I snorted. Pretty unlikely I'd go that far.

"Something funny."

"The door wasn't latched," Carter said in that quiet voice. "You really should be more careful about security."

Mrs. Rinaldi again, though if I were a better landlord, I would have replaced the latch by now, too.

"My tenants. You have something for me? I expected to hear

from you sooner."

If Burton were alive, information about Marty Laird could be very useful.

Carter followed me up the stairs.

"You didn't mention this was time-sensitive."

"No. It's fine." Maybe I could use the information to get Burton to surface. "Come in."

I keyed open my locks and let him precede me into the apartment. I turned on a lamp, low, in the living room.

"Let me know if that's too much. Drink? Coffee? Ginger ale?"

He pushed the hood of Celtics sweatshirt back off his head and smiled, white and wide.

"Ginger ale would be excellent."

When I returned, his back was to the room and he was running a finger along my LP collection, some of which dated back to my father's youth.

"Amazing," he said. "Some of these are valuable. I take it you're an audiophile?"

I owned a turntable but it wasn't a religious choice: without one I couldn't listen to a lot of the older music.

"Not really." I sat and pointed to an armchair. "I hope you've had some luck."

"The residue of design," he said. "Lots going on right now, and I do like to work."

He pulled out the leather-bound notebook and handed me a flash drive.

"Everything I'm going to tell you is backed up on there. In the sense of verified, as well as electronically copied. I'll give you the high points?"

I set the memory stick on the coffee table and sat back.

"Martin Feinberg Laird," Carter began. "Born in Mattapan, June 9, 1949. Parents both deceased, father of heart failure, mother . . ."

"Rasmussen." I realized belatedly I was dealing with a completist, maybe someone on the autism spectrum. "I'll read the deep background later. Tell me the most recent stuff."

He sipped the ginger ale with the stiff self-control of someone holding his temper.

"Maybe." His voice was mild as a milkshake. "You could tell me what you'd like to know."

"Recent events. Anything to do with Bousquet, real estate, finance, sweat shops, illegal immigrants. Russians."

I knew I sounded snippy but it was late and I was tired.

He paged through to the last pages of his notebook.

"You know about the Hyde Park development? The medical building. Since your housekeeper was involved."

"Yes." Though I was impressed he'd gotten that deep.

"After that, Laird stepped back from the public side of those developments, but kept his capital in various projects like the revamp of infrastructure in western Mass. After Tropical Storm Tammy."

"So he's still got a fair amount of money."

Carter nodded.

"Family money, to start. His father was a diamond dealer, with a store in the Jewelers Building. None of those guys are losing money."

"OK. What else?"

"He took on the cable show about three years ago, uses it mostly to promote his business interests and his political pals. He draws enough of an audience that the station doesn't care he's an asshole."

"Bousquet connections?"

"Laird owns two of the buildings in Chinatown that Bousquet leased for his manufacturing."

"Sweat shops, you mean. How many buildings did Bousquet have down there?"

"Three, at the time he was arrested. He'd leased as many as six, five years ago. And Laird owned five of those."

"So Laird was getting out from under? Was Bousquet's business failing?"

"Not so you'd notice. I looked at his corporate returns and for the last three years, his gross has doubled. Weird thing is, the net was about the same. Maybe up ten per cent."

I didn't want to know how Carter had gotten hold of the tax returns.

"Something funky, then."

"If I had to guess?" Carter said. "Money laundering. The gross doesn't match up with cost of goods sold, either. If he was selling as many suits and shirts as raw materials he claims to have bought, it should have been higher."

"Money from where?"

"Good question." Carter looked troubled, then went on. "Laird also maintains a very active social life. You know Bousquet had a half-Chinese mistress?"

"Viktoriya Lin." I rubbed my wrist. "We've met."

He frowned as if I'd stepped on his lines.

"Bousquet supplied girls to Laird. And Laird also has lady friends around the city. Married and not."

I thought about Laird's age and his hound-dog features.

"What's the attraction?"

"The usual, I assume." Carter finished his ginger ale and set the glass down on the coffee table. "Access. Money. He is sort of a media figure."

"Minor league."

"There's always someone looking for a step on the first rung. He takes advantage. As did Bousquet."

"Anything else?"

"As I said, they partied together. Both of them with a taste for high-end clubs, private rooms."

"Rumor?"

"Not dance clubs. More like Bijou."

"In Chinatown. What about the hookers?"

"Bousquet turned at least one of his seamstresses out to Laird for money." He checked his notes. "Kuan-Yin Zhao? I couldn't find out what the financial arrangement was."

He sounded apologetic, despite the deep detail he was bringing me. And, I hoped, Burton.

"Anti-cop bias? He went after a friend of mine on his show a couple weeks ago."

"Busted for OUI at least three times and wound up in the tank overnight once for mouthing off to a motorcycle cop."

"Lot of people don't like authority," I said.

"He was carrying a weapon and refused to surrender it. Cop had to subdue him."

Rasmussen lifted his head and looked at me, or I assumed so, since the dark shiny lenses pointed in my direction.

"The rest is background and details. Both Bousquet and Laird had a case of what's politely referred to as yellow fever. And Bousquet's sewing rooms were the source of the women."

Mickey Barksdale came to mind, as did Dmitri and the Russians. "Does he have any OC connections?"

That flat-lens stare again.

"OC."

"Organized crime."

"I know what it stands for," Carter said. "I'm wondering why you'd bring it up now. That's one area I don't go near and you didn't mention the possibility before."

Touched a live nerve there.

"I don't know that there is one. I was asking if you'd come across any."

He shook his head so hard he had to push the sunglasses back up his nose.

"I have not. I don't expect to. And I won't."

"That's all you have, then?"

He bristled.

"Fairly comprehensive for a week's work, I'd say."

More like a week and a half, but I was more interested in his touchiness, the need for approval. Lots of participation trophies growing up?

"Sorry," I said. "It is more than I expected. Is there a chance of going deeper? On the financial stuff, particularly?"

More evidence would be better for Burton, assuming I could find him.

Carter removed his dark glasses and regarded me with those creepy colorless eyes. He was accustomed to using the condition to bully people a little, keep them off balance. I looked at him squarely.

"That might get us into places where I'm driving without a

seat belt, so to speak." He tipped his head. "I can do that without endangering myself but you will then possess information you could not have obtained legally. Are you prepared for any consequences?"

It was a thoughtful question but yes was the only good answer. I was assuming Burton was alive and I was doing my best to help him out. And the fact that one day soon I'd be moderately rich, at least I'd be able to afford a good lawyer.

"I'll worry about that if we get there," I said. "I'm betting on more answers, deeper in the details." My gut was saying that greed outweighed lust as a motive in all this. "And while I respect that you don't want to brush up against any gangsters, it would help to know if a connection exists."

He raised his hands.

"I don't need you to get into it," I said. "I just need to know if it's there."

I needed to know specifically if Laird had any connection to Mickey or to the Russians. Carter didn't like it, but he wrote himself a note.

"That's all I have," he said.

"Excellent." I stood up, the fatigue flowing back into me. "I'll let you have the rest of your night back."

"Do you need timesheets or invoices from me?" he said. "Any of that?"

"Nope. Do you need more money?"

He pulled a face, as if I'd said something rude.

"I would like some further retainer."

"How much? I don't keep any cash in the house."

"Check is fine."

He named a figure that would have given me pause if he'd uttered it ten days ago. Bait and switch? Or a canny business model.

I stepped over to the Hepplewhite secretary, the last piece of furniture from my parents' house, dropped the top, and wrote him the check. He raised his sunglasses to read it.

"Blue ink," he said. "The shades make it invisible."

He tucked it inside his notebook and stood up.

"I am enjoying this, Mr. Darrow. It's a pleasure to work on

something that could achieve positive results for this city."

As he walked out of my apartment, I thought about what he'd said. Was that what I was trying to do? My motives weren't anything that grand. Mostly I was trying to haul Dan Burton out of whatever sticky quicksand he'd wandered into this time around.

# 36

The FedEx driver knocked on the open door of the Esposito around ten the next morning and yelled down the stairs.

"This the Esposito? You have an Elder Darrow down there?"

The little sign in the bricks must have been too subtle.

"Me," I called. "What have you got?"

He bounded down the stairs, wearing the dark blue company-logo wind shirt. I got a package maybe four times a year, so I didn't recognize the driver, a thirty-something Latino with wet-curls and the head of a dragon tattoo peeking up out of the neck of the pullover.

I tensed as he jogged across the floor toward me. He handed me an envelope and the electronic signature pad.

"Nice place," he said, looking around. "I didn't know you were here. Maybe I'll bring the wife in some night."

Then he jogged back up the stairs and out. I heard his truck start and grind away.

The offhand comment pleased me. People had the idea that jazz was too intellectual a music, also dated. Old people's tunes. But I was going to have to attract all kinds to keep the place going.

I turned over the envelope, my name and address in block letters on the waybill. It was probably paperwork from Attorney Markham in advance of cleaning up Thomas's estate. The three of us had an appointment Friday but there must be things I needed to do ahead of time.

When I zipped back the cardboard strip, though, what came out was a thick wad of computer printouts and photocopies, held together with a black steel clip.

The first document, a half dozen pages stapled together, was a police report of a burglary investigation, which didn't make sense until I scanned down and saw the name Kathleen Crawford in the middle of the page.

The investigator's account described the burglary of a second home in Burlington, Vermont, that belonged to an obscenely wealthy New York City real estate developer, someone whose name I recognized as a possible candidate for President the next time around. The cop-speak on paper was turgid but intelligible. All facts, no speculation.

City officers responded to a silent neighbor complaint at North Prospect in the Old North End of the city, home owned by S. Kahan. Premises secured by responding officers, front door ajar. Tire tracks indicated a 26-foot straight body truck backed up to the front porch.

Premises empty except for dishes and flatware (See Attachment A for inventory). Homeowner states no one in residence since previous Thanksgiving holiday.

I leafed back to the front page. The burglary had taken place in February, two years ago.

Owners also state premises fully alarmed and inspected weekly by local property management company, though burglary unreported for seventeen days. (Ref. loss of alarm service calendars, Attachment B). Property management firm states only engaged for remote temperature monitoring, not in-person visits, and payments in three months' arrears. (See interview at Attachment C.)

Home owner states loss of painting and antiques of approximate value $3.75 million USD. (See value inventory at Attachment D). Also furniture and electronics worth estimated $100,000 USD. (No inventory supplied.)

The report's tone was terse and unentertaining but the amounts made me whistle. If this was the work of a gang, they'd perfected the art of the major heist: one or two huge gigs a year in different parts of the country and no attempt to be selective about what they took. They simply loaded the entire household into a truck and drove it away, sorted out the details later.

I read past the technical details of how the alarm had been

bypassed and reattached without alerting the security company, then returned to the paragraph where Kathleen's name appeared. This part of the report must have been written by a different investigator, a wannabe novelist: the section on her was long, detailed, and couched in occasionally purple prose.

Extended consultation with other LE personnel via national databases raises the possibility this was one in a ten-year long series of approximately twenty-five high-end burglaries perpetrated in random cities of the United States. Modus operandi in all cases essentially the same, victims generally in the 1% class and only part-time residents of the burgled properties. Through collaboration with investigators in other affected cities, I was able to enumerate the following commonalities:

Use of a particular style of truck (See Attachment E for technical specifications)

Alarms disabled and reenabled in similar ways (See diagrams at Attachment F)

Common presence of one Kathleen Crawford in the geographical vicinity within the week before the crime (See photos, alias, and narrative at Attachment G)

My curiosity was raging by the time I folded back to Attachment G, the first page of which was a laser-printed color still that, from the angle and quality, had come from a security camera mounted above head height. Kathleen's gray-threaded hair was as familiar to me as the taste of Scotch, even allowing for the questionable resolution of the printer. Her face was turned to one side but I could make out a silver half-moon earring and the rounded bump at the bridge of her nose.

I took a deep breath and turned the page for four more sheets of densely-packed biographical detail, including the particulars of a long criminal life.

Kathleen was left in the care of a single mother at the age of twelve when her father reported to MCI-Framingham for a long sentence. Convicted of financing a minor armored car robbery in western Massachusetts, his sentence was extended by a rumored connection to another robbery in which a guard had been shot.

The prosecutor pushed for maximum penalties, even though prior crimes were not supposed to factor into a trial as evidence.

Kathleen, whose favorite alias seemed to be Nicole, was partway down her father's path by that time. Small for her age, the sweet little girl with the Hello Kitty backpack who went into the local package store to buy her gum and her mother's cigarettes was also shoplifting cans of Colt .45 to sell to her middle school classmates. Only when she upgraded to a larger backpack to increase her profit per trip did she discover that eight 24-ounce cans were too heavy to carry. I was sure the arresting officer thought she was cute as a kitten, pinched her cheek, and remanded her to her frustrated mom.

Who immediately packed Kathleen/Nicole off to Catholic school, which taught her to act more innocent when she was guilty. At this point, the biography settled into excruciating detail, cobbled from other reports of crimes she'd been arrested for or implicated in, all rewritten in the officer's florid prose. Then, about seven years ago, she'd disappeared from law enforcement view, the only remaining sightings in those towns about to experience a major burglary.

As I flipped over to the last page of the last attachment, a pale green post-it note in Burton's handwriting gave me a shock.

*Told you there was something off about her, didn't I?*

I spread out copies of news clippings from New Orleans, Atlanta, and several other cities in the eastern half of the country. The common theme was that the burglaries were all of ultra-rich homeowners in those cities. Was Kathleen acting like some kind of half-ass Robin Hood?

Burton must have thought the information would put me off Kathleen but in fact she intrigued me more than before. I'd always been interested in women who were more than they appeared to be.

I looked at the date on the waybill, two days ago, after the death photo of Burton had arrived. Could I take this as confirmation he was alive?

Marina walked out front.

"What's all that?"

I handed her Burton's note.

"You got this today?"

"Postmarked day before yesterday."

"So he might be alive?" She brightened. "What's the rest of it?"

I collected the papers into a bundle and reclipped them.

"Nothing important," I said. "Some information I asked him to get me a while ago."

# 37

On Friday, I picked Marina and Carmen up half an hour early for our appointment. Attorney Markham had agreed to meet us before his usual office hours so I didn't have to close the Esposito or open late. We would sign over her inheritance to Carmen and incidentally, release mine, closing up my father's estate. The money had been hovering out at the edge of my consciousness like a broken tooth the tongue goes back to again and again. Try as I might, I hadn't been able to forget it.

The two of them were standing out on the stoop of their building as I drove up, Marina in a navy blue car coat with toggle buttons and Carmen in a dark brown fur, a wool scarf tied over the top of her head.

"Morning," I said as they climbed in but no one replied.

I wondered if Carmen had had a bad night, not that anyone would tell me. Marina grunted from the back seat as I pulled away from the curb. Carmen stared out the windshield.

It felt more like we were taking the bus to visit someone in jail rather than heading to a law office we would all leave richer than when we went in.

When Carmen finally spoke, her voice was quieter than a message from outer space.

"Marina is not your father's child, Elder Darrow. You should know that, at least." She looked at Marina. "So, it's all right if you two want to . . . you know."

"Mother!"

Marina's face turned dark red. My neck was hot. I wondered

how tenuous Carmen's hold on reality might be, and how particular Markham would be about witnessing the signature of someone who might not be completely there. I opted to pretend she'd said something noncontroversial.

"Thank you, Carmen. That's good to know."

Marina shook her head and sat back in the seat.

The usual late-morning rush hour traffic had Shawmut Ave. blocked like a glutton's arteries, despite the fact that construction on Easy Berkeley had finished weeks ago. So when the car behind us tapped my bumper, neither of us was moving fast enough to hurt anyone. The worst that could happen was that I'd have to replace that whole goddamn vintage bumper again.

A big square black Gelandewagen loomed in my mirrors, supporting my theory that the more expensive the vehicle, the more likely the driver was an inattentive entitled asshole.

The 'wagen put its hazard lights on, so apparently the driver intended to further clog traffic by exchanging papers. I sighed. A tap like that wouldn't touch the Mercedes's deductible.

I shifted the Cougar into Park and unbuckled my seat belt. The door on the passenger's side opened and Marina screamed. Halfway out the driver's side, I could only watch as the red Chevy van in the lane to our right slid open its doors.

Big hands reached into the Cougar, popped Carmen's seat belt, and dragged her tiny body out of the car. Marina shrieked again, trying to claw her way out of the rear seat. The door slammed on her.

A squashed-face man in an orange jumpsuit, bald as a boulder, hauled Carmen into the van and the door slid closed. The van accelerated out in front of me, where the traffic had started to move, and shot down Dwight Street. The other vehicles from the right lane cut in and I could only watch the tail of the van disappear.

"Do something!" Marina screamed.

The Gelandeswagen was empty when I walked back to check, the monotonous clicking of its flashers infuriating me enough to want to break something. Whoever had kidnapped Carmen must be expecting a big payday to abandon a vehicle that retailed for a hundred and a half. A siren sounded, a few blocks over, far too late to do us any good.

\* \* \* \* \*

By the time I sorted it out with the patrol cops, we were too late for our appointment and missing one of the principals anyway. I called Markham to explain and told him what had happened. His voice conveyed relief that one day soon he would be done with the affairs of the Darrow family.

"Let me know when we can reschedule." He didn't seem curious about what had happened and when he hung up, I got the idea he was off to research how to close out the estate without Carmen. Just in case.

The police supervisor at the scene, one Liam Kelley, wanted to tow the Cougar and ferry us all down to headquarters to sort things out. I slowed him down long enough to let me call Biggs. No one in Boston had any reason to kidnap this old lady except as a way to pressure me, and through me, Burton. I was relieved when Murray did not answer.

"Professional Standards, Biggs."

I sketched out what had happened, Kelley standing so close I could smell the old coffee on his breath.

"Do whatever the officers tell you," Biggs said. "I'll try and have someone meet you at the station."

He hung up before I could say anything. Murray would have been more help and I warned myself not to assume Biggs was on Burton's side.

"My car's not going to tell you anything," I said to Kelley.

If the Cougar disappeared into the system, it might be weeks before I saw it again. Hotter heads prevailed.

"Taking his fucking car away isn't going to help my mother!" Marina shouted at the tow truck driver from a circle of cops.

Kelley turned his back and spoke to me.

"You know the detectives need to talk to you. And her."

I nodded.

"The woman's mother was just grabbed in front of her. What do you want me to say?"

"Look, I know Burton. And he knows you. If I can make it so you can leave, you'll be where I need to reach you? And hustle your ass to headquarters as soon as someone asks you to?"

I nodded gratefully. Marina was weeping now and the men around her were backing away. Kelley stepped into the street to talk to the tow truck driver, who eventually shook his head and left without my car.

The stress afterburn made my head ache, so when I spied the pale choirboy countenance, the thinning sandy hair, out on the edge of the spectators, it didn't immediately register. The relief flowed through me—Burton wasn't dead.

Nor was he in uniform. He wore baggy jeans and a black T-shirt that read "Duck of Justice" under a red and black checked flannel shirt. He stepped out of the crowd and tapped Marina's elbow.

When she saw him, she collapsed into his arms, leaving the cops who were standing close by at a loss. Burton stroked the top of her head and spoke into her ear as she cried, all the time surveying the crowd. He met my gaze and nodded.

"Isn't that Burton now?" Kelley said. "I thought he was on suspension or something. What the hell does he have to do with this?"

Only everything, Liam. Only every fucking thing.

\* \* \* \* \*

Burton's magical reappearance did not automatically make things easier. There was a considerable amount of milling around and testy conversation before Kelley could make good on what he'd promised me. We would be under Burton's supervision, from which I gathered the street cops were more comfortable with the way he operated than the brass was.

The traffic jam was the most difficult part of escaping. There were plenty of crime-fighting whizzes but no one who understood untangling vehicular confusion. It took the better part of an hour to clear all the cars out of the way and for me to get up to the intersection with East Berkeley and turn around.

"Leave the car out front," Burton directed before I could turn into the alley behind the Esposito. "I told Kelley it would be where they could get at it if they wanted to look it over."

I slotted the Cougar in next to the curb, a dozen feet down Mercy Street from the entrance.

"Now what?" I said.

Marina's tears were dry, her face a mask of worry and anger. Burton got out and leaned the seat back forward, helping her out of the back.

"Now," he said. "We have some breakfast. We make a plan. Someone just stepped across a big red line."

I unlocked the door, shut off the alarm, and we tromped downstairs. There was no place I less wanted to be right now, and though I was trying to control myself, I was furious with Burton. When Marina disappeared into the ladies' room, I turned on him.

"What the fuck, Burton? You keep disappearing and the people around you keep catching the heat. Did you fake your own death too?"

"Say what?"

"I've got a photo of you, looks like you've been shot in the head. Dmitri took credit for it."

"First I've heard of it," he said. "I've been trying to keep you two out of it." He slumped onto a stool. "Give me a shot of something. Rye. I've been awake for two days."

"No." I didn't want him drinking while we had to figure out what to do about Carmen. "Not on my account. But Marina? She's been so worried she can't see straight. And now her mother?"

He rubbed his hands down over his stubbled chin, leaving pale marks on his jaw.

"I thought I had this under control."

Marina appeared and banged her fist on the bar.

"You start drinking and I'll slap you so hard you see stars."

"Marina."

"Don't you Marina me. What are you doing that gets a ninety-year old woman kidnapped? You have an explanation for that?"

I stepped back to give them some privacy but not so far I couldn't hear.

"I was doing a favor for a friend," he said. "Her sister had gone missing."

I wondered if he knew yet that Kuan-Yin wasn't really Vicky's sister.

"That doesn't tell me why my mother's been kidnapped."

"She—the sister?—was smuggled in to work for Antoine Bousquet."

"So you went out to beat him up again?"

He shook his head.

"When I arrested him, he pushed a button. I smacked him. But I never saw him after that. He sold the woman, Marina. Like a slave."

"To Marty Laird," I said.

Burton's look mixed approval and supplication.

"You knew that?"

"Only recently. And by the way, Kuan-Yin is no relation to Viktoriya Lin. They're lovers."

Burton turned white. Marina looked concerned, like she thought he might faint.

"That clears a couple things up," he said.

Now he had to be wondering if Vicky sleeping with him was more power play than pleasure.

"So why is my mother involved in all this?" Marina demanded.

"It's got to be something else completely," he said. "Other people have been looking for me, trying to leverage my friends. Right, Elder?"

I nodded. Marina inhaled sharply.

"No one believed me when I said I didn't know where you were," I said. "Including Dmitri. And Mickey Barksdale."

"Smirnov." Burton snorted. "Which is Russian for meek, if you can believe that."

"So this Dmitri is holding my mother? Why? So he can talk to you?"

Burton shook his head.

"Doubtful. Tell her why."

"Dmitri sent me the picture. He thinks—or thought—Burton was dead."

"Someone convinced Dmitri I screwed up the Russians' deal. I think they had something going with Bousquet."

Marina's anger spun up again.

"Then who the fuck has my mother?"

Two "fucks" in one day? I'd never seen her so hot.

"It's such an asshole thing to do," Burton said. "It has to be the stupidest person in the mix."

"Marty Laird," I said. "About whom I have some information for you. But what's his motive?"

"I heard you basically kidnapped his girlfriend. His property, bought and paid for. Correct?"

"Viktoriya did. I was along for the ride."

I left out the part where she'd wanted me to impersonate a cop.

"But you were the only male there, right, except for Edward. And Marty's not taking on the toughest opponent. You were the guy who stole Kuan-Yin. Not Viktoriya."

Marina stepped up beside me and focused her rage on Burton.

"You know, I don't care who was fucking with who. Is he holding Carmen for ransom? Or revenge?" Her voice wavered. "Is she going to get hurt?"

"The cops are on it," he said. "I promise you, we will get Carmen back and she will be fine. No question."

Her stare was hard as iron.

"You'd better fucking be right." She slammed back into the kitchen.

\* \* \* \* \*

"So we need to call Biggs and Murray in, too? They're the only cops who have the whole picture."

"Jesus, no," Burton said. "They have one focus, whether I did or didn't do whatever they started out investigating me for."

"Just working for Viktoriya? No matter what else you happened to be doing with her?"

"Not proud of it," Burton said. "Getting played like that."

"To help her find Kuan-Yin."

"I found Kuan-Yin once. She and Marty were in a condo up on Rye Beach. She talked me out of telling Vicky."

"And she's not part of the IA case?"

"Doubtful. They're only interested in protocols. There's a process and a format for every situation. No room for independent thinking. And I violated several. Look, I get it. Freelancers cause confusion. But I like to think for myself."

"Then what next?"

"We find Marty and get Carmen back. Then I need to get Dmitri calmed down—I don't understand that bullshit with the picture. I'm pretty sure he's not the one who killed Bousquet, but the Russians are crazed about something."

"Bousquet was into them for money? Or was laundering theirs?"

"Something like that." He looked at me sideways. "You've done some work, then."

"You don't remember asking me to do research into Marty?"

He shrugged.

"I didn't know he was involved then."

"That's how you treat your friends, give them make-work to keep them out of the way?" Now I was hot. "Trouble comes to you and you disappear? Don't give anyone a chance to help?"

He closed his eyes and shook his head.

"If I could have fucked this up any worse? I don't know how."

"Then run the whole thing down for me, will you? On the off chance Marina and I will forgive you."

"What did I do?"

"Besides disappearing? While we were worrying about you? Wondering if you were dead. I know it's all about solo effort for you, but still."

He looked stricken. I pulled a bottle of beer out of the cooler.

"I don't want to say anything in front of Marina."

"Because of Vicky?"

He grinned like a seventh-grader peeking up his teacher's skirt.

"Can you imagine someone like that with me? I'd probably do it all over again, even if she does play for the other team."

I grimaced.

"Two words for you, friend," he said. "Jacquie Robillard."

My infatuation with the woman who'd talked me into buying the Esposito, Marina's predecessor in the kitchen.

"Burton. Forget that. What are we going to do about Carmen?"

He tilted the bottle to his mouth, as if it helped him think.

"We can't do anything. Until we figure out who did it."

"So? Who?"

"I don't know, Elder. Smart money might be on Marty, because he's so unpredictable. The Russians? Dmitri's still pissed that I supposedly screwed up their financial thing with Bousquet. But he thinks he killed me, too, which I don't get. Vicky's got no real reason."

"She's not that tightly wrapped," I said.

"Agreed. But she's been focused on finding Kuan-Yin. She was on fire at Bousquet for turning Kuan-Yin out. And Marty, for buying her."

"So. Laird or the Russians."

"I guess. I don't see Mickey Barksdale kidnapping old ladies."

No. If he were going to send a message, he'd have shot Carmen.

Marina carried a plate of fried egg sandwiches out of the kitchen, plucked away Burton's beer, and poured him a glass of water.

"Eat," she said. "Then we're all going down to police headquarters and camp out until we find out what they're doing to locate Carmen."

Burton gave me a helpless look. A loud pounding sounded on the emergency door out back. My head snapped up and Marina whipped around to look.

I slid the pistol out from under the bar and held it down by my leg, walked back through the kitchen and down the hall past my office. Burton followed close behind, but did not, I noticed, take the lead. Marina picked up the big cleaver on the way through the kitchen.

The pounding stopped as we reached the door, then restarted, weaker. I wished I'd thought to install a peephole but I never expected the door to be anything but egress.

Gripping the gun, I pushed the panic bar to unlatch the door, which pulled open so quickly I almost fell through. I was glad I didn't give in to the impulse to raise the pistol.

"*Gesù Cristo*," Carmen barked. "Where have you all been?"

# 38

Marina pushed past me and threw her arms around her mother, which only aggravated Carmen. She shook off her daughter's embrace with a vague shooing motion. Any other woman might have been deeply frightened by what had happened but Carmen only seemed angry that we hadn't come and picked her up. As if we'd known where she would be.

She spat a long sentence in rapid liquid Italian at Marina, who stared at her mother.

"What did she say?" Burton said.

Marina smiled.

"Believe me, you don't want the verbatim. Something to do with the strength and intelligence of your collective parentage."

A small beige envelope was pinned to Carmen's coat like a child's lunch money. I unfastened the stationery—fine linen, not something from the drug store—and pulled out a small stiff note card.

*See how easy it would be? I still need to speak to Mr. Burton, since he appears to live.*

A rage-flush threatened to black me out. No innocents for the Russians, I supposed. The note was signed with an ornate cursive *D.*

It hadn't been all that easy since Dmitri had paid the kidnappers and lost an expensive SUV but I wasn't going to quibble with him.

Carmen was behind the bar, assembling a pot of coffee. Burton was on the phone alerting the rest of the force that the kidnapping was a moot point for the moment.

"Caffeine, Ma," Marina said.

Carmen had misplaced her English momentarily. She fired off another thunderbolt of Italian and Marina backed away with her hands in the air.

If the Russians were dragging civilians into their mess, the trouble on that front was intensifying. It was one thing to threaten Burton, whose actual work was dealing with violence, crime, and murder. Or even me—I accepted that my association with him had brought me notoriety, even some vulnerability. But laying hands on an old woman? Beyond the pale.

What frustrated me was not knowing what Dmitri wanted, beyond another conversation with Burton. He'd originally pressed for information about the investigation into Bousquet's murder, I assumed so he could punish whoever had broken up the sweet money laundering deal the Russians had had with Bousquet. But I was beginning to realize I didn't have the imagination to guess what was in the man's tiny vicious mind.

"Carmen." Burton called to her, closing his phone.

She leaned against the back bar, waiting for the coffee to drip through, and in that unguarded moment, looked older than her years. At the same time, inside the wrinkled face and thickened body, I saw the ghost of a beauty that could have attracted my father. And wondered all over again.

"What do you remember? Did they hurt you in any way?"

She lifted her chin and scoffed, as if she'd survived much worse. For all I knew of her history, maybe she had.

"They just drove me away and put me on the Red Line," she said. "Paid the fare and told this nice young man to walk me home."

"You walked here from Downtown Crossing?" Her grit amazed Burton. Me, too. "And that was it?"

She shook her head, aggrieved.

"They're acting like I was crazy," she said. "Talk to me like I'm furniture."

Exactly what old people looked like to some. But now I was confused. This was the extent of Dmitri's threat?

"Was this an older man?" Burton said. "Russian, maybe?"

"Russian, yes. But young. Very handsome and polite. Tall. Dark-haired." She smirked at him. "Big shoulders."

Ermolai. Who had even less to gain by provoking Burton or me. Probably just following orders. I squeezed Carmen's hand carefully.

"I'm glad you're all right but we don't have any idea what else could be going on." I looked at Burton. "I think we'd better put the two of you up in a hotel for a few days."

Behind Carmen's back, Marina shook her head. I wondered what I'd said wrong. Carmen brightened and said something else in Italian to Marina.

I raised my eyebrows.

"She wants to know if we can stay at the Parker House."

I had to wonder how a nice old woman living in a modest apartment building knew enough to want to stay in one of the finest historic hotels in the city, but if it contained our concerns while Burton and I figured out how to deal with Dmitri, it was worth it.

"Fine," I said. "Take a taxi and I'll call over with a credit card."

Marina spoke low and intensely to Carmen, still in Italian. What a useful thing a second language was around people who did not speak it. Carmen dropped her head, as if chastened.

"What?" I said.

"Nothing." Marina filled mugs with coffee and passed them around. "I just told her you weren't going to pay for room service."

Standing in the doorway to the bar, Burton snorted like a horse.

\* \* \* \* \*

It was inordinately slow for a Friday night and I figured we could all use a break, so I decided to close early. I taped a paper sign to the front door lying about a plumbing problem and headed back to my apartment. I was wrung out and I wanted to be alone to breathe, shake off the strangeness of the day, and figure out our next step. Burton had left the Esposito around dinnertime without a word about where he was going.

I circled the Cougar in front of my building three times before deciding to wedge it into a loading zone and take my chances. It was after ten but I'd have until nine in the morning to move it. I could manage to get up that early. And my bad ticket karma had to end sometime.

Rain pelted me as I jogged the half-block to my front door. The outside door was latched and locked for a change and water dripped down my collar as I fumbled with the keys. A neck-crawling feeling that had nothing to do with the rain shivered me. I stood in the open doorway and looked up and down the street and saw nothing. But as I turned to step inside, a bulky presence rushed up the stairs beside me and passed into the foyer.

My feet tangled as I flinched, then I caught the fleshy part of my hand painfully on the edge of the door jamb.

"Sorry," a familiar voice said. "The door was unlocked the last time."

"Jesus, Rasmussen."

"Sorry," he said again, in a not-sorry voice. "I didn't mean to frighten you."

My breathing and heart rate slowed quickly, maybe because they'd had so much practice lately. I pulled the street door closed, making sure the latch caught. I was a little tired of Carter's studied oddity—I almost wished Markham had connected me with an honest-to-god private eye: fedora, rubber-soled shoes, and a drinking problem. That cliché at least I could understand.

The door on the ground floor landing opened, spilling light across the stairs. Carter stepped back into the shadow.

"Is that you, Mr. Darrow? I thought I heard someone speaking."

Carter probably couldn't see my irritation in the dim light. I hated disturbing Mrs. Rinaldi.

"It's fine, Mrs. R. Sorry if I woke you."

Someone—probably she—had solved the dead light bulb problem by plugging in a night light at the bottom of the stairs. It spread a muffled cone of light around my ankles.

"Oh, no," she said. "I hardly sleep these days."

Into that pause, I was supposed to drop an invitation for a visit some time. I remembered how I'd once had the time to spend with her and Peter Voisin, the second-floor tenant, before he'd gone off into assisted living. We'd have a drink occasionally, play backgammon.

I knew I'd have to make the time—Mrs. Rinaldi wouldn't be around forever. And she'd lived in Boston all her life. There were stories I knew she had for me.

Her door closed firmly and sadly, as if she hadn't expected anything more.

"Quietly, please." I gestured to Carter to precede me up the stairs. Despite his dark glasses, he stepped as confidently as any night creature, as noiseless as if he wore slippers.

I threw my keys down on the side table and dropped into an armchair. The only reason he'd returned so quickly was that he'd found something important.

"I'll be quick," he said.

"You couldn't come out in the day time?" I regretted it as soon as I said it.

"This may be the last time you'll need to hear from me," he said.

I pointed to a chair.

"Sit. What do you have?"

He turned the dark glasses, a fine mask, on me.

"I could come back tomorrow."

I rolled my hand to get him moving.

"Your subject, Mr. Laird? Not only owned the buildings Bousquet's sweat shops were in? He was part owner of the business itself. When Bousquet had to close factories two years ago? Laird took a multimillion dollar loss."

"But they still partied together? Shared the women?"

"They were estranged until about a year ago. I couldn't get the details but the story was that Bousquet made up his loss."

"Proof?"

"Not of everything. Ownership and loan documents for the buildings. Much of this is not public, by the way. You don't want to have to testify about where it came from."

"Understood. You've taken this about as far as it can go?"

"Probably. Unless you want the kind of documentation that will hold up in a lawsuit. Or a prosecution." He smiled loosely. "Hate to give this up, though. It's much more interesting than most of what I do."

"If you think there's more, go for it. Do you need more money?"

"We're square for now, but let me poke around. I did hear one other thing. About your friend the cop."

I'd been thinking how Burton could use all this to leverage Marty Laird. Now I gave Carter back my full attention.

"Laird has been telling people Burton's out of the picture, whatever that means."

"No more detail than that?"

Marty had either picked up the rumor of Burton's death or he was connected to the Russians somehow.

"Nope. Just that he's not going to be a factor anymore."

"OK. I'll be sure to let Markham know what a help you've been." He shrugged.

"That's my bread and butter, but it is kind of boring. You come up with anything else like this you need help on, let me know."

He stood up, pointed his finger at the ceiling.

"One thing? I heard they're bringing back *Eric in the Evening*."

"Excellent." But my mind was already on getting this information to Burton so he could use it to pressure Laird.

"Jazz is," Carter said, and walked out.

I followed him downstairs, made sure the street door was locked, climbed back up, and went to bed. My body was screaming at me about the fact it was three in the morning.

# 39

I always tried to get in early on the Saturday closest to the beginning of the month to catch up on paperwork and do the books, but I'd missed last week because I'd thought Burton was dead. It was usually quiet enough at this hour to check in on the business side. The deliveries for the weekend had all been made the day before, so there weren't usually any interruptions. I cleaned up the office and set the DVD the mysterious Eileen had left in her purse on top of the laptop to remind me to look at it when I had time.

After confirming that I wasn't going bankrupt this month, I walked out front, remembering that I'd left the house pistol under the bar. I took it out from under a pile of bar towels and dropped the magazine to check inside. I wasn't going to fool myself. I might be able to use it to threaten someone but I doubted I'd ever be able to shoot anyone with it.

It was still only nine-thirty when I sat down at the bar with the *Globe* and a mug of coffee. I'd started drinking it black, aware that sugar was as much an addiction as anything else. The bite of it was growing on me, though I'd given up the cheap bitter Dunkin's beans and started buying fresh-roasted from Suffolk Grounds, a couple blocks over.

The street door was propped open for air, maybe not the safest idea right now, but I couldn't pretend being Burton's friend wasn't dangerous anymore. That was one of the reasons I kept the pistol out front.

The flow of cool air and the traffic sounds up on the street were interrupted by someone stepping into the doorway. I swiveled on my stool and watched Ermolai stomp down the stairs, the hard heel of his boots ringing the steel risers.

I walked around the bar and set my hand on the checkered grip of the gun.

Ermolai held up his hands as he reached the bottom of the stairs.

"We have nothing to fight about, Darrow. Really. I come in peace." He grinned. "Not in pieces."

Nothing could fool me into thinking he was funny. Or harmless. I recalled Dmitri's warning, that Ermolai might want to avenge his orphanage brother Anatoly.

"How about you stay right up there at the end of the bar?" I said.

I didn't flash the pistol at him but Ermolai would know I wasn't playing pocket pool under the counter. He dropped his hands, pushed back the skirts of his brown leather coat, and showed me he was not carrying the big ugly pistol he'd toted in the alley the day he'd beaten up Burton.

"You're old enough, you've heard this term *détente*, am I right?" he said.

Though I'd pegged him as a thug, his voice was unaccented and conversational. It hinted at an education beyond the streets or steppes or wherever he'd come from in Russia.

"Nixon and Brezhnev?" I said. "They didn't teach you that in school."

Ermolai looked to be about thirty, too young to have lived then.

He grinned, showing teeth so white and square they had to be false.

"I always liked to read," he said. "Anyway, I'm bringing you *détente*. Or the offer of, at least."

"Really. So Dmitri isn't coming by after to kick my ass?"

He shucked his heavy coat, shaking his head, and looked at my mug.

"Is it too early for coffee? Plain and black?"

"Not tea?"

He pouted. I poured him some and he tasted.

"Thank god. You're not one of those Starbucks drones."

I was still wary of his peaceable nature.

"You're not here on behalf of your boss?"

He raised a shoulder. His head was shaved, as everyone who wanted to look tough these days had it, his eyebrows plucked to a narrow line. The tattersall L. L. Bean shirt stretched around his torso.

"Things are always changing," he said. "You know this." He gestured at the *Globe*. "You read the newspapers. Politics, sports, the financial world. One has to deal with change."

He seemed to imply that included the criminal world, but I didn't think I wanted any details.

"Let's just say that Dmitri and I used to work for the same entity. Now we have different responsibilities and different goals."

I suspected something like the age-old story of the young buck easing the old man out of a position of influence. If it happened everywhere else, why not in the mob? The energy and confidence of the young pitted itself against the slyness and craft of the old.

"What could either one of you want from me?" I said.

He continued explaining, as if I hadn't spoken.

"Dmitri was what you would call an old-schooler. Threats, intimidation, succession by hierarchy, all of it happening in a physical way. As in kidnapping old ladies. Or beating up police officers. No room for subtleties. You understand what I'm saying."

All of those were activities Ermolai had participated in. Was Dmitri aware of the chameleon dancing in his entourage?

"But you and I both know, Elder Darrow, there are fears and there are *fears*. A person who's experienced physical pain, someone who injured themselves playing sports, might respond better to a psychological threat. Or an arm's length attempt, something that threatened his business or his family."

I reached back under the bar. Ermolai wrinkled his broad nose as if I'd farted.

"Please. As I said, the old woman was Dmitri's brainstorm. I tried to talk him out of it." He set his hands flat on the bar. "I haven't come to threaten. Merely to try and create a mutual trust."

"Is that so? Then tell me straight what you want. Conflicting desires are floating around and confusing the issue."

Ermolai coughed.

"Would you have something for my throat, perhaps? Maybe Metaxas?"

Why anyone would drink that Greek kerosene was beyond me, though I had a tall thin bottle someone had given me when I opened the Esposito. I doubted it could have spoiled. I reached down the bottle and wiped off the dust.

"Pour yourself one," Ermolai said. "On me."

I gave him a dark look but he didn't seem to be trying to goad me. If I were going to have a drink, it sure as shit wouldn't be Metaxas.

"I don't drink."

"Probably wise," he said.

I poured brandy into a cordial glass.

"Why was Dmitri so interested in the Bousquet investigation? Was he one of yours?"

Ermolai waved a hand, then put his nose down into the glass and sniffed.

"Another weakness of the old-timers' approach. Burton had nothing to do with our problem with Mr. Bousquet."

"Which was?"

He danced around this question too, something that was starting to annoy me.

"Dmitri considered the death of Antoine Bousquet a loss. For his entity, if you will. I prefer to see the opportunity."

He picked up the stemmed glass and sipped. His eyes watered.

"Potent." He exhaled. "You won't join me?"

My turn to ignore a question.

"If I understood your entity's connection to Bousquet? I might follow. As it is, I'm paddling in yoghurt."

He pointed a finger, flashed his store-bought teeth.

"Good one." He sipped. "Let me try and explain. Without telling too much you might find uncomfortable."

I was already uncomfortable and I still didn't know what he wanted.

"Go."

"Mr. Bousquet, until four or five years ago, he had a very successful business operation in your fair city. Can we agree on that?"

I didn't pay much attention to the rag trade but what he said

213

correlated with what Rasmussen Carter had told me. I nodded, if only to keep the conversation moving.

"And, in fact, everything about his business up until that time? As the newspaper stories and the testimonials say? He was legal, legitimate, paid his workers living wages, and housed them at market rates."

Not that a living wage would support a market rate, but I wasn't going to argue with him.

"An unfortunate confluence of temporary cash flow problems, a canceled contract, and an unfortunate review of his forthcoming line stalled his progress." Ermolai tilted his head. "You understand? No one liked his new clothes."

I wasn't sure I believed that confluence was random.

"So his business was under threat."

"Worse, really. Antoine was one of those fellows who thought of the business as himself, as his identity. So he felt in danger of being erased. Personally. That psychological fear."

"And Dmitri saw an opportunity."

He finished the brandy, shuddered a little, then corrected me gently.

"To say the entity saw an opportunity is more correct. But because of Dmitri's old-timer way of doing things? We didn't get involved until a year or so ago."

"Money lenders in the temple," I said.

Ermolai beamed, as if I'd been an apt pupil.

"We did lend him some money, yes. And no, we did not gouge him, as you would say, on the terms of the loan. These were market rates."

"And your advantage now," I said. "Let me guess. You had a place to launder your excess cash."

He looked surprised I knew so much, then nodded.

"We have a very wide range of business activities, expanding every day. There is always a need to make the proceeds of some transaction appear more legitimate, yes."

He pushed the glass away. I wondered if Mickey Barksdale knew all this.

"The illegal immigrants for Bousquet's business? One of those transactions?"

He shook his head.

"Using them brought us a level of scrutiny we were not prepared for. But still, we had to protect Bousquet's operations."

"So your entity had no reason to harm Bousquet? Is that what you wanted to tell Burton?"

Ermolai leaned across the bar.

"Your friend knows who caused these illegal immigrants to enter the country. Because they were not here legally, Bousquet thought he could take certain liberties. Further jeopardizing our relationship."

Liberties. Like rape and turning young women out as prostitutes.

"And you want to know who brought the people in? Why?"

He wasn't going to hear Mickey Barksdale's name from my lips.

"Burton knows," he said. "And we need to know. Wasn't Burton looking for one of those women?"

Time to cut off the conversation. The news Burton was alive probably hadn't made it public yet.

"Burton is dead, Ermolai. Dmitri is claiming he did it."

Ermolai roared with laughter.

"He would have like to kill Burton, yes. But instead, he asked me to take care of it. More old-timer business."

"You were the one who phonied up the picture?"

Why hadn't Burton said so, then?

Ermolai puffed out his chest.

"Technology, yes? I am a whizzer at it. But Burton is alive. Because of me."

"He's in hiding," I said. "Using the fact people think he's dead to stay low."

He frowned, not sure whether to believe me.

"So the police will come to speak with Dmitri probably?"

"Your opportunity?" Because I had a damn good idea what he was thinking.

"Then." He stood and slipped on his coat. "You and I have had a pleasant drink together. Nothing more."

"I will convey your wish." And I was sure Burton would deny it.

"We don't have anything to discuss," he said.

He gave me a threatening look, then jogged up the stairs at a noisy clip.

I picked up the cordial glass, sticky in my fingers, and ran it under very hot water.

# 40

After Ermolai's visit, it was useless to pretend it was going to be a regular Saturday. I queued up music automatically, a couple three-hour playlists with nothing too loud or challenging, and brought my laptop out front to start checking figures for my tax returns. I'd been ignoring some of the practicalities of running my jazz joint, and despite the fact that I was going to have more money than I knew what to do with in a couple weeks, I didn't want to get sloppy.

As usual, the first customer appeared at the top of the stairs around eleven-thirty. People talked themselves into starting their drinking a little earlier on Saturdays—my deepest fantasy for the Esposito was that the three-martini lunch would make a comeback.

But when I saw my first customer of the day was going to be Marty Laird, I turned the lights up high and reached under the bar to touch the pistol.

He walked across the black and white linoleum floor with a limp, a sign of age not injury, and in the bright light, he looked at least seventy. The shaved head was a bad look for him, highlighting the droopiness in his ears and jowls, the wild eyebrows and ear tufts. His shoulders rounded forward and his face was hangdog. Whatever Kuan-Yin had seen in him, assuming she'd stayed with him voluntarily after Bousquet died, it wasn't sexual magnetism.

I tensed as he approached the bar, carrying his battered briefcase as if it held diamonds or Cold War secrets.

"Mr. Laird."

"I'm not holding anything against you," he said. "Viktoriya Lin is a rabid cunt."

He laid the case flat on the bar, ignoring my frown of distaste for the word.

"I need a favor. But first I need a drink. You have any Blue Label?"

Johnny Walker Blue, one of the world's great marketing gimmicks, claimed to be a blend of rare and exceptional whiskies but it was, indeed, a blend. It had no singular character, only a mélange of the tastes and flavor notes of everything J. Walker threw into the vat. Give me a straight-ahead single malt anything—Scotch, Irish, rye— over the bastard child of too many parents.

"Nope. How about a nice cask-strength Macallan?"

Laird shook his head.

"Jack Black, ginger ale on the side."

As I poured the drinks, he unlatched the case.

"I'm not here to cause any trouble," he said. "I just want Kuan-Yin to come home."

I placed the two glasses on coasters and swept away the twenty dollar bill he'd laid down. Unless he was playing a darker deeper game, Laird had it bad for her.

"What makes you think I can do anything about that?" I said. "I was only there because Vicky insisted."

I regretted smart-assing him on the way out of the Bee Stack the other day. He tried for a glare but the hound-dog face couldn't manage it.

"I don't know what that crap with her was all about," he said. "Kuan-Yin's been with me for a couple months. It started out one way but now it's real. And exclusive. Vicky doesn't know she's fighting a losing battle. Kuan-Yin likes cock too much to settle for her."

Any sympathy I might have felt washed away with his assumption, not uncommon, that all a lesbian needed to change her orientation was a dose of penis.

"Shouldn't you be talking to Kuan-Yin about this, Marty? Or even Viktoriya? I was incidental."

And wishing I hadn't been there at all. He looked as abject as a puppy without a biscuit.

"You must have some pull with her, Darrow. You were there. I love Kuan-Yin. You must know how that is."

I thought of Kathleen, though nothing we'd had rose to the level of Marty Laird's infatuation.

Marty lifted the top of the case and displayed rows of banded bills, a ridiculous amount of money, if they all were hundreds.

"Maybe Viktoriya would accept a gift, in exchange for Kuan-Yin?" He looked pathetically earnest about buying his love back. "This is not a love thing for Vicky—it's all about possession."

"Marty. I don't buy and sell people. Unlike you and your pal Antoine, all right? So at the risk of being insulting, why don't you drink your drink and get the fuck out of here?"

His face turned feral.

"You don't think I could make trouble for you? This shithole? You think I'm some schmo with a cable show?"

That summed it up as well as I could, but I wasn't going to inflame him by agreeing.

He snapped the case shut and leaned over the top of it.

"I know some things about your family that wouldn't go over so well in this town, you know. About your father, for example."

The pistol was up and pressed against his forehead before I realized it. Marty sat very still, his only sound a liquid swallow.

"I would be very grateful if you took your sleazy, slave-trading ass out of my bar, Mr. Laird. Along with the blood money. Threats may be useful sometimes, but I'm in a mood to act. Take that how you will."

The hairless rodent scurried up the stairs without looking back.

I couldn't remember the last time I'd lost my temper so completely. As the door closed behind him, I shoved the pistol back under the counter and leaned on the bar. My hands shook and I barely recognized myself. What the hell kind of person was I turning into?

# 41

One Saturday in the Esposito was just like another if I didn't have live music, and the rest of that afternoon was indistinguishable from another day, which was all right. I'd had enough strange visitations for one day. I only turned on the news at six o'clock because I was bored with making drinks and taking money, bored with the conversations along the bar, even bored with the music, which I couldn't seem to get right. Worse, I didn't have anything to blame it on, though in retrospect, I can see the mood was prophetic.

I paid little attention to the lead stories—bombings, terrorist attacks, and school shootings were adding the same kind of numbing background music to the world that the Afghanistan and Iraq wars were. Modes and methods and political stances shifted all over the place, but the apparently unkillable desire of people to fight over power and religion didn't ever seem to abate.

As the news returned from one of the interminable commercial breaks, the boredom blew out of my mind the way a hurricane clears a stink. A serious male in shiny hair and a shirt that clashed badly with his polka-dot bow tie put on a grim face as a picture of Burton in uniform displayed behind him.

"Marina!"

The half dozen people along the bar looked up at the panic in my voice. She ran out of the kitchen, drying her hands on her apron.

"What?"

I pointed at the screen.

"Jesus Christ." She grabbed the remote off the bar and pushed up the volume.

"In city news tonight," the newscaster intoned. "A decorated police officer from Boston's Homicide Unit is under arrest tonight for the alleged murder of Antoine Bousquet, the well-known Boston businessman and philanthropist whose mutilated body was discovered ten days ago."

"No." Marina was shaking her head.

My petty little mind fastened on the fact that it wasn't the murder that was alleged but Burton's involvement in it but shock kept my mouth shut. What kind of evidence did BPD have that Burton killed Bousquet that they didn't have a week ago? None of us, Burton included, had seen this coming.

"Our correspondent Constantina Mulcahy is at the jail tonight for this report."

The visual shifted to a leggy Latina standing in front of the Nashua Street Jail, dressed as if she were on her way to a cocktail party.

"Thank you, Rob." She stared into the camera and licked her lips, unconsciously, I hoped. "Sources inside the Boston Police Department tell us that Daniel Burton, the Homicide detective seen in this clip from February, has been arrested and charged with the horrific slaying of Antoine Bousquet."

The media moguls would never have denied themselves the opportunity to run the choice bits of video showing Burton punching Bousquet in the face. Of course, the clip, without sound, didn't show Bousquet's provocation. My first thought was that the video would make it hard to empanel a jury almost anywhere but here in the city. Too many people would look at a place on this jury as a chance to make a statement about cops.

"Burton, a fifteen-year veteran of Homicide, was arrested at his apartment tonight."

Subsequent footage showed uniformed officers perp-walking him through the back door of the jail, his head high, looking straight ahead. I could only imagine his rage and embarrassment.

Marina leaned heavily against the bar.

"Now what do we do?"

I was stunned, as well. My barflies watched us with interest, having connected whatever was happening on TV with our concern. Eddie Dracut, a printer, called down the bar.

"Everything OK, Elder?"

I nodded and smiled.

"Sure, Ed."

"Then how about another round before you lose your shit again."

I shook up another Tequila Sunrise for him and thought about who to call first. Marina stared at the TV, unable to move, though the newscast was on to another story. I delivered Ed's drink and pulled out the phone.

"Biggs, Professional Standards."

"You're there." I was relieved, afraid I'd end up with Murray.

"Who is this?" Frosty as January.

"Elder Darrow. Burton's friend?"

"What can I do for you? Pretty busy here."

No doubt.

"Burton," I said.

"What about him?"

"What happened? Why was he arrested?"

"Wrong department, Darrow. You want Media Relations."

"Wait."

He exhaled so loudly my ears hurt.

"Decision was made elsewhere. Not my bailiwick. Or my choice, for that matter."

"They must have some evidence."

"I can't discuss this with you, Darrow. Talk to Burton. Or his lawyer, if he has one. I'm on the wrong side to be any help."

I got the clear sense he didn't like what had happened, that he'd help if he could. I wondered if I could trust him.

"Tell me one thing, then," I said. "Or better? Don't say anything if I'm right. Is this primarily a political move? Someone covering their ass?"

Silence may not have been golden but it was eloquent as a hallelujah.

"All right. Thanks," I said, and hung up.

* * * * *

It was after seven on a Saturday night but Attorney Markham was in his office. I forewent any jokes about his work ethic—Burton needed legal help. He wouldn't be stupid enough to fall for the canard that lawyering up meant you were guilty, but I doubted he'd hurry to do it.

"Attorney Markham. Glad to catch you in. Have you seen the news tonight?"

I'd been in his office with my father a couple of years ago when Markham had a small set turned to CNN, when the Democratic presidential primary had been in doubt, but he probably thought TV frivolous.

"No." He sounded impatient, and I wondered what it would be like to always anticipate, not be able to focus on the here and now. "Are you and the Antonellis prepared to reschedule?"

Oops.

"No. Carmen's been . . . indisposed." I didn't want to complicate that situation. "I'll let you know when we can do it. No. I need a reference for a criminal defense lawyer."

"For yourself?" He coughed. "No. Never mind. Assuming it has no impact on our business together, I don't need to know."

Or want to, certainly.

"Agreed. Do you have a name for me?"

"Jacob Gundersen," he said immediately. "We matriculated together at Harvard, though he didn't complete his undergraduate there. Boston State, I believe. But his practice has taken him in that direction. Please give him my best when you speak to him."

He rattled off a phone number but I was ready for him this time.

"If there's nothing else," he said. "I'm trying to get a handle on my taxes."

"Thanks." I hung up.

Working on his taxes in March? Either he was making too much money or his finances were too complicated. Since he was a lawyer? Probably both.

The number he'd given me got me to an after-hours answering service with, *mirabile dictu*, a human voice.

223

"Would you please ask Attorney Gundersen to call whenever he can, please? I'm a late night person."

"Certainly, sir." The crisp voice repeated my number and wished me a pleasant evening.

Marina was still staring into space. Two tables of drinkers were coming up to the bar to cash out and my stool sitters all wanted refills. I put an arm around her shoulders.

"It'll be fine," I said. "Not perfect. But it's going to be all right."

She pulled away.

"Don't you blow sunshine at me. None of this is right and you know it."

The phone rang and anything else I might have said to calm her down flew out of my head. I motioned for her to ring up the people leaving and held up a wait-a-minute finger to the bar sitters. Getting Burton help was at the top of my list right now.

"Esposito."

"I'm looking for an Elder Darrow?"

The voice was mild and tentative.

"Is this Attorney Gundersen?"

"It is. Are you Darrow?"

"I am. I'd like to hire you. A friend of mine has been arrested for murder. Which he did not do, obviously."

"Obviously." The reply was tinged with humor, which irritated me, though I supposed the cliché would have it that everyone arrested claimed their innocence. "This would be the Burton case? Danny Markham just called me."

"Yes. And if you spoke to Markham, you know I can afford your fees. And bail."

"Just so," he said. "Though if this is a capital case, I'd be surprised there was a bail provision."

"That's your province," I said. "Assuming you'll take on the case."

"I will. I'll bring over a written contract in the morning, but in the meantime, I'll speak to some people, see if I can gather some background. Can we meet at your establishment at, say, ten A.M.?"

On a Sunday morning? No bankers' hours for this man.

"Of course."

"I'll see you then."

I recharged my drinkers, then walked out back to tell Marina what I'd done. Her face was damp and mottled and she scrubbed the cutting boards like she was sanding them down.

"Look," I said. "We've done what we can do for now. The lawyer will be here in the morning."

She shook her head and looked away, as if she didn't dare speak. There was nothing I could do but leave her in the grip of her emotions.

* * * * *

Jacob Gundersen was the first customer in my tenure at the Esposito who used the freight elevator that I'd had to convince the city egress inspector doubled as my handicapped entrance. He must have figured out its operation without any help because the first notice I had of him coming was the groan of the elevator cables in the wall. He emerged from a small creaky door next to the stage and I was astounded that the elevator actually worked.

"Not exactly ADA-approved, is it?" He whirred a minimalist black carbon fiber wheelchair up to the open space where the bar led into the kitchen. "Can we talk at one of the tables or do I need to ask you to hoist me up onto a bar stool?"

He was smiling as he said it, though, and my first impression was of a good-natured man, not much bigger than a jockey, with a bald pate and a scruff of graying hair pulled back into a skimpy ponytail behind his neck. A chunk of turquoise the size of a pea punctuated his left ear. He was dressed in a white linen suit over a maroon shirt, open at the neck to display one of those Hawaiian bone fish hook necklaces. I wondered how his sartorial style went over in the courts of the Commonwealth, which tended to the conservative.

"*Mahalo*," he said.

I wiped my hands and pointed to a table at the far end of the stage. "Soda? Water?" I said. "Drink?"

"Coffee wouldn't go amiss. Espresso for a choice but black coffee would do as well."

He pivoted the chair and powered over to the table, a black

backpack hanging from the back of his chair. I filled two mugs and followed him over. As I sat across from him, he pulled a folder of papers out of the backpack.

"Jacob Gundersen." He held out his hand. "As you've no doubt inferred."

"Have to like a man who knows the difference between inferred and implied," I said.

He frowned at me, then slipped a three-page contract across the table, along with a black Montblanc fountain pen.

"Standard agreement," he said. "But we don't go any further until you sign it. In lay terms? Small initial payment to take on the case, hourly rates and lump sums if we have to go to trial. Big ones."

I leafed through the first two pages, which were understandable, then fetched up hard at the last page and whistled.

"I should say. This is serious money."

Gundersen wasn't fazed—he'd had the reaction before. But he also knew that by the time most people got around to hiring a criminal lawyer, they'd be too worried to quibble about money.

"Only if we go to trial," he said. "And based on preliminaries? I have serious doubts that's going to be necessary."

I cocked an eyebrow.

"Burton's not going to plead on a lesser charge to something he didn't do."

Gundersen waved the idea away like a bad smell.

"I don't make a habit of having my clients plead guilty to anything. Bad for my reputation. But understand this: even if you sign the contract, Burton is my client. Not you. Just because you're paying the fees doesn't mean you're buying the right to direct what happens. Or even know. You OK with that? Because you have the reputation of someone who's used to getting his own way."

I wondered who he'd been talking to—it was a view of me I hadn't heard.

"Why don't you think it will go to trial?"

He put both hands around the mug to lift it, his grip tremored, though he didn't spill. When he looked at me, I could see the serious lawyer behind the hair and the earring.

"As a mark of my willingness to help," he said. "I've done a little research. Without, I'd remind you, any agreement to be paid for it."

He nodded at the papers. I uncapped the fountain pen and scrawled my signature across the bottom of the page.

"There is some serious contention within the Commonwealth's legal system as to whether the assistant DA who brought the charge and the investigator who built the case against your friend are pursuing an agenda other than solving a homicide."

"You're talking about Murray? The Professional Standards guy?"

Gundersen nodded, showing the liver spots on his scalp.

"Which is the largest part of their problem. Typically, a Professional Standards investigator is not tasked with assembling a murder case. That would be Homicide's purview."

"So why not this time?"

"Apparently Inspector Murray did an end-around the usual process and found an ADA with some unpleasant history with Burton, convinced him that Homicide would close ranks against an investigation of one of their own."

"Cynical."

"Even for Professional Standards. Who trusts nobody." Gundersen chuckled. "Needless to say, Homicide wasn't thrilled."

"I'd think Homicide would be more inclined to punish one of their own if he committed a murder."

Gundersen nodded.

"What complicates things is that, despite his stellar closure record, Burton has become a little too maverick for the department. He's pissed off so many people by now that no one's even vaguely amused by him."

His head twitched right, an abrupt jerk that shook his ponytail. I hoped I didn't have to find out what kind of impression he made in court.

"You think the department is trying to make him quit?"

"Possibly, though it would be an incredible misuse of procedure to do it this way. More likely someone decided they needed an answer to who killed Bousquet, for the public. Murray could be being manipulated by someone further up the chain."

The bad faith in that possibility was breathtaking.

"Don't they have any internal controls? Can they break their own rules that way?"

Gundersen snickered.

"Like the ADA in question, the law is an ass."

His right hand shook more and he did not try and pick up his coffee again. As if to distract me from that, he concentrated his gaze on me, a deep and dark focus. I saw how a jury could ignore his physical being and listen.

"You ever work for anyone? Besides yourself, I mean?"

I thought he was making a comment about being a rich man's son and my neck got stiff.

"No."

"And just as well, I suspect. You've made a success of this place. No one wants to work where they're not wanted, Elder. And after you swallow a certain amount of crap, you can't."

"You're saying the price of Burton's freedom might be his job."

He nodded, nothing uncertain about it this time.

"Exactly. And you and I both know what that would mean to him."

"You've known Burton for a while?"

"Quite a while, in fact. We've always been on opposite sides in the courtroom, but he's one of the few who's retained my respect. He doesn't play games with people's lives. If Markham hadn't called me, I might have called myself."

He pushed his papers together, the tremors gone. When he gave me his hand to shake, it was soft, boneless-feeling.

"You're a good friend to do this," he said. "I'll do my best not to bankrupt you."

I dropped his hand. He whirled the chair and motored toward the door next to the stage.

"Joke, Elder. Joke," he called over his shoulder. "Crissake. Can't anyone take a joke anymore?"

# 42

After Gundersen left, I shut the place up and went home, figuring I'd done everything I could for now. I worried about Burton in jail with people he might have put there or, at least, people who knew he was a cop. Would they isolate him, for his own safety?

Monday night was deader than a haddock until Mickey Barksdale dropped in, descending the staircase like a conquering general. All he needed to complete the picture was his hand tucked between the buttons of his long black topcoat with the velvet lapels. He took off a black Homburg as he walked across the floor, my few customers sneaking looks at him as if he were someone they should know. I had to laugh—I'd gentrified the Esposito so much I was the only person in the place who knew Mickey was a gangster.

"Mickey. Welcome to the Esposito. Again."

He unbuttoned the coat and looked behind him, as if expecting someone to take it off his shoulders.

"Darrow. You heard?"

It was never good practice to assume you knew what Mickey meant. You might give something away you didn't mean to.

"Heard what?"

He shucked the coat and folded it carefully, set it on a stool.

"Let me have a Sombrero."

My face must have shown surprise—it wasn't a tough guy's drink.

"What?" he said. "You curate the drinks, too? This is a shebeen, as you liked to call it?"

"No problem, Mick. Just not much of a sweet drinks guy."

He subsided onto another stool.

"The way I hear it, you're not much of a drinks guy at all. Or maybe that's too much of one?"

The anger washed through me and out again. Nowhere was it written I could win an argument with the city's most powerful gangster or that it would be worth anything if I did. I pulled down the Kahlua bottle and went to the little refrigerator for the cream.

"Much as I appreciate the business," I said. "I have to believe you're here for something other than a cocktail."

He sipped, nodded thanks.

"Never had any stomach problems until last year," he said. "What I meant was, you heard Burton was arrested?"

"Bullshit," I said. "Departmental politics."

He leaned over the bar confidentially. Half the Sombrero had disappeared while I wasn't watching.

"You would tell me if you had an in with the cops, yes? Someone to talk to? I could say this to Burton directly but they won't listen to him in the current state. They'd only think he was trying to save his own posterior."

"Possibly." Biggs had been ambiguous about offering help. "Can't guarantee it, though."

Mickey looked up and down the bar, pure theater since no one sat within five stools. He spoke low, so I had to lean closer, into his breath of mint and Kahlua.

"I have an acquaintance who believes this Martin Laird character— you know who I mean?"

I played dumb; it was never good to seem smarter than Mickey.

"Cable TV guy? Big mouth, semi-professional asshole?"

"That's the feller. My friend believes Laird might be responsible for what happened to Bousquet."

"On what evidence?"

Mickey looked at me as if I were a not-very-bright child.

"Money, of course. Bousquet cost Laird some significant money he'd invested in the clothing business. And there was the broad, of course. The one Laird bought from him?"

"Kuan-Yin," I said. "We've met."

If he hadn't heard about her rescue, I wasn't going to bring it up. He slurped down the rest of his drink.

"Word is Bousquet got there first, then turned her out. Laird didn't like . . ."

If he said "sloppy seconds," I was going to spit.

He shoved his glass toward me, but Burton had cured me of taking that kind of hint. If he wanted another drink, he was going to have to use his words.

"I'm surprised you'd let anyone else run hookers," I said.

Mickey shook his head.

"Smallest part of my business. And not a profitable one. But anyone who wanted to help Burton out, pointing the cops at some other dude is going to help."

"What's in it for you, Mick? And why come to me?"

"You're Burton's pal, aren't you? And you're straight. No one's going to think you're lying. I go in with information like this, some yoyo starts pulling on my business ties and I'm tangled up with lawyers and cops for the next ten years."

"No. That I get. But why help out someone on the other side of the fence? You know Burton wouldn't bail you out of a legal jam."

"You understand loyalty, Darrow? We have a history. Burton and I have been friends since grade school. That means something to both of us. You and I both know he didn't kill anyone."

"Laird seems like a wimp."

Mickey raised his ginger eyebrows.

"Fool for love," he said. "If you've never seen that, you haven't been paying attention. Laird has connections in my world, you know. He wouldn't need to be hands-on."

It was as likely a possibility as anything, though Biggs would rightly demand corroboration.

"What do I say when they ask where the evidence is? They're not going to take my word for it."

"Find the cop who already believes he didn't do it, man. There's always someone who's not with the program. Whisper in his ear. The proof will turn up."

Meaning Mickey had evidence, or would manufacture some, when it was needed. I didn't like it. If it backfired, Burton would look guiltier than ever.

"Guaranteed."

He shot me a grin.

"I can't guarantee a goddamned thing, bucko. What I will guarantee is that if they get off their asses and look at some other alternatives, Dan Burton will be out of the pokey in no time."

And burning Biggs would trash whatever skimpy credibility I might have. Mickey was as Machiavellian as any prince, with other agendas I didn't know about.

"Let me see what I can do." I assembled another Sombrero and set it in front of him. "You know I want him out as much as you do. Maybe more."

He stared over the rim of the glass at me.

"You're sure you're up for it? Because I do have alternatives."

Then why bother me, I wanted to ask him. But having been to prep school, I could recognize the smell of peer pressure. What Mickey didn't know was that I owed Burton enough to move mountains off his back.

"I said I'd pass it along." I stared at him. "If this fucks Burton up, though? I'll be coming for you."

"Whoa." He laughed out loud, as if he'd seen a dachshund try to mount a Great Dane. "Relax yourself, young fella. We're on the same page here. Truly. You're telling me a hoodlum isn't allowed a benevolent impulse once in a while?"

He drank the Sombrero like it was straight milk and put on his coat.

"Talk soon," he said, and headed for the stairs.

# 43

I wanted to talk to Biggs about what Mickey had proposed and I left him a message. The next morning, when the bar phone rang, I assumed it was him. But Ermolai was asking me to meet.

I didn't want to taint the Esposito with more people who'd make it look like I worked with gangsters—the bar's original reputation as a bucket of blood wasn't so far removed that people would ignore something that looked like a connection to the Russian mob. In the public eye, in fact, the Russians were the new criminal bogeymen of the city, replacing the Italians, which I'm sure made the good citizens of the North End happier. The fact that most of the real power in the Boston underworld belonged to a native Irish gangster was generally ignored.

Nine A.M. was still early morning for me, though I'd only slept about six hours a night all through the winter. I wanted to see that as a positive sign, my body repairing itself after the decades of abuse, but it might only have been that I was getting older.

Ermolai hunched over a tiny cup at a two-top inside the door at Mr. Giaccobi's, where the cold breeze would hit him every time the door opened. None of the other tables were occupied, so Giaccobi must have insisted he sit there.

Ermolai wore a thick brown roll-neck sweater, jeans, and black elastic-gored boots. He looked about as threatening as a male model in the L. L. Bean catalog.

Mr. G stood guard behind the counter, eyes on the thug. When he saw me come in, he raised a hand and started the bean grinder. I nodded at him and sat down opposite the Russian.

"What's the occasion, Ermolai?"

The dregs in his cup were dry, which meant he'd been sitting here a while. I wondered if he knew about Mr. Giaccobi's pistol, which had been sufficient to run Edward Lin out of the place.

"Mr. Darrow. I do appreciate your coming out. We need to discuss."

Mr. Giaccobi carried over my espresso and set it down in front of me, patted the bulge in his apron pocket. He was having a very good time with all of this.

He raised an eyebrow at Ermolai, who shook his head. One of Giaccobi's double shots was a quad anywhere else. The old man retrieved the empty cup and saucer as if worried that Ermolai might steal it.

I sipped, put the cup down. Superb, as always.

"You called me," I said.

"Your friend Mr. Burton is in the jail for something he didn't do." Ermolai's fingers danced on the tabletop like he was reading Braille.

"That much I know. What's it to you?"

"It is bringing us too much attention." He inhaled deeply. "I will tell you a story. For the obvious reasons, I can't repeat it anywhere else, but maybe it will help your friend."

I guessed this was my week for running into people who wanted to save Burton's ass. I felt like a baby who'd found out a spoon can contain castor oil as well as sugar.

"Because you're a saint," I said.

His eyeballs bulged, but he controlled himself. I considered whether I shouldn't stop being a smartass and listen.

"First off," he said. "You must understand what Antoine Bousquet's business offered to Dmitri. When Bousquet had his cash flow problems, several years ago? It was Dmitri who bailed him out, with large cash."

So they'd been in Bousquet's business that long ago.

"Cash," I repeated.

"Bousquet's enterprise was crashing. He'd expanded too fast."

Rasmussen Carter had told me Laird had had to sell a couple of buildings in that time frame. Had Bousquet hidden the Russians' cash and stiffed Marty Laird? It made a dandy motive for murder.

234

"In return for which, Dmitri gained access to the money-laundering machine."

"Dmitri's into drugs?" I said.

The one criminal enterprise I knew Mickey Barksdale shunned, as too prominent an issue for law enforcement right now. Though he might be charged an access fee or a usage tax.

Ermolai rolled his shoulders under the thick sweater.

"Probably better I don't say that kind of detail."

"Good enough. Though I do notice Ermolai is not in this story anywhere."

He sucked in a breath and regarded me, questioning how much he could safely reveal.

"At that time," he said. "Up until a few days ago, in fact? I am a soldier in the army of Dmitri. Nothing more than that. Do what I'm told, go where I'm supposed to."

"And that's changed."

He inclined his head but didn't elaborate.

"The problems began when Bousquet started to cut on the corners. Instead of people with green cards, he imports the undocumented. Saving money."

"Not so large a problem, though?" Immigrants from many countries overstayed their visas or disappeared into the shadow economy. It was one of the ways cities—the entire country, in fact—refreshed itself. "More or less how this city was built. Other places, too."

Ermolai nodded.

"That was fine. Until we find out Bousquet is making these people slaves. Pay them almost nothing, charge high for passage and housing and food and any other little thing he can think of."

Ermolai was outraged. I saw the thing whole for the first time.

"Which brought undue attention to Bousquet's business and thus to Dmitri."

"Thus," Ermolai said. "And then, of course, Bousquet killed those two girls."

Steam hissed over by the plate glass window as Mr. Giaccobi relieved the big Rancilio machine.

"You're telling me Dmitri had Bousquet killed?"

He shook his head.

"I cannot say for sure. He tried to reason with Bousquet but the egos were too big. And I have seen Dmitri apply his kind of solution to a problem before."

The duct-taped chair, the pool of blood on the floor of my cottage. "Torture," I said.

He nodded.

"Makes no sense," I said. "Wouldn't Dmitri already know everything? He was the one controlling Bousquet. Was it revenge, for screwing up the laundry?"

"The old man's style. He wouldn't just kill him."

I stared at the framed signed photo of the current Pope Mr. Giaccobi had hung behind the cash register.

"You have any evidence that Dmitri killed him?"

Ermolai raised a hand and Mr. Giaccobi turned on the grinder again.

"My stomach says yes, but no, I have no proof. Which is why I come to you."

I snorted.

"I know. You want me to put a bug in the ear of the police department about Dmitri. That the rumor mill thinks he might have killed Bousquet. Your intuition, Ermie? It's not worth shit to them. If I had any credibility, it would disappear as soon as I told them that story."

Ermolai laced his hands together.

"On top of which," I went on. "The primary beneficiary of this story that takes Dmitri down? Surprise, surprise. It's the one telling me the story. You see the problem?"

For an instant, I thought he might come over the table, but Mr. G, delivering his coffee, pushed the heavy right side of his apron against Ermolai's shoulder. The thug did some complicated breathing and dropped his shoulders.

"I bring you what I have, Elder Darrow. Whatever else you need to know, this uncertainty you have, this bullshit with your cop friend? All of it complicates my business. Anything I can do to resolve . . . well, yes. It's a bonus to me. But whoever got your friend arrested?

That is a fake thing, nothing to do with Bousquet or me. But if everyone is nervous, no one's doing business."

Which was as cold and convoluted a reason for solving a murder as I'd ever heard, but a mobster like Ermolai or Mickey Barksdale was no different from a CEO when his income stream was threatened.

He sipped the espresso and made a face.

"How do you drink this shit, anyway?"

"Taste and class, Ermie. Look. I'll make sure Burton's lawyer knows what you said. But I'm going to give him the context and the source, too. My guess is you care more about taking Dmitri down than anything else."

Ermolai looked grateful, even if the support was qualified. All he had to do was tell his bosses Dmitri was under investigation. Attracting attention was the plague of the contemporary mob.

"I would appreciate it." He tilted the empty cup on its side in the saucer.

I stood up.

"I have a bar to run. But you should understand—when Burton gets out? No claim you had anything to do with it will cut any ice with him. He will not belong to you, even a tiny bit."

"Yeah, yeah, Mr. Elder. I know."

Expansive now, having squeezed what he wanted from our meeting.

I walked up to the cash register where Mr. G stood, a sly up-curl to his smile. I reached for my wallet.

"*Nyet.*" He pointed at Ermolai. "He'll pay. And he'll leave me a nice tip, too."

# 44

Biggs and Murray had been sitting at the bar for a couple of hours and I had no idea why. If they were killing time, it wasn't clear to what end until Jacob Gundersen called me around two.

I stepped as far away down the bar as the long cord on the receiver would allow me and turned my back on them, in case the Professional Standards skill set included lip-reading. I didn't trust either of them, Murray even less than Biggs.

"Esposito."

"Your world-class defense attorney speaking." Gundersen was jaunty. "This is where I tell you I saved you several hundred thousand dollars and settled some justice on the world, too."

"You got Burton out on bail?"

"Oh no. Released. Charges dropped, with a personal apology from the head of Professional Standards for the overreach of one of his men. I would have tried for the Chief of Police, but that might have been pushing it."

"Fabulous. Where is he now?"

"Processing out. He said he'll be by as soon as he's free."

"Tell him to stay away from the bar for a while. Murray and Biggs— the cops from Standards?—have been sitting here for a couple hours."

"Drunk?"

He sounded hopeful.

"No, like they're waiting for something."

"Or someone. They probably found out he was being released. I'll tell him to stay clear. Though it would be sweet to nail that Murray prick."

"Thanks. And thank you, Attorney Gundersen."

"You can call me Jacob, young fellow. And don't worry. The bill is in the mail."

* * * * *

Thinking about it later, I should have realized warning Burton that Biggs and Murray were here would be more of a goad than a caution. When I hadn't seen him by seven, though, I figured their presence was keeping him away. They'd been taking up space at the bar for four or five hours now and only consuming two beers in all that time. I tried moving them along.

"Don't believe he's going to show, gents. Why don't you settle up and try again tomorrow?"

"And why don't you go fuck yourself," Murray snarled, passing his empty glass back and forth between his hands like he was performing a magic trick. "We just wanted to congratulate him, you know? For getting off again. Slip-sliding away."

I plucked the glass from his grip and set it in the bar sink. Murray's anger-blotched face made me wonder what Burton could have done to make the man such an enemy.

"Another? I assume you two aren't on duty."

Biggs was watching me, to see how I'd react to Murray's anger. He was the more dangerous of the two, being in control of his feelings.

Murray shook his head. Biggs tilted his head toward the far end of the bar and I took his advice, stepping to the sound system to change out the music. It wasn't a terrible idea anyway. Gato Barbieri was all tangled up in some big band mishmash I couldn't fathom. As I moved away, I heard Biggs tell Murray it was time to go.

"No way." He shook off his partner and charged down the bar toward me.

I froze. The little pistol was right under my hand, but it would have taken a far stupider human than me to pull it on a cop. Murray thrust out his jaw.

"You fucking civilians. You just don't get it."

239

His breath was sour with the beer and a darker odor like tooth decay.

"You watch a couple of TV shows and then everyone's a fucking expert on cops, how we're all lazy and cynical, how we give in to temptation every chance we get. Cover for each other all the time. You think it's an easy call."

He paused as if expecting an answer. I took three or four seconds before I said anything.

"That's not my experience, Murray. And I might know a little more than your average civilian. When I started out here?" I pointed at the bar. "I had police officers in here almost nightly. Vice cops, other undercovers. Patrol officers responding to fights. I never had a problem with any one of them." I took a risk, naming the one cop I knew he had a hard-on for. "Burton included. He's always been scrupulous about keeping his job separate from our friendship."

Not a complete lie, if it elasticized the truth.

Murray blew out an angry snort. Biggs was watching us, prepared to intervene if things got heated. To protect Murray, no doubt.

"Burton." Murray said his name as if it tasted bitter. "Good cop. Maybe a great one."

The praise surprised me.

"Yeah." Murray pointed at the bar back. "Give me a shot of Jack. You're surprised I have anything good to say about him?"

"You haven't said much, so far."

"Well, he is a good cop. No one's disputing that." He leaned over to take the shot glass. "But the only way an organization like BPD survives is if there's discipline."

He looked around the bar, the framed black and white photos of jazz greats, the black walls that faded to infinity when the lights went down, the tiny stage.

"Guy like you. Businessman? An entrepreneur?" He said it like a curse. "Whatever. You make all your own decisions. You tell people what to do, how to do it, when." He picked up the shot glass and licked the rim. "With the cops? We have to have discipline. Consistency. Stability. It's fucking chaos if everyone's running around doing their own thing."

Burton's weakness was always his tendency to fly solo, but I'd always thought he did a good job dancing the line between going his own way and pissing off his bosses irretrievably. I was looking at it from outside the organization, though.

"Well, he crossed someone's line, if you guys arrested him. Or was this supposed to be his wakeup call? Fall in formation or get the hell out?"

Murray tossed back the whiskey, then slammed down the glass.

"We had evidence. Motive and opportunity. Ask him—he would have arrested himself."

How dumb was Murray that he couldn't hear how stupid that sounded?

"Then how did he get released so fast, Murray? Maybe because your case was shit?"

"Politics." He spit the word. Odd that he'd blame it for Burton's release when it had been the cause of his arrest, too.

"You don't really believe he killed anyone."

His small nod admitted it.

"Even so," he said. "He needs to stand up and answer for the way he operates. Either he's part of the department or he's not."

Murray's predilections must have dictated his career path. People who liked to judge other people, force them into line, tended to be black and white on everything. They worshipped systems, rules of law, rigid schedules, and inflexible values.

Burton's undeniable advantage was that results trumped rules. He cleared more homicides than anyone else in the department. Until his independence threatened that fact, he was likely to stay employed.

When the street door opened into the quiet, I realized I hadn't replaced Gato on the sound system. And I wished I'd been more successful moving Murray and Biggs along when Burton started down the stairs. His head was down and his shoulders slumped, from fatigue not depression, I hoped. His coat was wrinkled, like he'd used it for a pillow.

At least, since he'd just come from jail, he wasn't armed. From the bottom of the stairs, he threaded his way through the occupied tables, not looking at me. Murray, warned by a dark light in Burton's eyes, got up off his stool.

"Look, Burton . . ."

Without a greeting, warning, even a blink, Burton threw a right hand from somewhere down by the floor and uppercut Murray square on the chin. The impact decked the cop and then Burton was straddling Murray's chest, pistoning punches. Murray thrashed a couple times, then went fetal to ride it out, until Burton stopped abruptly and stood up, breathing hard.

Biggs sported a tiny grin, which said his partnership with Murray had changed irrevocably. He moved down the bar and eased Burton away, then knelt next to Murray, who groaned, half-conscious.

Burton turned his back on both of them and leaned against the bar, inspecting a torn flap of skin on the back of his right hand.

"How stupid do you have to be to punch someone in the head?" he said. "Best way I know to fuck up your hand." He clenched the fist and flexed his fingers. "Don't think I broke anything, though."

His thin sandy hair was mussed and his smile mad and wild. A rush of brotherly warmth swept me. Any kind of cop in any kind of jail was in a precarious situation. Seeing him free and whole made me think maybe things would be all right.

"Is this place still a bar?" he said. "Can a man get a drink?"

I matched his grin.

"I'll even buy, you tell me what you want."

As Biggs levered Murray up onto his feet, the beaten cop folded in on himself as if his ribs hurt. His face was a mess, black lines of blood trickling out of both nostrils. His tie was askew and his suit jacket ripped at the shoulder. Burton looked through the door into the kitchen.

Holding his partner up with one arm, Biggs lectured Murray. He beckoned at Burton, who sighed and looked at me.

"Nice fresh whiskey sour, please. I'll be back in a minute."

He stepped down the bar. Biggs asked a quiet question and Burton spread his arms in a who-me? gesture. Then Biggs said something to Murray, who shook his head and limped for the stairs, a handkerchief held over his nose. No brokered peace for him, then.

He hauled himself up the stairs using the handrail. I wasn't too happy about the return of fist fighting to the Esposito, but it hadn't fazed any of the dozen or so customers in the place. Maybe I hadn't civilized things as much as I'd thought.

In honor of Burton's freedom, I composed his drink from fresh lemons, muddling the juice with the sugar, shaking it up with an artisan rye from a distillery in Portland, Maine. I wondered if he'd notice the difference.

Biggs passed a few more peaceable words with Burton, then followed his partner up and out. Burton came back up the bar, tugging his collar open. His posture was straighter than when he'd walked in.

"Sorry about that." He was bright and buzzed as a hummingbird. "I know you like to think you're running a respectable joint here."

I set the foaming glass in front of him.

"It's fine. Just don't let it happen again or I'll have to call the cops."

He snickered. Marina stepped into the kitchen doorway, saw Burton sitting at the bar, and turned back inside. He bent and sipped the foam off the top of the drink.

"Well, at least you were glad to see me," he said.

"I'm assuming you didn't shoot your way out of jail."

I didn't know if Gundersen had told him I'd paid for his lawyer. Burton hooted.

"As good as. Do you have any notion of the ass-puckering that takes place in the DA's office when Jacob Gundersen rolls in? The ADA working with Murray had to swap out his shorts. So, thank you. What do I owe?"

"I shook him off. Gundersen implied this might have been a ploy by the brass? Someone trying to send you a message?"

"Possibly. Message not received, though. He also said there was barely enough evidence to justify suspecting me. None of which I saw."

"Who'd want you gone that badly?"

"No idea. I've pissed off enough people over the years it could be any one of about a dozen. I always thought getting the work done was enough. Guess not, anymore."

Truth be known, I was starting to be surprised he'd lasted this long.

Any time a job hinged on politics, performance seemed to be the last thing that predicted success. Which made Burton something of a romantic.

"No harm, no foul?" I said. "You're back to work?"

"Pending yet another departmental review. Probably *pro forma*. If someone up the food chain really wants me gone, I'm gone."

He sounded resigned and my stomach flipped at the prospect of his not being a cop. He had nothing else.

"What about finding out who killed Bousquet, though? You come up with that, won't it buy you some juice?"

He sighed heavily and sat down.

"I'm not sure I care anymore, Elder. If I'm not allowed to bring in the actual killer I find? How do I answer to the victims? I'd do more good working on a garbage truck."

I hoped this was only evidence he was weary and disturbed by his night in jail.

"Drink up. I'll have Marina make you something to eat. Relax and get yourself back to normal. It'll get better."

Knowing how unlikely a candidate I was to be purveyor of sunshine, Burton gave me a baleful look, the capillaries of his eyes stained red.

"Better?" he said. "What the fuck is that?"

# 45

There were a few short days when I thought all of us—Burton, Marina, and I—were well out of the Antoine Bousquet case, Burton by departmental fiat, the rest of us by inclination and the press of other business. He'd had his second hearing with Professional Standards yesterday, but we hadn't heard how it went. Marina was talking to him again but avoiding me, the question of when we were going to get to Markham's office, and everything else that didn't involve garlic, heat, or vegetables. My gut kept twinging prophetically, though. I wasn't sure we were all the way out of the tunnel yet.

This Thursday afternoon was pleasantly quiet. In fact, now that the business was running smoothly and the bar so much more civilized, the Esposito was starting to bore me. It was as if the problems of converting the bar to a decent club, all the issues I'd had to grapple with, had been more absorbing than the day-to-day running of the place. If one of the side effects of taming my desire to drink was boredom, I might have to find something else to do. Or I might end up where I'd been three years ago, hanging by my fingernails to a cliff over an abyss.

The *Globe* sports section was all I had today to counter my mood swings. Opening Day of baseball season was only a few weeks away and though the Sox were opening the season in Texas this year, baseball was always a good subject to bitch about with my patrons. That and the weather, a conversational gambit for all seasons.

What caught my attention this afternoon, though, was a small headline on an inside page reporting that an alleged Russian mobster—how the newspapers loved that word—had been shot execution-style (as dead as any other style) and dumped off the Charles River Esplanade, the floating corpse discovered by an eight-man scull from Harvard doing drills. Good way to ruin a peaceful morning on the river.

The story had few details but I would bet the corpse was someone I knew and that it would open up the whole Bousquet business again.

About three, Burton wandered down the stairs into the bar, wearing what I'd come to think of as his homicide detective uniform, a tailor-made fine cotton shirt and silk tie under a shabby pilled-out polyester sports coat. He'd never said so, but I assumed the jacket was to protect the shirt and tie from crime scene matter.

"You've been reinstated."

"Provisionally. There's still bureaucratic crap."

He pointed at my newspaper, as I started to mix him another whiskey sour.

"You read it yet?" he said.

"Not the whole thing. Got stuck on the curly-headed boyfriend's column this morning. He thinks Youkilis should go play in Japan."

Burton blew a raspberry.

"The Russian gangster shooting."

"Anyone we know?" I said.

"Depends. You know a Dmitri Smirnov?"

"The one who . . ."

"Beat the winkie out of me in your back alley?"

"Well, shit. Doesn't this put you right back in the line of fire?"

He shook his head.

"For once in my life, I was in the right place at the right time. According to the ME, Dmitri was perforated about the time I was sitting down to my departmental review."

"I have a good idea whodunnit," I said. "If anyone cares."

"Not my case. It's being written off as goon on goon."

"You remember Ermolai, Dmitri's apprentice thug?"

Burton touched his rib cage.

"Hard not to."

I recounted the conversation I'd had with him about Dmitri and his old-school way of doing things, the implication that Ermolai was superseding Dmitri in the hierarchy.

"He offed Dmitri in a power struggle?" Burton took out his phone. "I could see that happening."

He thumbed out a text, presumably to the detectives assigned to the case.

"Feels a little obvious," he said. "Though sometimes things feel obvious because they're true. You think Marina will talk to me if I go back in the kitchen?"

The topic shift startled me.

"I thought the two of you were back talking again. Did she find out about you and Vicky?"

"Somebody told her about that?"

I held up my hands.

"It wasn't me."

"That's why she's been stonewalling me?"

He stood up, ready to storm the kitchen.

"Don't barrel in there, Burton, all right? She's had a rough couple of weeks."

It wasn't my place to tell him about the inheritance, but he'd seen for himself that Carmen was getting shakier.

"I need to straighten her out on that score. Carmen's OK, after the kidnap?"

"You could ask Marina," I said. "Calmly."

He shook his head and walked out back.

Their voices rose and fell, but conversationally, not loud. I relaxed as I scrolled through the playlist on my iPad. They'd figure it out.

Still tender about Kathleen fleeing the city, I'd forgotten to ask him about the dossier. Did he think she'd been planning a major burglary here? Or had this been a home base? Even if a relationship with a professional thief wasn't the right kind of thing for me, she still had me interested enough to wonder if she'd be back.

I wiped down the bar, dumped the rest of Burton's drink. If he and Marina were talking again, the last thing she'd want to see in his hand was a drink.

Then I poured myself one of an endless line of club soda, squeezing in some lime, recognizing my vague discontent. When I'd first bought the Esposito, monitoring my shaky sobriety and rehabbing the bar kept me too busy to drink. But now that things were stable, the idea of staying here in Boston and running a bar the rest of my life, even the upscale-ish jazz nightspot I'd dreamed about, didn't feel like enough. Though I didn't have the slightest idea what I'd do otherwise, despite the fact I was going to have enough money for pretty much anything.

Burton returned to the bar as I turned up the Count Basie, hoping to lift his mood. He slapped my shoulder and looked sadly at the bar.

"You threw it out? And that was the good stuff. I wasn't finished."

"You didn't pay for it, either."

"All the more reason not to waste it," he said. "Why didn't you tell me about your father's will? That's good news for Marina, isn't it?"

"Not my story to tell." Had she also told him she and I might be related? "You must have known I'd inherit from Thomas."

He leaned across the bar.

"You wouldn't believe how happy she is that Dmitri's dead. Because of what he did to Carmen."

"Jesus. You don't think . . ."

"You ever see her really angry?" Burton said. "Why didn't you tell me he was leaning on you, too?"

That was the Dan Burton I knew, more worried about his friends than himself, regardless of what it cost him. It reminded me to be grateful for people who looked out for others, for reasons no one else might think important.

"You were a little busy your own self," I said.

Basie faded out and Marcus Roberts kicked into "Ain't Necessarily So." I relaxed, feeling as if things might have finally settled down. Even a fool would have known better than that.

# 46

Burton stayed around for dinner, though he didn't drink anything more than another beer with his chicken sandwich. When Mickey Barksdale appeared at the bottom of the stairs, Burton stiffened up, put down the heel of the bread, and walked over, asking loudly enough for me to hear, what the fuck he was doing here. I didn't know if Burton was worried about the bar's reputation or his own but Mickey's reply calmed him enough for Burton to lead him to a table over by the stage, farthest in the place from any customers.

Marina carried a bowl out of the kitchen, sat down at the bar, and crumpled a handful of crackers into the soup.

"Uh-oh," she said. "Burton's not going to like that."

Seeing the two of them together gave me a feeling of cognitive dissonance almost as acute as I'd felt the previous year during Hurricane Katrina, watching the local, state, and federal governments all look at each other and say: "Dunno. What are you going to do about it?"

Mickey's reappearance made me more curious than annoyed. The last time he'd been here, he'd lectured me on the right way to do illegal immigration. Then a shiny penny dropped into a rusted slot in my brain and I recalled that a pushy Russian gangster had been permanently removed from the game yesterday. Maybe Mickey had come to confess to the one man he thought wouldn't take him in. Wrong about that, Mick.

Then Burton waved me over. I shook my head. I had no desire to link into their odd relationship. He insisted.

I wiped my hands and walked over.

"Sit for a minute," he said. "I need a witness to this, in case it blows back on me."

Mickey looked as if Burton had lost his mind.

"You really trust this man that much, Danno?"

"It's the only way I'll be able to prove I didn't make this up." Burton pointed at Mickey. "Our relationship, yours and mine. It's too well-known. I can't have people saying I cut you any breaks."

Turning toward me, Mickey dropped his eyelid in a wink. A group of softball players—rabid ones, since it was all of forty-five outside this afternoon—clattered down the stairs in their cleats.

"Let's make it quick, gents. I've got a bar to run."

Mickey turned a blank black gaze on me, letting me know without a word that I was on his schedule. Only when I nodded did he speak.

"You fellows know of a boyo name of Smirnov? Erstwhile leader of a small rebel band of the Russian criminal variety here in the city?"

My heart flopped. I'd assumed correctly there was a connection between Mickey and Dmitri. Burton raised an eyebrow at me.

"Met the man," I said. "Your point?"

"He was recently removed from the pitch, you'll pardon a football metaphor."

Still pretending he was a loyal son of Eire.

"As the *Globe* reported this morning."

Burton was silent.

"I want it known clearly," Mickey said, "that neither I nor anyone employed by me, had a thing to do with the execution of that poor benighted fellow."

"OK," I said. "That it?"

Mickey favored me with a flat reptilian look that made me question myself. I got up to go wait on my customers.

"Consider it witnessed."

As I drew pitchers of beer, I watched the two of them from the corner of my eye. Mickey stood and walked out as I changed the music to something less challenging. As far as I could see, he and Burton had said nothing else to each other after I left the table.

The softball players pushed tables together and were pouring glasses of beer by the time Burton walked over to the bar. He nodded and I built him another whiskey sour.

"So. You think Mickey did it?" I said. "Dmitri?"

Burton nodded.

"The only reason he came was to see if I already knew."

"What did you tell him?"

Burton's relationship with Mickey was unfathomable but I was sure it didn't include letting the gangster slide on a criminal act.

"Oh, I played dumb. Mickey doesn't think I'm very bright anyway, working for a salary when I could earn untold riches being his partner. I'll pass all this along to the people on the case."

He looked down at the floor.

"Though he had to be desperate to get his story out, to be seen in public with me."

"How long until your next hearing?"

"Hearing's done," he reminded me. "Waiting on full reinstatement paperwork, though they don't seem to mind I'm working.

He tasted the drink and grimaced.

"How can it taste so good one day and so bad the next?"

"No answer. So, a couple of weeks?"

"Days." He tapped the side of his nose. "I've still got friends in low places. Not everyone in the department is trying to pee down my leg." He emptied the glass all at once. "Right now, though? I've got some business to take care of."

# 47

I didn't expect to see Rasmussen Carter in the light of day, nor did I expect Marina to be standing outside the Esposito's door the next morning, her hand on his arm, laughing at something he'd said. I stepped between them to unlock the door, irritated somehow by his familiarity.

The sky was low, gray, and thick, but Carter wore his sun shades anyway.

"That's how he came out." He finished the story to Marina in a soft confiding voice.

She laughed again and gave him an approving look as they passed in front of me to head down the stairs. She said something I didn't catch and Carter's laugh was rich. It was silly to be jealous on Burton's behalf but I couldn't think of another reason why I was irked.

I flicked on the light over the back bar but when Rasmussen flinched, decided not to turn the overheads on yet. Louis Armstrong stared at us out of the gloom.

"We don't serve breakfast," I said to him.

He stood beside the cash register and shook his head, the light glinting off the pomade slicking his hair. He placed his body at an oblique angle so I was blocking the light.

"I can't stay long," he said, as if I'd offered to cook for him. "I wanted to conclude our business. I have to assume you have no further interest in Marty Laird."

"And why is that?"

"You haven't heard."

Carter apparently liked knowing things other people didn't, which made sense considering what he did for work.

"No to whatever you're talking about. Why don't you spit it out?"

The radio turned on in the kitchen, salsa. He looked back that way, then nodded as if he'd figured out why I was being crisp with him.

"Oh," he said. "I didn't mean anything by it. We were just chatting while I waited for you to show up."

I folded three one hundred dollar bills and held them out.

"Let's hear it, Carter. Though I agree that our work together is done, regardless."

He straightened up and the smell of mothballs wafted from his sweater.

"Marty Laird is dead," he said. "I don't know what it was you were hoping to find but whatever it was, your point is probably moot."

I was so shocked I got angry at him, which was stupid.

"You don't tell me what's moot and what isn't," I said. "For one thing, it's a bad way to run your business."

He gave me the cool look that deserved.

"If I assumed too much, I apologize." His head bobbed in a way that reminded me of the young Stevie Wonder. "But I also told you I didn't want anything to do with organized crime. And he did have such a connection, however loose."

I forced myself to calm down. Shooting the messenger was a classically stupid way to respond to bad news.

"What happened?"

"I'm not sure they've ever had a drive-by shooting on upper Boylston Street," he said. "By the parking garage?"

"Gangs?" Which would account for his stated nervousness.

"The cops are looking for Mickey Barksdale. Which is why I'm stepping away. Even if it isn't moot."

I leaned on the bar, wondering what experience he'd had with gangsters to make him so skittish.

"It's their theory that Laird killed Antoine Bousquet?"

"My sources have their limits," he said. "I don't have access to what people think unless they tell me."

I passed over the bills.

"You're correct, then. We are done. Unless you came up with anything deeper on Laird?"

"Nope. You got it all." He tucked the bills in his shirt and buttoned the flap, then glanced into the kitchen again.

"Seriously," he said. "Are the two of you together? Because if not . . ."

I shook my head. There was one other question I had for him.

"No mention of Dmitri Smirnov in all this? That Laird might have been connected? Because Dmitri was killed yesterday, too."

Rasmussen Carter turned pale as a bar rag.

"Jesus shit. You're telling me the Russians are involved in this, too?"

And he turned and bolted up the stairs as if his feet were on fire.

I raised my eyebrows as the street door swung shut and wondered what fresh hell was descending now. More murders, no suspects. No live ones, at least.

# 48

Burton wandered in later that afternoon, looking beat. He was back on duty but he hadn't been assigned a case yet. I thought what I was seeing was the accumulated stress of the last five weeks.

"Jesus," he said. "Losing my stamina. Too many afternoons lying on the couch watching Perry Mason."

I popped a beer and set it in front of him, ignoring his whining. I was interested in his reaction to my street gossip.

"You hear about Marty?" I said.

He saluted me with his beer.

"I did. I suppose once again I was lucky to be somewhere people could verify my presence, or they might be trying to fit me up for that one, too."

His bitterness was running deeper than usual.

"Then whodunnit?"

"Damfido," he said. "Tec-9 recovered at the scene."

"Isn't that heavy artillery for a single victim?"

"Nobody actually knows how to shoot anymore. They treat it like power-washing a house."

"Seems strange, so soon after Dmitri. Think they're connected?"

"Possibly. I have no clue. Both of them had a finger in Bousquet's business dealings, but that's flimsy. Maybe one of them killed Bousquet and the other one killed him for messing up that business."

Nowhere to go with that. I changed tacks.

"Kathleen Crawford."

"Your sweetie from the People's Republic of Cambridge?"

The innocence was too studied.

"You sent me that dossier."

He tapped his bottle on the bar top.

"I thought I'd run into her name somewhere. The Robbery guys were keeping an eye on her."

"Because of her father?"

Burton shook his head.

"All on her own. She bought that house in Cambridge right after he died. You've seen it."

It didn't surprise me he knew.

"She paid one and a quarter mil for it in 2000. Cash money," he said.

"So her father left her some money. I can relate to that."

He gave me a cockeyed look.

"Not that the IRS was aware of. She had to do a deal with them to get forgiven."

"So. Nothing illegal, then."

"Elder. The property taxes alone are fifteen K. On a bank teller's salary?"

I gave up, not sure why I was defending her anyway.

"Did you ever say anything to her about your inheritance?" he said. "You might be seeing her again soon. I know some people who'd be interested if that happens."

I shook my head—she was a thief, not a con artist.

"Not going to worry about it," I said. "You want another?"

The bottle was empty. I'd never liked beer but the sharp clean smell of hops and the alcohol were singing a little song to me.

He shook his head and started out to the kitchen.

"Still trying to mend those fences?" I said.

"Why? You have any advice?"

I shook my head and slotted the empty into the cardboard case.

"Good luck."

# 49

After we closed and I got home to bed, the possibilities whirled, keeping me awake. My monkey brain kept trying to parse out how the two most recent killings fit in with Bousquet and who in the cast of characters had the most to gain or lose here.

Prone as he was to violent solutions, Dmitri was the one most likely to have canceled Antoine Bousquet's ticket. Bousquet's cost-cutting measures—using illegal immigrant workers and treating them like sub humans—had brought excessive attention to what had been a useful money-laundering operation for the Russians. And I could make a reasonable case for Ermolai killing off Dmitri as part of a power struggle, even under orders from his bosses. They might have punished Dmitri for intensifying the scrutiny into their businesses. Contrary to popular lore, intelligent gangsters ducked notice as much as possible. None of the Russians had a good reason to kill Marty Laird, though.

Could Mickey Barksdale have killed Bousquet, then Dmitri? He'd been unhappy with how the immigrant-smuggling part of his business had suffered when clients found out they'd be slaving in sweat shops and living eight to a room. But the Laird problem surfaced there, too—Mickey couldn't have cared less about him.

I gave up, performed the slow-breathing exercises that helped damp down the worst of the alcoholic cravings, and started to feel sleepy. My busy-brain subsided and I sank into the mattress and slept.

Until the phone rang and bolted me upright, shaking off the afterimage of a very bad dream. The red numbers on my bedside clock read three thirty-four.

I fumbled my way out of bed and walked to the living room, the small bones in my feet crackling.

"Hello?"

"Is Burton with you?"

I wasn't so foggy that I couldn't hear the worry in Marina's voice.

"No. Was he supposed to be?"

"No." Her voice skied. "He was supposed to be here a couple of hours ago. He was going to his place to pick up a few things and we were going to have a late dinner."

They must have patched up whatever they had to patch up, which made me feel better.

"When did you talk to him last?"

"He texted me when he left his apartment, but he never got here."

Anyone could text a message, but there were also all kinds of legitimate reasons for a homicide cop to be diverted. Sweet reason didn't calm her down.

"What do you want me to do?" I asked finally.

"It isn't like him. We were going to try and talk things through."

A relationship talk would have been enough to send me screaming from the prospect of that dinner, but that was not Burton's style. He wasn't always a stand-and-take-your-medicine guy, but with Marina, he tried. It was unlike her to panic, though—something in the last year had made her less dependent on his approval.

"You know if he got sidetracked, it was important, right?"

I hoped I wasn't lying to save his ass. If he'd blown off dinner to go chase Viktoriya, for example, Marina wouldn't feel better.

"I suppose." She wasn't in complete agreement, but she had to remember how Burton's job put us through paces before.

"It'll be fine, Marina. He'll turn up, probably right around the time you get back to sleep."

"And probably drunk." She still sounded like someone trying to convince herself the sky wasn't falling.

"Don't worry about him. I don't, anymore." I yawned so loudly my jaw creaked. "OK? I've got to get some sleep."

"OK. But if I don't hear from him tomorrow . . ."

"Why don't we worry about that tomorrow?" I said.

The bang of her hang-up was louder than it had to be.

* * * * *

So of course I was awake by seven, hours earlier than usual. I sleepwalked my way through a shower and a shave, made coffee in the French press, and toasted a bagel. The first bite tasted like wet cardboard and I realized Marina's worry had well and truly infected me. One thing Burton was not was cruel. Even if some other woman had turned his head, he wouldn't allow himself to be mean to Marina.

I tossed the rest of the bagel on the plate and reached for the phone, tried his home number first on the possibility that he'd gotten drunk and passed out in his own bed. No joy there, not even voice mail. I hadn't known you could still get phone service without it.

I punched in the digits of his cell phone and it rang long enough for me to wonder how he'd gotten the same non-service on his mobile. Finally his voice growled in my ear.

"Burton. Leave a message. Make it short."

I clicked off without obeying. The cell was his primary connection to the world, especially when he was working. The fact he hadn't picked up, now that he was back on duty, wasn't normal. Unless he'd seen my name on the caller ID and decided he didn't want to talk. Which he'd do if he were in the middle of something very personal.

I banged the heel of my phone lightly on the tabletop, unable to ignore a mounting worry. I got myself dressed and instead of the soft shoes I wore for comfort behind the bar, tied on the steel-toed boots, grabbed a jacket, and locked the apartment door behind me.

I stepped out onto the stoop in brilliant sunshine and warm air, one of those rare March days when the sweet hints of spring made you stop and breathe, take pleasure in having survived another winter. I wouldn't need the jacket at all, but rather than run all the way back up the stairs, I tied it around my waist and headed up the block to where I'd parked the Cougar.

Ticket under the windshield wiper, of course. I scanned it—not close enough to the curb—and tossed it onto the passenger's seat. Enforcement had gotten tougher in the city as the economy improved.

Back when I was drinking, I could park my car halfway up on the sidewalk and not draw attention.

Even without evidence, my sense something was wrong grew as I took North Washington over the Charlestown Bridge and wound my way through the back streets to Burton's building. He'd never moved far from the neighborhood he knew and, in fact, the low brick building on O'Reilly was only four blocks from the house he'd grown up in, on the back side of where the Bunker Hill Monument sticks in the air like a middle finger.

I pulled up in front of 59 and parked behind Burton's pickup, his motorcycle chained in the bed. He'd recovered the vehicle, apparently. The blue tarp covering the bike flapped in the breeze and I tucked it back in. I didn't think he had the use of an unmarked car, so if he wasn't home, he was out walking. And Burton hated walking.

The street door was ajar, reminding me of my own building. I climbed the stairs to the third floor and rapped hard on the reinforced steel door. There was no smell of cooking in the hallway, no trash, no bicycles, strollers, or plastic milk crates. It wasn't a fancy building, but the occupants had pride. And/or they didn't want to piss off a cop.

"Burton!"

A door on the floor below opened.

"The fuck are you?" A sleep-rusty voice called up the stairs.

"Looking for Burton. You seen him?"

"Could you do it quietly? I'm on nights."

"Seen him or not? It's an easy answer."

I sensed the slow swell of anger, the decision it wasn't worth climbing the stairs to kick my ass.

"Burton's a good guy." Suggesting that was the only reason he wasn't coming up. "I think I heard him go out around midnight."

"Thanks," I said. "Go back to bed."

"Fuckin' A."

Burton and I were not the kind of friends who exchanged house keys. There'd never been a reason to, though I wished I had one right now to reassure myself he wasn't lying on the other side of the door bleeding to death. And there was no way he'd leave a spare anywhere obvious.

I started back down, trying to be quiet. Where could he have gone if he wasn't on the bike or driving? Taxi? Or had someone picked him up? Marina would want an answer, but I did, too.

When I emerged onto the street, it took me a second to register someone sitting on the hood of the Cougar, someone thick through the torso, straining a bright blue and carmine Hawaiian shirt. Edward. Vicky's brother.

His back was to me. I scraped my soles on the sidewalk so he'd hear me coming. He turned his head.

"Thought you might show up."

It was the longest sentence I'd heard him say. I stopped ten or fifteen feet back, not even sure that was safe enough.

"Edward, right?"

Safest response I could think of.

He slid down off the hood and opened the passenger's side door, looked over the top of the car.

"Let's go."

"You're kidding me, right?"

He stared, his small eyes, soft features, and dull conversational skills making me wonder how small his brain actually was.

"I'm not going to jail for killing some cop," he said. "Let's go."

When he climbed inside, that whole side of the car bottomed out on the pavement. I started the engine and we pulled away from the curb, Edward yanking the seat belt to make it fit.

"I assume you're talking about Burton?"

He inhaled, grunted, and the latch clicked shut.

"What?"

One thing at a time for old Edward's brain.

"You're talking about someone trying to kill Dan Burton?" I sounded like a first grade teacher.

"Don't know the guy's fucking name. But he shouldn't have messed with Kuan-Yin."

The mental gears started to mesh. As I'd seen with Marty Laird, no one messed with Kuan-Yin but Vicky. But Burton? Could I trust Edward not to be leading me into a trap?

I drove to the end of the street.

"Which way?"

He pointed left, then right onto Medford.

"Pull up over there."

The playground and the ball field were the last things this side of Route 1. On the other side, I could see the channel and the Navy Yard. I slipped the Cougar into a parking space—plenty of them this far from downtown—and looked where Edward was pointing, off to the left.

"Far dugout."

The other side of home plate, over on the ball field. We climbed out of the car, the traffic noise loud enough that I didn't think of trying to be quiet until after we'd slammed the car doors.

"Follow me." Edward's diction, if not his verbosity, had improved.

We followed the sidewalk toward a round concrete entryway with stairs down to the field level, then along the asphalt path that curved out behind the near dugout, then fifteen feet or so in back of home plate. The turf looked muddy and wet, faintly green, not ready for play. The back walls of the dugout that we passed were ribbed with metal louvers.

Edward held up a hand like a scout as we neared the second dugout and we slowed, walking as quietly as our footwear and the hard surface of the path allowed. As we neared the back of the dugout, the rise and fall of a female voice bespoke a certain amount of upset.

Edward got down on his hands and knees. I frowned but followed suit and we low-crawled across the wet grass up to the structure. The louvers allowed enough space to see and hear what went on inside.

Burton wore a pair of muddy jeans, sneakers, and a red quarter-zip sweatshirt from UMass-Boston. His eyes shone in the dimness but his face was so deep in shadow I couldn't tell if he'd been beaten. At least he was conscious. His hands were high over his head, zip-tied to the highest louver on the short wall of the dugout.

Directly to his left sat Kuan-Yin, her hand moving in her lap. I couldn't see what she was doing but a strange sick feeling pulled at my stomach.

"Pretty-boy," Vicky hissed at Burton in a low venomous whisper. "Pretty boys always get what they want, don't they? Or they think so."

She waved a club, ash-colored and tapered to a handle, the broken-off end of a baseball bat. She held it by the splintered end and tapped Burton on the forehead with the handle, not too hard. The sun broke out again, lighting the scene more clearly. Burton's face was bruised and dried blood crusted next to his nostril.

"Could not control yourself, could you? Even though I was paying you to find her for me." She poked him in the chest, hard enough to make him grunt. "Even after I told you she was my sister. Even after I told you."

Her voice seesawed. Some strings on her piano had snapped. Kuan-Yin eased toward Burton on the wooden bench and threaded something through his belt, the metal reflecting dully, like greasy bicycle chain.

"She didn't want to come with me, Vicky." Burton's voice was rough but still strong, reasonable. "Tell her the truth, Kuan-Yin. Nothing happened with you and me. You wanted to stay with Marty. Or anyone else."

Kuan-Yin loosed a high watery laugh, as surreal as Vicky's. Neither one of them was in possession of herself.

Edward shifted his weight and showed the butt of his pistol, what looked like a baby Glock 40. I pointed at it.

Burton grunted, harder this time.

When I looked back inside, Viktoriya was waving the bat end again. I pointed at Edward's pistol urgently, trying to get him to intervene before Burton got seriously hurt. Even if he had to shoot his sister, we couldn't sit here and let her beat Burton to death. Wasn't that why he'd brought me here, to save him?

But Edward shook his head. Vicky poked Burton again. He yelped and winced and blood dribbled down his arms from where the plastic ties cut his wrist.

"She's going to kill him, Edward," I whispered. "Do something."

Edward pulled the pistol from his belt holster and handed it to me, then back-crawled across the muddy grass to the asphalt path.

He stood up there, and watched to see how things would come out.

"Chickenshit," I muttered under my breath. My pulse was Taiko-drumming and my throat felt as if I'd swallowed a rock. The pistol felt familiar—Burton and I used to target shoot together—and I knew how to operate it. That wasn't the issue.

Vicky was getting pleasure from poking various places on Burton's torso. His body jumped in hopeless reaction, as involuntary as a frog being prodded in a lab. Kuan-Yin watched primly, a thin smile across her mouth: interest, not sympathy.

I held the pistol in close to my chest to muffle the sound as I racked the slide. A cartridge popped out onto the ground but I couldn't assume Edward would carry the gun hot.

Vicky heard something. She bent over and peered through the louvers. I flattened myself in next to the dugout's concrete foundation.

"I'm cold, baby." Kuna-Yin's voice was whiny, total tired child. Any pleasure she took from seeing Burton punished was overcome by her own discomfort. "Can't you just do him? Then we can go home and have a nice hot bath."

Viktoriya dropped the bat and I relaxed, thinking we might be done. Then she flicked open a long thin knife, the blade shooting yellow shards of light in the sun. She stepped in close to Burton, Kuan-Yin leaning forward almost drooling with excitement.

I raised Edward's Glock and aimed for Viktoriya: center body mass, the way Burton had instructed me.

Then a gun went off behind my ear, so close it deafened me on that side. Vicky spun and crumpled on the dugout steps, half in and half out. She twitched, once, twice, three times, then went still.

Kuan-Yin slid off her bench and went for the knife, but Burton managed to kick it away. It skittered down the dugout floor and under a trash barrel.

Stunned, I stood up and turned around, Edward's pistol at the ready. Mickey Barksdale's gloved hand pushed it down and away. He looked self-satisfied, like anyone who's brought a satisfactory end to a difficult endeavor. I had no idea how he'd come to be here.

"Not bad shooting, eh?" he said. "I was afraid I was going to hit one of those louvery things."

Coming in the only working ear I had, his voice sounded flat. Kuan-Yin wailed from inside the dugout. Mickey replaced Edward's pistol in my hand with the chrome automatic he'd shot Vicky with.

"Better cut him loose before the other one comes around." His tone was conversational, as if we were in a bar.

"How did you get here?" I was sure I would have noticed anyone trailing us from Burton's place.

"I was never here, boyo. Was I? Burton would never forgive me."

I nodded. He held my wrist and made me fire the pistol into the ground. Then he took a last look at the dugout as if recording a memory, then walked away.

Beyond Mickey's retreating back in the Harris tweed coat, Edward started running down the sidewalk. He'd managed to do half a right thing, but not a whole.

# 50

Things went quickly from there on, probably because along with the patrol cars the ball field's neighbors called in—people in that part of town knew the difference between gunshots and car backfires—Biggs showed up. And because Burton was a cop, the uniforms were happy to secure the scene and let Biggs do the heavy thinking.

I'd cut Burton loose with Viktoriya's switchblade. He groaned from the pain in his ribs and his wrists, raw from the zip ties. Over his objections, the EMTs sent him to Mass General for a once-over and likely a new tape job on his ribs. He had a cut over one eye that was going to leave a scar and he was woozy enough that I suspected a concussion.

"Tell Marina I'm OK," he said as the EMTs closed the doors on them.

"Sure, Dan. Don't worry about it."

The Medical Examiner's van carried Viktoriya's body away, once the uniforms had pried Kuan-Yin loose from her dramatic performance over the corpse. She went into custody, though I doubted there were criminal charges that would stick to her.

Biggs held onto an evidence bag containing the chrome pistol Mickey Barksdale had given me. We stood on the mud behind the dugout. His unmarked car was the last vehicle left at the field.

"You need a ride?" he said.

Something about the scene was bothering him but there wasn't any evidence to back up the feeling.

"No, thanks. My car's parked up there."

I pointed up the street.

"Tell me one more time how you just happened to show up?" he said.

"Phone call. He hadn't shown up for a date with a friend of mine last night. And there's been a fair amount of crazy shit going on. As you know."

"Hmmph."

"Talk to Burton. He'll corroborate that much."

Biggs shook his head.

"Of that I have no doubt."

"How's Murray going to feel about all this?"

"Don't let it make you cocky." He stepped off toward the plain car. As he spun his tires, digging divots in the turf along the third base line, I thought that was pretty good advice.

# 51

From the car, I called Marina and told her I'd found Burton and that he'd be all right. I asked her to put a sign on the door that the Esposito was closed until Monday and I went over to the hospital to see Burton.

They wanted him to stay overnight but as he said, all they could do was tell him not to cough or laugh for a month or so. He took seven or eight stitches over the eyebrow and the nurse said there were no signs of concussion. I'm sure the E. R. was happy to see the last of him. I pushed his wheelchair out to the exit doors and walked him to the Cougar.

"Scar's going to make you look like a tough guy." I pointed at the eye.

"And lose what little advantage I had. The innocent boy."

He was in a decent mood, once the doctors told him he could choose between alcohol and painkillers as long as he didn't mix them. I'd had a nasty experience once with Scotch and Tylenol and told him about it in detail on the off chance he'd take my advice seriously.

"So it was Viktoriya all along," I said once I had him in the car. "Killing Bousquet, snuffing gangsters right and left?"

"Bousquet, for sure."

"That I get. He pulled Kuan-Yin out of the sweat shop and turned her into a hooker."

"Pulled Vicky out, too, remember. She said she killed him for selling Kuan-Yin."

"To Marty Laird. Which explains his demise."

268

"Paid for his sins. By all accounts, he did love Kuan-Yin and Vicky couldn't take the idea. Anymore than she liked the idea Kuan-Yin would . . ."

"No baseball metaphors. Please."

He grinned.

"I should have told Vicky she hit like a girl. Though it might have gotten me killed faster." He shifted in the seat and winced. "That was a pretty fair pistol shot, by the way. From behind the dugout and through those louvers? You been practicing without me?"

I'd considered not telling him, but I didn't know what his thinking I'd saved his life might do to our friendship.

"Wasn't me," I said.

He raised his eyebrows.

"Mickey B."

I explained the sequence, including the fact that Mickey hadn't wanted him to know.

"Don't ever tell him I do know," Burton said. "He's sure to want something in return."

"Done." I wasn't getting near that relationship anyway. "So did Vicky have something to do with Dmitri? Bousquet supplying girls to the Russians or something? In addition to the laundering service?"

Burton shook his head.

"Everyone I talked to is pretty sure it's the younger thug taking over, what's his name."

"Ermolai."

"Yep. Changing of the gangster guard. Which means nothing's really changing."

"We'll always have the thugs."

"Truer words never spoken," he said. "Which is why I'll always have a job. Assuming I don't fuck up again."

I parked outside his apartment.

"You want a hand?"

"Nah, I'm fine."

But he groaned under his breath as he pulled himself up out of the Cougar. I let it go. He looked back inside the car before he shut the door.

"Thanks, Elder."

And that was that.

\* \* \* \* \*

I thought about Burton as I walked up the steps to my apartment, wondering if he would be able to find a way to protect himself professionally and still do the work he loved. Sooner or later, someone higher up was going to decide it was more important that he work within an organization than that he close cases. I hoped it wouldn't happen soon.

My brain was too full to cycle down and I knew I wasn't going to sleep any time soon, between the excitement of the day and the way sobriety had messed with my sleep patterns. I changed into sweats and lay down on the couch with *Common Ground*, J. Anthony Lukas's history of the bussing crisis in Boston. It was readable and I knew it probably wouldn't put me to sleep but I'd been very young during that time and the tales of what the South End had been like back in the Sixties and Seventies intrigued me.

The prose didn't distract me enough. I got up off the couch and prowled, sat down at the little table in the den where I kept my laptop. Something mindless, maybe. A game of Scrabble against myself.

When I connected, my mail program put a small red 1 up in the corner. I would have ignored it, since most of my pertinent email arrived to the account on the Esposito's office machine. I clicked on it anyway.

The return address looked like spam until I read the Subject: line: *Brunch at Pedro's?* Someone would have to know an awful lot about me to construct a teaser like that. I opened the message.

One line: *Got DVD?*

I made the connection immediately and started searching the desk drawer for the disc the bourbon-drinking Eileen had left in the bar a couple weeks back. I set it in the tray, let the drive spin up, then pushed play when the icon appeared.

Kathleen's face came into view, her mouth moving without sound. I paused the clip, unmuted the speakers, restarted it. A sadness filtered

270

in as I admired the auburn riot of her hair, the smile that detonated in my chest.

"Elder."

She looked directly into the camera, directly at me.

"What can I say, except how bloody sorry I am. I suspect your good friend Burton found me out and wouldn't leave well enough alone. That's not why I ran, though.

"I've found myself around a fair number of men, my friend."

Schoolboy moment—jealousy punched me in the gut. She pinched the bridge of her nose, a gesture I used myself to keep from crying.

"You surprised me," she said. "We surprised me. Something better than I expected, even if it was short. But I feel like we lost something, and that hurts."

Her eyes glinted. Did I dare believe the tears?

"Unfortunately for both of us, I'm a thief. Pretty good one, too." She laughed. "Like father, like daughter. I'm sure Burton has details."

She took a long shaky breath. The disc clicked in the tray.

"Even more unfortunately? I stole something from someone I shouldn't have. Something extremely valuable, of course. What would be the point, otherwise? And these are not people who'll be happy just to retrieve it. They're going to want a pound of flesh."

My heart bumped. Was she talking about someone here in Boston? The Russians? Mickey Barksdale?

The image on the screen pixelated, then resolved.

"Don't try and figure it out. Please. I know you'll want to help and this is not in your skill set."

She sounded confident she'd survive, which made me feel marginally better.

"Suffice to say, any gangster-looking guy with an accent comes by, you don't know me. Never did."

If she was talking about Dmitri, he was dead. Maybe Ermolai could help.

"No." She shook her head, jingling the silver moon earrings. "I can read your mind from here. This is nothing words, time, or money can cure. Hence the disappearing act."

Now she was crying.

"If I saw a way around this, Elder? I would try and do it. We had a good beginning and it might have gone someplace. But for now? Down the road, my friend."

She blew me a kiss and the screen went dark.

I sat back in my chair, as sad and angry as the day Burton sucker-punched Antoine Bousquet. I closed the video, dragged it to the Recycle Bin, and shut down the laptop. If I'd had an ounce of Scotch in the house, I would have used it to put myself to sleep. Peppermint tea did not do the job so well.

# 52

St. Patrick's Day fell on a Friday that year but I didn't break my
rule of not acknowledging it at the Esposito. There were enough
Irish bars in Boston that would festoon themselves with shamrocks,
plastic hats, and green beer, that I thought people might want a
place to hide from all of that. It was one of the several holidays in
the year—New Year's Eve, Cinco de Mayo being others—ruled by
amateur drinkers and sloppy ones. I put a spring training game up
on the tube and everyone seemed reasonably happy.

The last couple times Burton and I had been tangled up in one of
these messes, I'd tried to collect all the parties involved—the ones
who weren't disappeared or in jail, at least—at the Esposito for a
minor celebration, a summing up, something like a collective purge
of all the leftover emotion.

But on Sunday, even after everyone who could make it showed
up, no one seemed up for a party. Maybe it had to do with the
violence and the vulnerability being too close to home this time.
Key figures like Kathleen were missing and most of the rest had
shown up out of duty.

When Burton arrived, Marina disappeared into the kitchen.
Something serious had ruptured between them. He took his usual
stool to the left of the cash register.

"Back to work tomorrow?" I said. "You're back in the rotation?"

He nodded without enthusiasm, watching Joey Blanco noodle
on his guitar and chat up Carmen and Mrs. Rinaldi at a table by
the stage. They were all drinking from tiny glasses of homemade
limoncello Mrs. Rinaldi had brought. Blanco had asked me this

morning if I'd ever thought of having a house band. He was always trying.

"Full duty. Off the desk, thank god. At least they didn't put me back in the bag." He looked over the top of his glass. "I am thinking about quitting, though."

I didn't know what else to do but crack wise.

"Finally broke your spirit, did they?"

He looked bereft.

"You're serious?" I said.

He nodded, pushing the empty glass toward me to reorder. I grabbed it, realizing my tea-scalded hand no longer hurt.

"I'm losing whatever chops I had," he said. "I didn't do shit to solve Bousquet's murder. Vicky surprised me."

His voice vibrated with self-loathing. I mixed him another drink and wished I could join him in one. For solidarity.

"It got done, though. Justice."

"It happened that way because I didn't care enough what happened to him," he said. "Because of what he'd done to those women. If I'd been paying better attention, I'd have gotten there sooner."

His eyes were dull, the gray blue of winter light.

"If I let myself believe someone matters less than someone else? That a person's murder is less important because of who he was? I've got nothing."

That rigid integrity strapped him too tightly. For me it was enough that the responsible party was punished, some rough equity restored.

The upstairs door opened and Rasmussen Carter walked downstairs, removing a tweed cap. His sunglasses were shiny and black as polished coal. Burton looked at him incuriously.

I slipped down the bar to meet him, worn out with trying to buck Burton up. I poured Carter a ginger ale and offered to introduce him around. He offered an enigmatic stretch of the lips and walked back into the kitchen.

"OK, then," I said.

Joey Blanco bounced up to the bar, guitar case in hand.

"Elder, gotta bounce. But thanks for the invite. Next Friday, right?"

Because the Esposito would continue on, regardless.

I nodded, he dapped me, and headed out.

Burton looked up as I returned with a fresh drink. He was putting it away like someone planning to get drunk. The thought opened a black hole in my gut.

"You'd really quit the cops?"

He screwed up his mouth.

"Marina said you got the money thing straightened out, Carmen and her? They're rich."

No answers for my questions today, then. I nodded at the corner where the two old ladies chatted.

"All set."

The meeting with Attorney Markham had been comical, Carmen pulling the Italian grandmother act on him, asking why such a good-looking man wasn't married, whether he attended Mass, what parish he belonged to. I kept my amusement to myself, not sure the dotty old lady thing was entirely an act.

But Marina now had signing authority over a five-million dollar trust and had made arrangements for Carmen at a very nice assisted living facility in Newton. It was just in time—Marina said Carmen was showing further slippage.

"Big relief for Marina," I said.

Burton nodded. Marina came out of the kitchen with Carter and shook her head at the two of us leaning on opposite sides of the bar.

"We're taking Carmen home," she said. "She's getting tired."

I looked over. Both of the ladies waved and smiled.

"She looks OK to me," Burton said. "Like she's having a good time, in fact."

Carter stepped up behind Marina and put his hands on her shoulders. Burton stiffened.

"And we have reservations," Carter said. "Would you like us to drop Mrs. Rinaldi off?"

"Ask her," I said.

We watched the four of them get into their coats and head out.

"I've got reservations, too," Burton said.

"You and me both, brother. Almost always."

The atmosphere didn't get any lighter with just the two of us there, Burton slipping down into that black hole he'd found earlier in the season, where all the energy turned over and he became a sucking vortex for people's love and concern and comfort and fellowship. This place ate all the light.

He lifted his chin and drank. I saw him trying to fight it, trying to argue against his own fractured sense of self—I could see it because I'd done it myself. He sat up and shook himself like a dog.

"Ah, fuck. I couldn't quit. What the fuck else would I do with my time?"

That wasn't even somewhat convincing but I gave him credit for trying. Without the counterweight of his work, though, the one thing that took him out of himself, the thing that gave him his right to take up space on the planet, he might spin himself right off earth.

He tapped at his glass with his fingernails.

"What about you, sport? Young, handsome, and rich?" He swiveled on his stool to regard the empty bar. "One out of three isn't bad. This is it for you? Enough to keep your big brain occupied?"

The very question I'd wrestled with since I'd sat in Attorney Markham's office and found out what awaited me. The enormity of it hadn't penetrated until I'd seen the actual number.

I took a deep breath, feeling like I owed him an honest answer. Any ideas I had about what came next were scraps, so fragmented I wasn't sure saying them aloud wouldn't scare them away. My attempt was interrupted by the street door opening.

"We're closed," I called up.

"Is he here? That bastard?" Sharon's little girl voice cut through the long slow of Grant Green's guitar like a machete through soft cheese.

I cringed. Burton's smile widened as Sharon's boot heels pounded down the stairs.

"Daniel X. Burton, you fucker. Are you drinking up your whole pension before I get my share?"

He sighed like a horse settling into its stall after a long day.

"Yes, Sharon. That's exactly what I'm trying to do. Come on down and give me a hand."

Then he winked, surprising me. He'd been avoiding the woman

he called his soon-to-be-ex-wife for the better part of two years, to the point I'd assumed they weren't done with each other yet.

She bounced down off the bottom step, stunning in a black cocktail dress with a demure V in front, a faux-fur wrap around her shoulders. She clicked across the black and white linoleum in her knee-high black boots, and slapped down an envelope on the bar. She gave me a nasty look, reminding me I'd failed to get him to sign the last set.

"Finally I catch up with you, you black Irish bastard."

Burton used his pinkie to push the envelope away. Signing the papers would be his final acknowledgment he'd failed at something important. I didn't see him doing it.

"My parents were married when I was born," he said. "You've met them. Remember?"

She looked shocked, as if she'd expected return fire, then glared at me again.

"Jesus Christ, Darrow. Is this a bar or not? Is making me a Cape Codder too much of a challenge for you?"

Trust Sharon not to notice it was Sunday. Or that this had been a private party. And trust her to order a drink only teenagers on Spring Break drank.

I went to work on it, alert for the sounds of breaking glass or slaps on flesh.

"I had my boobs done," she said, not quietly.

Burton looked over at her, undid the metal clasp on the envelope.

"You want to see them?"

Talk about mixed messages. I turned back to my drink mixing. Sometimes it was a bane people thought bartenders were invisible. She was entirely capable of dropping her top right there.

I set the drink in front of her.

Burton slid the papers out of the envelope, yellow sticky notes bristling along the edges. He slipped his hand into his shirt pocket.

Did Sharon look stricken suddenly? Or was that just surprise?

"Don't have a pen," he said. "Elder?"

I wouldn't have said anything if I hadn't seen how depressed he was five minutes ago.

"You sure?"

He lifted his chin, all the answer I got. I found a ballpoint in the junk drawer and slid it down the bar.

He uncapped it and methodically signed all the places in the documents, stacking the yellow sticky notes on the bar beside him. When he'd signed the last place, he recapped the pen and slipped the sheaf of documents back into the envelope.

Sharon beamed at him.

"About the boobs," he said. "If I said they looked pretty good on you, would you hold them against me?"

Her eyes stretched wide for an instant, then she cackled.

"Jesus, Burton. You can't even get an old joke right?"

She looped her arm through his and tugged him off the stool. He wore a goofy grin and it wasn't because he was drunk.

"I'm not promising you anything," she lectured as they started for the stairs, her ankles wobbling. "They're still kind of sore. But you should see how tiny the scars are."

At the top of the stairs, Burton turned and waggled his fingers at me. That was all I needed to know that things would be all right with him, eventually. Only children and fools believed they could ever be perfect: no pain, no happiness. No uncertainty, no love.

And for me, on that one day at least, I was happy to be alone in the place I'd created out of my dream. After I locked the upstairs door, I came down and poured myself a Scotch and water—a weak one—sat down at one of my tables and pretended I was a customer.

I looked at the photo of Dizzy Gillespie, his cheeks puffed out like balloons, and thought about friendship and love, about losing Kathleen, whether there was any use trying to find out where she'd gone. As Burton had said, I was neither young nor handsome anymore—assuming I'd ever been—but I was rich. And so most of the troubles from here on out were likely to be ones I made for myself. Solo troubles, mine and only mine.

# About the Author

Richard J. Cass is the author of the Boston-based Elder Darrow jazz mystery series.

The first book in the series, Solo Act, was nominated for a Maine Literary Award in 2017. The second book in the series, *In Solo Time*, is the origin story for Elder and his friend, Boston homicide detective Dan Burton. *In Solo Time* won the Maine Literary Award for Crime Fiction for 2018. Burton's Solo continues the story of Elder and Burton and the Esposito Bar and Grill.

Cass's short fiction has been published widely and won prizes from *Redbook, Writers' Digest*, and *Playboy*. His first collection of stories was called *Gleam of Bone*. He blogs with the Maine Crime Writers at https://mainecrimewriters.com and serves on the board of Mystery Writers of America's New England chapter.

He lives in Cape Elizabeth, Maine with his wife Anne, and a semi-feral Maine Coon cat named Tinker, where he writes full time. You can reach him on Facebook at: Richard Cass – Writer or on Twitter at: @DickCass.